The McGunnegal Chronicles

The McGunnegal Chronicles

Book 2 – Taming the Goblin

Edition 2.1

Edited by BZ Hercules

To Janet,

Enjoy!

9-11-16

For Sam, Luke, Rachel and Katie.

All my love.

– Dad

ACKNOWLEDGEMENTS

Thanks to everyone who helped me with editing, ideas, and encouragement, especially Frederica, Mary Beth, Sharon, my mom, Doris, my daughters Katie and Rachel, Julia, Jannie and others.

Thanks to BZ Hercules for their great editing help on this second edition.

Special thanks to my dear wife, Janet, who has been so patient with me on the journey of writing The McGunnegal Chronicles.

And thanks to all of my heroes of ages past, whose teachings whisper through these pages.

Chapter 1 – Journey to the Lake

Frederick Buttersmouth twitched and mumbled in his sleep. His hooded face was hidden, but his gray arm lay uncovered at his side. Black spidery veins radiated outward from the goblin bite he had received the night before.

Suddenly he cried out, “Stop! Stop!”

His eyes shot open and he jumped to his feet, shaking himself and looking around. The nightmare scene of his dream faded, and the dim interior of a cave formed into waking reality.

Now he remembered where he was – in a strange land that he and his cousin, Colleen McGunnegal, had blundered into by accident through a mysterious passageway in her grandfather’s basement. She was here, along with a collection of little people that they had somehow picked up along the way.

Colleen reached out and touched him. “Frederick, are you all right?”

He wiped the sweat from his face and nodded.

“I’ll be okay,” he said. “It was just a nightmare - a terrible nightmare.”

“Want to talk about it?” she asked.

He shook his head, and then remembered the fight with the goblin. His wounds still throbbed.

“How's it doing this morning?” asked Colleen. “Any better?”

“Why isn't your hair ever a mess in the morning?” he asked grumpily, avoiding the subject.

She smiled at him and shrugged, then took a good look at his arm again.

“We better get going soon,” she said gravely.

They ate a breakfast of nuts and berries and a stew of roots that Cian the leprechaun cooked up for them. Everyone else ate it with relish, but Frederick thought that it tasted a bit woody.

Cian sat cross-legged before them, his two-foot tall body hunched over his bowl of stew.

"For us wee folk, the Lady's Lake is at least a ten-day march," he said. "It's said that she is gathering the remnants of the little people who still fight on against the Spell and the goblins."

"What is she like, Cian – this Lady Danu? We have old legends back home about someone with such a name. They say she once gave a great sword to a king," said Colleen.

"She is a beautiful and terrible sight to behold," said Cian. "I have known her for many a year, although we have rarely spoken in these later days."

"Is she dangerous?" asked Frederick.

"Dangerous?" mused Cian. "Yes, dangerous to those who hate what is good and right and full of light, and dangerous to the goblins and to the Witch and all her minions. The Lady does not answer to any of us, although she watches over us, and, I think, many other places as well."

"Is she human?" asked Frederick. "Or one of these... *spirits* that seem to inhabit this world?"

"Not human, I think," replied Cian. "Nor wholly an immaterial spirit either. She seems to be something else, and she appeared in our world before the Witch came. I remember long, long ago, when the world was young, and life was simple, I first saw her at that very lake. So bright and beautiful and big! She was the first of the big people that I ever saw, if it is right to call her that. But she did not stay here then. She only greeted me with a smile and disappeared beneath the waves of the lake. It was only after the goblins came that she remained for any length of time. Her power is very great, although now she contends against a great tide of darkness. There are times when I fear even for her."

He sighed and shook his head.

"At any rate, you should get on your way. Mal will return soon after her long night of trying to find me, and she may lead others back here as well."

Humble, Nemon, and Zelo, the three gnomes they had met along the way, inched their way forward, heads bowed.

"Begging your pardon, Mr. Cian, sir," said Humble. "We would love to stay with you and hear the tales of when the world was young and all that, but we would also like to go with Colleen and Frederick to see the Lady."

Cian laughed and said, "Of course, friends, you should travel with them. They may need you along the way. Who can say what they may face, and you should see the Lady too."

So they packed up their things, and the three gnomes decided to ride in the back of the cart with Dvalenn, the sleeping dwarf whom they had found in the forest, while the Wigglepoxes sat on the seat between the children. Oracle just went about banging on things with his stick and occasionally giggling.

Frederick wondered for the hundredth time about the odd leprechaun. He seemed crazy at times, doing or saying ridiculous things, and yet at other times, mysterious things happened when he was around. In any event, he seemed not to be touched by the Spell, unless it was the cause of his strange behavior.

"Farewell for now, my young friends," said Cian.

Oracle gave a snort, at which Cian smiled and said, "Perhaps we shall meet again in better times."

The two big leprechauns looked each other in the eye, and Frederick thought he saw Oracle wink.

“Until then,” said Cian.

They said their goodbyes and started out once again, a strange band of two children, four leprechauns, three gnomes, and a sleeping dwarf, all riding behind Badger, the shabby old farm horse turned magnificent warhorse by a leprechaun's wish.

Colleen, in her green cloak, and Frederick in his blue, looked like young nobles riding off to an important engagement, and Oracle, a little midget of a man, grinned a goofy grin at the little people and Cian as they pulled away. Waving goodbye, they pulled out of the strange cave, leaving behind the little hermit they had found in this sleepy wood. But, in their hearts, they were fearful at leaving their newfound friend, and they wondered what the new day would bring.

The sun began to rise in the morning sky, and as it did so, a beam of its rays shone down on their little band. Immediately, Frederick let out a cry of pain and grabbed at his arm.

“What's wrong?” said Colleen.

“The sun is so bright! It hurts my arm,” he said, and pulled his cloak over his wounds.

Colleen said nothing, but Frederick could see the obvious concern on her face.

He lifted the cloak, being careful to keep his arm shielded from the sun. His arm looked terrible, and the grayness and black spidery veins seemed to be creeping steadily outward, toward his hand and elbow. He shut his eyes and took a deep breath, trying to calm himself and not think about what was happening to him. Cian had said that those bitten by goblins became goblins. He hoped they would find help before that terrible fate took him.

As the day passed, they rode on deeper and deeper into the forest, following the remnants of the old road that led south. Often it was overgrown, and Badger valiantly heaved his way through tangled underbrush. Frederick wondered at the great horse's power and endurance, marveling that it had been so transformed from a bony old thing to a fabulous warhorse by Lily Wigglepox's wish back in the Hall of Sindri. Great trees, many of which had a sickly look about them, lined the road. Twisted trunks and sagging branches surrounded them, and the bare canopy of the forest was a knotted tangle that cast weird shadows across their path.

"This place is spooky," said Frederick after a time, looking up at a great black tree with huge knots on its trunk that gave the illusion of a frowning face with closed eyes.

"Yes," said Humble, one of the gnomes. "But more sad than spooky. Sad that where there was once so much life, now there is only the long Sleep filled with nightmares, and if that doesn't snare you, the goblins probably will."

"It's hard," said Nemon. "You've got to always remember that they are there, maybe just around the next tree. They don't forget about you, you know."

"That's right," said Zelo. "Most of them don't seem to tire of trying to hunt you down and cart you off to their black pits, so you've got to be ever vigilant and watch out for them."

"And even if you've escaped their nets and traps for a hundred years, never think that you can just relax and that they'll never get you. Don't get all proud and think too highly of yourself, like you're somehow special and won't get caught," added Humble.

"Right," said Nemon. "That happened to poor old Bumble a few years ago. He had managed to keep himself from the goblins for decades. But one day, he said that he was tired of worrying about them and just wanted to take a walk in the woods. After all, we hadn't seen any in months. So off he went, all alone, and, wouldn't you know it, that just happened to be the day that the goblins were setting traps. Bumble walked headlong into one, and they scooped him up and took him away. Poor Bumble, he should have been more watchful."

As they chatted on, telling stories of other little people whom they had known and who had been snatched away by the goblins, Frederick thought that his eyes were beginning to play tricks on him. The shadows in the forest seemed to shift and flit about, as though they were dashing from tree to tree.

When he was sure that he *had* seen something dart behind a big old oak, he nudged Colleen. But she was already looking into the woods.

"Over there, Frederick," she whispered. "Watch the shadows between the trees. But don't stare! Just pretend you're talking to me, but watch."

"What is that?" he said.

"Just watch!" she said.

Mrs. Wigglepox overheard, and stopped telling a tale of her great cousin Eldred and gazed into the woods as well.

"Cluricauns!" she said in an urgent, hushed voice.

The gnomes all stopped talking and climbed to the rim of the cart to have a look.

"What are cluricauns?" asked Colleen nervously.

"More spies of the Witch!" said Mrs. Wigglepox. "They are little people who have given themselves over to her, and she has granted them powers like the Shadows to spread the Spell."

"Will they try to harm us?" asked Frederick.

"Not as long as we stay together," replied Mrs. Wigglepox. "But they will try to summon the Spell with renewed strength and have us all fall under it. They may try to separate us from each other. Once they do that, then they have great power."

"Well, let's stop them," said Frederick, trying to sound brave.

"Easier said than done," said Zelo. "They're like fleeting shadows and can hide most anywhere."

"Well, I'm going to try," said Frederick, and he jumped down from the wagon and drew his sword.

"Frederick!" said Colleen. "Just what do you think you're going to do with that thing?"

"Scare them off, of course. After all, they're just little things," he replied, and he let the wagon pass and ran into the woods, brandishing his sword.

"Wait!" cried Mrs. Wigglepox. "We must stay together!"

But Frederick did not heed her warning, and as soon as he stepped off the road, the shadows converged around him, pressing in from the surrounding trees. The view of the wagon rolling away was swallowed up by the night, and the air grew thick and oppressive.

Within the sudden darkness, Frederick could see tiny faces – scores of them, peering out from roots, in the branches, on the trunks of the trees, and in the air, and all of them looked at him with scorn and hatred, as though he were some loathsome thing.

Fear swept through his mind, and he could hear them putting thoughts in his head. "*You are nothing. We will take you away. Drop your useless weapon and surrender to us. We will take you to the Witch, and you will serve her. You know that you wish to be a goblin – you are already becoming one!*"

He sank to his knees and only just managed to hold onto his sword. His injured arm began to feel strange, as though a will other than his own were moving it. He struggled against it, and his mind whirled with a sea of thoughts and images that seemed to come from the faces in the darkness all around him. He did not know how long the voices howled, only that he fought them, resisting the temptation to drop the sword.

Just as he was about to let go, the sound of thunderous hooves and a great neighing burst through the tumult of noise in his head. Through the circle of darkness burst Badger, with Colleen riding on him, her golden-red hair and green cape whipping in the wind behind her as the great horse galloped into the oppressive night. Badger reared on his hind legs, neighing wildly and kicking at the darkness in defiance.

For a moment, the faces wavered and looked doubtful, and their clamor was broken. The voice of Colleen parted the tumult like a mighty ship plowing through a storm.

"Take my hand!" she shouted, and she bent low and stretched it out to him.

Numbly he stood, and then reached up with his pained left arm. She grasped his wrist, and with strength he did not think she possessed, she hefted him up on the saddle behind her.

But the darkness recovered from its momentary distraction, and began to close in again.

"Light, Frederick," came Colleen's voice from somewhere. "We need light!"

With all the strength he could muster, Frederick lifted his sword in the air and shouted something that he could not even hear himself say.

There was a brilliant flash from somewhere above him. Badger reared, throwing him backward. His head struck the ground hard, and the last thing he saw was Colleen leaping from her saddle, sweeping his fallen sword into the air, and then her whole visage seemed to burst into flaming light. But the darkness took him, and he knew no more.

When he finally awoke, he was lying beside Dvalenn in the wagon as it once again bumped along through the woods. The three gnomes sat on the dwarf's chest, their worried faces staring at him.

"What happened?" he asked, pushing himself up. His head pounded, and he groaned.

"Just lie down, Frederick Brendan, and I'll tell you," scolded Colleen.

"You acted like a foolish boy, that's what!" said Mrs. Wigglepox.

"Braviculous Fredersmouth!" said Oracle, and whacked him on the top of his head with his cane.

"Ouch!" said Frederick.

"Frederick, you ran into the woods and vanished into the shadows. It grew dark all around you, and you started to move away, deeper into the woods," said Colleen.

"Yes," he replied, "and there were terrible faces in there!"

"As soon as that happened, we couldn't see you. We called and called, but you didn't seem to hear us. So, I jumped down, unhooked Badger, and went riding after you. Badger is marvelous to ride! He charged right into the darkness as if he wanted to fight it himself. But then I saw the faces too, and they were shrieking. I pulled you onto the saddle, but Badger went wild at their sound. You lifted that sword, and then it happened."

"Then what happened?" he asked.

"The sword – it started to shine with a brilliant white light!" she replied. "The faces all shrieked louder than ever. Then you were thrown from the saddle, and dropped your sword. I jumped down after you and grabbed the sword, and suddenly they all fled. It was the strangest thing. I thought they had left, but in a moment, they started to return. Their rage was terrible, Frederick. I was really afraid, but Oracle came strolling in among them, singing some silly song and started chasing them with his cane. They ran away and didn't come back. And, I might add, I had to drag you all the way back to the cart and get you in by myself. You're rather heavy, you know."

Frederick felt at his side and found the sword was missing.

"Don't worry, its right here," said Colleen, and she handed it to him.

Frederick took it. The blade was bright silver and engraved with symbols and runes, and the handle was inlaid with smooth green and blue gemstones.

"I think there's something special about that sword, Frederick," said Colleen.

"I'd say," said Zelo. "A blade that drives cluricauns away and shines like that is more than special. You just hang onto that, Frederick. We may need it again."

Frederick looked at the sword again. Had it heard his cry for help? Was it a magical weapon? And who had forged it? Elves? Dwarves? Someone else? Then he remembered that Doc the dwarf had said that he had a hand in its making, along with all other armor and weapons in the House of Mysteries. Who was that old dwarf anyway? More than he seemed, that was for sure.

He lay back in the wagon and rubbed his head, and then realized that he felt in control of himself again. But he looked at his arm, and the grayness and spidery black tendrils had spread even more. He sat up and looked into the woods. Strange shadows flitted this way and that.

"They're still there, aren't they – the Shadows, I mean?" he asked.

"Yes," said Colleen, "although they've been keeping their distance."

"Don't underestimate them," said Mrs. Wigglepox. "You can be sure they won't forget what you did back there, Frederick, and I think they'll be looking to get at Oracle too. We need to be sure we stay together from now on."

Frederick climbed out of the back of the cart and sat down next to Colleen. Oracle sat perched on Dvalenn's beard, singing a nonsensical song, and the little people sat in the hay, listening to him.

“Are you okay?” Colleen asked him.

“I’ll live,” he said. “Thanks.”

He glanced back at the little people who were riding behind them and said, “I suppose I should thank Oracle too. That's twice he's done me good. But he's a weird chap, isn't he? I mean, he seems like a total loon at times, and then strange things seem to happen when he's around. Where did he get that pot of gold from back in that cave? And back in Doc's Crystal Cavern, I saw him put his hands on the wall and lights started flashing. Then he chased those cluricauns away with his cane. Now he's just acting odd again.”

Colleen looked at the old leprechaun, who seemed to have suddenly fallen asleep. She shook her head, then shrugged, unsure what to think.

“You scared me back there, Frederick. Still, I think what you did was very brave,” she said.

He blushed and turned away.

“Thanks,” he mumbled.

They rode on down the ancient road for some time, but as the sun climbed high and then began to sink, the sleepiness in the forest around them began to grow once again, and they could see the shadows in the wood deepening.

“There's a heaviness about this place,” said Colleen, rubbing her eyes.

Frederick was slouching in the seat beside her, Badger's great head began to sag, and Mrs. Wigglepox yawned.

“Cluricauns!” she said sleepily. “As the sun gets lower in the sky, their power gets stronger. We've got to keep moving!”

Onward, they slowly went, and it seemed that the further they trudged on, the sleepier they got, until before Colleen realized it, they had stopped altogether. Badger was asleep on his feet, the Wigglepoxes were out cold, and Frederick was sitting hunched over, his chin on his chest. But Oracle was awake again, and was once again singing an odd song.

Colleen rubbed her eyes and shook her head, and felt her eyelids closing. She forced herself awake, but the drowsiness was overcoming her.

"*You're going to fall out of the seat and squash Mrs. Wigglepox and Rose,*" she said to herself. "*Now wake up, you silly girl!*"

With a tremendous effort, she tried to open her eyes, but they would not obey her, and she felt herself slipping to one side.

"*Do something!*" that inner voice urged, "*Do anything! ... Sing, Colleen, sing!*"

With her last bit of conscious will, she forced her lips open and began to whisper.

"When the singer and the tree
Meet in a place that none can tell.
And there she whispers words that free
The sleeping forest from its spell..."

She did not know where the words came from, but they seemed to go along with Oracle's tune. As she sang them, her eyes fluttered open, and she rubbed them again, and, taking a deep breath, she sang louder.

"Oh singer come, oh come this hour,
Your voice can break the evil power
Of curses, spells, and darkest gloom.
Oh sing, oh sing and free us from our doom."

Badger snorted, tossed his head, and began to pull. Frederick, Mrs. Wigglepox, and Rose began to stir, and Lily yawned hugely in his pocket and opened her eyes. Colleen sang on, louder now, and stronger.

"Come singer over mount and sands,
And cross the wide sea 'tween our lands.
Come singer from a distant shore.
Come sing and free our people 'yor."

As she sang, the trees around them began to sway, their bare branches scraping and scratching one another, as if a wind were blowing, but no wind blew. Now another sound rose – a growling and whining rising from the shadows, and dark, angry faces appeared, glaring at them as they rode by.

Colleen stopped singing and, in a few moments, the trees grew still and rustled no more.

Mrs. Wigglepox looked up at Colleen with amazement.

"My dear child," she said in awe, "you have just wakened the forest with your song. For a moment, the spell of the Court Witch wavered!"

"I what?" asked Colleen.

"Please, child, sing more. I feel the sleep coming ag..."

But Mrs. Wigglepox did not continue. She was asleep again, and Colleen also felt her eyelids getting heavy. She sang on, trying to hear what Oracle was singing and letting his scratchy voice fill her mind.

The others woke once again. In fact, they found that as long as she sang, they felt almost fully awake, and as Badger carried them along, the trees all around them stirred, the shadows dispersed, and it seemed to Frederick's ears that along with Colleen's song, the trees were whispering – a strange sound like wind in the leaves.

"What are they saying?" Frederick asked.

"It is very sad," said Lily. "They are asking us to stay and sing to them. *"We have slept too long! 'Ere long we will not wake again, unless you stay and sing to us!'"*

"Frederick," said Lily, "I don't like this part of the woods. Something is very bad here. We shouldn't be so tired."

"Lily is right, Mother," said Rose, who had been listening in. "I don't feel so sleepy in our tree back home."

"Yes," said Mrs. Wigglepox. "You are both quite right. There is something terribly wrong here. The Witch's spell is so strong! It's as if she's put more effort into this place, and the cluricauns are whispering."

Frederick slowly, with great effort, pulled his cloak away from his injured arm and looked down at it. The grayness had spread all the way to his fingertips and up to his shoulder, and now a sickly green was blending with the gray. His fingernails were turning a dirty yellow, and his knuckles were growing knobby.

In despair, he let his cloak fall, and his chin dropped to his chest. He could not fight any longer, and he so wanted to let the Sleep take him. But something kept buzzing in his ear.

What is that? he thought to himself. *If it would just go away, I could get some sleep.*

Colleen sang song after song, sometimes seeming to follow along with Oracle, and sometimes he followed her, until she ran out of songs to sing and started over with the first one. One hour went by, then two, and her voice grew tired. When at last Colleen was only whispering her song, the heaviness of sleep began to overtake them once again.

"We all must sing!" said Mrs. Wigglepox with a yawn. "We must all sing and help Colleen!"

* * *

And so they all sang, and for a while, this helped. But when nearly four hours had passed, Lily and Rose were nearly asleep again and Frederick sat listlessly in the seat next to Colleen. Was he snoring, or was he croaking out some song that she could not make out? She could not be sure. But periodically, he would wave his injured hand as if shooing away a mosquito from his ear.

Badger was trudging slowly along, his head again drooping to the ground. Only Mrs. Wigglepox and Colleen and Oracle continued the songs, although Colleen's throat ached and was parched. She could barely speak, and the struggle to keep singing weighed her down like a stone. Again and again, she nearly gave up, but shook herself and kept on whispering her song, fighting with all her might against the heavy spell that the Court Witch had laid on the land and that the cluricauns made stronger with their evil whispers.

When she finally felt as though she could not utter another word, and it seemed as though even Mrs. Wigglepox had grown silent, and Oracle's words were just gibberish, they broke through the trees and walked out onto a grassy meadow that was covered with white and purple flowers, which led down to the edge of a brilliant shining blue lake.

Chapter 2 – Professor McPherson

All five of the McGunnegal children crowded into Professor McPherson's office.

He smiled as they all entered, and said, “Well, at last I meet the McGunnegal family... except I hear that Colleen has not yet arrived. I am so very pleased to make your acquaintance. Now, let's see. As you know, I am Professor McPherson, and let me guess your names.

“Aonghus, your reputation precedes you! The children are chattering like chipmunks about how strong you are. And Bran, fastest player on the rugby field. Pretty good in a fight, I might add.”

Bran started to reply, but the professor cut him off. “But never mind that for the moment. Let's see... hmm... Abbe. You are the oldest of the girls, correct? And you have a great interest in our lake, I hear. Perhaps you and I could walk around it later, and I will show you the various flora and fauna that live in and around it.”

“I would love that, Professor,” Abbe replied.

“And Bib,” he continued. “You've been spending lots of time in the library. Good, good. And, I have my own special collection of books here in my office and in my tower office that you are welcome to investigate. Just make an appointment.”

Bib grinned and said, “Thank you, Professor!”

“And, of course, dear Henny,” he said. “Henny who can melt the heart of even old Miss Fenny. And what would you like to learn about at our school?”

“I would like to learn about fairies and mermaids,” she replied innocently.

“Fairies and mermaids!” replied the professor with great enthusiasm. “Indeed you shall! But what makes you think we could teach you about them?”

“They live here, don't they?” asked Henny, her eyes inquisitive.

The professor grew serious and thoughtful and glanced out his window, which overlooked the field and the nearby lake. Then he came around his desk, bent down, and looked Henny in the eyes.

“My dear Henny, there are many things that are mysterious in this world – fairies and mermaids among them. Our lake and the grounds hold many surprises. Keep your eyes open. Who knows what you may see?” he replied.

He stood then and said, “Now then, as to the matter of the fight. Bran, please tell me what happened.”

Bib glared up at her brother and said, “You were in a fight already?”

“It wasn't my fault!” he said defensively. “We were just playing rugby on the field when this Ed fellow came up and accused me of stealing his girl, Mary. I'd never met her before then, but he tried to slug me.”

Bib now had her hands on her hips in a motherly way and poked her tall brother squarely in the chest.

“A likely story!” she scolded.

Professor McPherson cleared his throat and interrupted. “Perhaps you could allow me to ask the questions, Bib.”

“Oh! Sorry,” she said ruefully.

The professor continued. “That's what I thought I saw, Bran. Aonghus, is that your story too?”

“Yes, sir, and they tried to gang up on Bran. I held two of them back. Dad always said that if you have to fight, fight fair,” replied Aonghus.

"Thank you," replied the professor. "I think that will be enough for now. I do believe your story, Bran, and thank you for not hurting Edward – something you seem to be more than capable of doing."

"Dad taught us to fight really well. There's not a man in Ireland that can top him. But he said you don't hurt people just because you can. You only try to get them to calm down and keep your own cool while you're at it," replied Bran.

"A wise man, your father. I would like to meet him one day. Strength is not always found in the powerful, but often in the meek and lowly things of life, or in a patient man who bears with the rudeness of others without taking offense," he replied.

"Professor," said Aonghus after a moment. "Before we go, may we show you something?"

"Certainly," he replied. "I was wondering what was in the bag."

Aonghus reached into the bag and pulled out one of the white stones that had the markings carved into it and handed it to the professor.

He took it and examined it closely for a moment, and then said, "Aonghus, please close the door."

Aonghus did so, and the professor said, "Where did you get this? Are there more like it in that bag?"

Aonghus handed the bag to him, and the professor took them out one at a time and examined each of them briefly.

"We got them from our farm, sir," said Abbe. "There are thousands of them piled in a big wall."

"And there are more really big stones in our basement that have those carvings on them," said Bran.

"We think they're the reason why Rufus Buttersmouth is paying our way here – to get us out of the way so that he can get to them, and maybe take our farm as well," said Bib.

Professor McPherson was silent for a few moments as he examined some of the stones closer. He looked very thoughtful and finally said, "Children, this is of very great importance. You are to talk to no one else about this. Do you have more of these stones?"

"Yes, sir," said Aonghus. "Four more bags. Mabel was trying to steal them, and we took them from her trunk."

"I see," said the professor. "And are they in your room at the moment?"

"Yes, sir," he replied.

"May I see them as well?" he asked.

"Of course. I can get them now if you would like," said Aonghus.

"No, that will not be necessary. But I would like you to bring them to me after the evening meal. This will be your *punishment* for fighting on the field today – you boys are to come to my office with cleaning supplies – and those bags of stones – and tidy things up in here for a few days. You girls shall volunteer to help as well," he replied.

Aonghus grinned and said, "Right!"

"May I keep this bag of stones here and study them further?" asked the professor.

They trusted him instinctively, such was his noble bearing, and so they immediately agreed.

"I have also decided that I am granting all of you – and your sister Colleen – scholarships to my school. Rufus Buttersmouth will not be paying an English penny for your tuition or room and board," he added. "I shall also see to it that your travel expenses here and on the way home are taken care of."

"Professor, are you serious?" asked Aonghus.

"Entirely serious, son," he replied. "You do not realize yet what this means, and perhaps I do not either. But we must make plans to go to Ireland immediately, just as soon as your sister and Frederick arrive."

"But why?" asked Abbe. "We just got here!"

"Let me show you something," he said, and he walked over to the wall behind him, removed a brick of white stone from a shelf, and placed it on his desk next to the pile of stones that he had taken from the bag.

"Look closely," he said to them, and they gathered around.

The carvings were nearly identical.

"Where did you get that from?" asked Bib. "Did that come from our farm?"

"No," he replied.

"But those runes look almost exactly the same as the ones on our stones," she said.

"Yes," replied the professor. "It has been handed down through many generations in my family."

"But where did it come from?" asked Abbe.

"You would not believe me if I told you," he replied.

He paused, considering, and then continued. "But let me say this – these stones may well represent the most important archaeological discovery made on this planet in a thousand years."

Chapter 3 – The Lady Danu

Colleen rubbed her eyes for the hundredth time and urged Badger forward. Slowly, he walked toward the lake edge, but before they reached it, a new sound reached her ears. Someone *else* was singing too.

It was a sweet voice. *No, more than sweet*, thought Colleen. Words escaped her to describe its beauty, even to herself. It was a voice beyond a voice. Powerful as a raging river, subtle as a falling feather, deep as an ocean, high as the sky, rooted as a mountain, but also sweet as honey and gentle as a breeze.

As soon as they heard the song, they were all instantly awake, and no trace of drowsiness remained, and as they listened, their minds grew sharp, and their bodies felt rested.

In that moment, Colleen felt as though she had been awakened from some long winter's night and would never need to sleep again.

The voice sang in a language that she did not understand with her ears, but in her heart and mind, it became clear as crystal. When she would later try to recall it and put words to it, she would shake her head and be silent – such was the power of its memory.

Colleen and Frederick jumped down from the wagon and led Badger to the lake's edge. It was a crystal blue, bluer than the sky, and into its pure depths they gazed. Its center ran deep – too deep to see any bottom at all, and it fell away into a blue infinity that stretched beyond their vision.

Frederick pulled his cloak around himself as they neared the water, and he grabbed his arm as if a sudden pain shot through it.

The grass all around the lakeside was a brilliant green with many wildflowers merrily swaying in the breeze. Flocks of birds danced in the sky above, playfully soaring about, and their dance seemed to be to the song that spread itself out over the lake.

Then, all at once, they saw her. Sitting gracefully by the lake on a large rock was a lady dressed all in white, and she was singing.

She sat there on the horizon of the world where the land met the sky, but she seemed to be of neither land nor sky. She was, like her song, totally *other* than both, yet of them both.

She saw them, and without pausing in her song, reached down and cupped water in her hands. It trickled playfully between her fingers, sparkling in the bright sun, as it touched the surface of the water again. Its sound added to her music, and together they seemed like some mystical orchestra that had played for all eternity.

Then the lady paused in her song, although it seemed to still echo across and around and through the lake. She scooped water in her hands and drank, then smiled a deep, satisfied smile. Dipping in her hands again, she made a gesture of welcome that seemed to embrace not only the little group of travelers, but the whole land around them. To the grass and flowers and trees, and to all that would heed her invitation, she offered a drink.

Again, she sang, and in the depths of that song, they heard words of beckoning, "*Come, taste and see...*"

The words that followed struck some chord in their hearts, raising them to the song's eternal heights and fathomless depths. All fear, and even memory of fear of goblins and witches and the sleeping forest and its shadows, was washed from their minds as they went forward to the water. It seemed as though the very grass and flowers around the lake were singing as well, inviting the visitors to come.

Then they noticed that little by little, curious faces were emerging from behind the trees of the sleeping forest and were shyly creeping down to the water's edge to heed the singer's invitation.

Colleen and Frederick carefully put the little people down, and Oracle climbed over the side and slid down the wagon's wheel, tumbling head over heels in the bright grass and lay there.

All but Oracle and Frederick went to the water's edge, knelt, and lifted a handful of water to their lips. Even Badger bent his head and drank deeply. All around the lake now, the animals of the wood were gathered - foxes and rabbits and squirrels, birds and mice, and none feared the other, none pursued the other. All seemed to be joining in the song and drinking from the lake.

As Colleen drank, the water's cool sweetness flowed within her, and she knew that she would never be the same again. No earthly water would ever satisfy her, she knew, for she had tasted something that seemed heavenly, and she felt as though she could stay there by that lake forever. Deeply she drank from the waters until she was refreshed beyond her mind's and body's ability to comprehend. She looked at the little people, and their faces seemed aglow with joy and peace.

Gnomes danced, leprechauns twirled, and pixies flew high in the air, then low over the lake and back to shore again, and the light of their bodies seemed intensified to a piercing brightness. It was as if they were all sharing a dream, but it was realer than anything she had ever experienced.

"Colligal shines!" said Oracle with a gleeful grin, peeking over the grass.

"Frederick, you've got to taste this water!" she called.

He was watching them all, seeing the delight on their faces, and wondering if he ought to try it.

"I don't know..." he replied. "It's terribly bright, and, well, my arm is aching in this light. And the lady, she is ..."

But he fell silent and shaded his eyes, for now she approached them, and her flowing dress was radiant in the sun. She was tall and stately, and her graceful stride spoke of royalty. Her white limbs were perfect, her back so straight, her form lovely beyond measure, her hair golden beyond gold, her lips redder than the reddest rose. She seemed neither young nor old, but simply ageless. There was wisdom and restfulness in her eyes, and yet, beyond all of this, it seemed to Colleen that she bore a hidden power that also made her seem, almost, *worshipful.*

"*No, not that,*" said a thought that seemed to come from the lady herself.

"*Then, venerable,*" Colleen said to herself.

When the lady reached them, she paused in her song and spoke. "Welcome, friends," she said. "I am the Lady Danu. I see that you have traveled far and through many dangers. Stay for a time and you will find rest. No dangers from the sleepy wood can touch you here, and no goblin dares approach these waters."

Frederick stared at the Lady, his mouth wide open, and she smiled at him. He realized that he must look foolish, so he closed his mouth, blinked several times, and then said, "Who *are* you?"

She laughed a joyous laugh, and it seemed as though all the lake sparkled with a million shafts of light at its pure sound. "Why, dear Frederick," she said. "I have told you, I am the Lady Danu. I have other names as well, although I would tire you in the telling of them all. This is my home, and you are welcome to share it with me for a time."

"How... how do you... know my name?" he stammered.

"Why, you are as clear to me as the waters of the lake are clear, although there is a shadow on you," she replied. "Won't you come? Taste and see that it is good! Do you not see how Colleen shines?"

Frederick looked at Colleen and, to his amazement, she did indeed seem to be *radiant* somehow, like the Lady, yet far less so. In fact, all around them, the land and the little creatures seemed to possess that same radiance.

Frederick slipped his arm from beneath his cloak for a moment and looked at it. Immediately, it burned as though he had gotten too near to a bonfire. He flinched and hid it again.

The Lady saw this and said, “Ah, and I see that you bear a wound, young one. We shall speak of it later. But I ask again, will you not drink?”

“I... I don't feel... I mean, just the light of it hurts my arm. I'm afraid to touch it,” he admitted, ashamed.

“Ah, that is the way of it, child. These waters can either burn or brighten, blind or illumine, bring distress or comfort, hurt or heal. One could say that they show you just what you already are, deep down inside. That is their magic. But if you would chance this fire, it may burn away this hurt you have taken. Did you not try your own fire to staunch this wound, and it did not avail you?”

Frederick remembered the red-hot knife he had used to cauterize the wounds. He stared at the shining lake. But to him, it was like staring at a full moon on a clear night. It was too much, and it hurt his eyes. A part of him wanted to run forward and leap into its magical blue depths. But the more he thought of it, the more the ache in his arm throbbed and spread. It seemed to be moving upward now, toward his neck. He was about to say something more when a little voice broke the silence.

“My Lady,” said Colleen, “how is it that everything is so *alive* here, when the forest is so dead?”

Again, she laughed and said, “Ah, the old Court Witch has no power here. Her spells of gloom and sleepiness cannot overcome my song, nor the light of the waters. She has tried many times, but the magic here is far deeper than hers, and is beyond the knowledge of those that use her.”

She paused, smiling at them, and said, “Come with me, dear ones, let me show you something. But first, untie your horse and let him graze.”

Colleen unhooked Badger from the wagon, and he contentedly began to munch on the sweet grass by the lake.

It was then that Oracle popped his head out of the grass and shyly grinned at the Lady. She noticed him then, and a look of surprise and joy swept over her face. She curtsied to him, and some unheard communication passed between them as their eyes met again, for she nodded and said, "Welcome, good sir, to the Lake. Please, grace my home by drinking of these waters and refreshing yourself."

Oracle rose from the grass, picked up his cane, hobbled over to the shore, and took a long draught of the shining waters. He smiled broadly and said, "Ahhhh!" very loudly, then danced a little jig.

"He's a bit like that, you know," said Frederick to the Lady.

"Yes," she replied, "but do not judge by mere appearances."

She stared at Oracle for a few moments and then spoke again.

"But, come, follow me. And the invitation stands, Frederick. Taste and see..."

Frederick picked up the Wigglepox family with his good hand and put them in his pocket. The Lady turned and led them up a hill that looked over the lake. Its top reached just above the highest trees, so that they could see the vast brown expanse of the forest stretching out before them.

"Look around us," said the Lady as they reached the summit. "It would seem that the whole world is under the spell of the Court Witch. See, the forest sleeps, and many of its creatures have become her spies. Your coming to the Lake is known to them, so they strengthened the Spell against you. It may be that if you, Colleen, had not sung and the power within you had not fought against her, you would now be in her hands, captured by her dark servants."

"So that's why we were so sleepy," said Frederick.

"Yes," the Lady replied. "You were in grave danger."

"But how could I, just singing, make any difference?" Colleen asked. "And besides, the others sang too, even Oracle."

The Lady Danu gazed at her intently for a moment, and her eyes seemed to see right into Colleen's mind and soul, even beyond them to see in a moment's time her entire life.

"I see that you have not yet learned of your destiny, nor of your history, Colleen. The future is always dim to we who are created, but history, and the present – that can be looked into, at least a bit. I can tell you that your coming here was no accident, and you have great deeds to accomplish before your journey ends," replied the Lady. "You have many songs yet to sing. Is it not true that you can sing the songs of all things that you are near?"

"I'm not sure what you mean, Lady Danu," she said.

The Lady extended her arm and, with a sweeping motion, indicated the brown forest. To the north, east, and west, the trees stretched to the horizon, brown and dead, and to the south, it spread out for many miles until it reached long, high hills.

"All this lies under the Witch's spell, my friends. Yet each of you possesses power to fight that spell. Not the whole thing, of course, not yet, at least. But for yourselves and those around you, a song of hope will wake the sleeper. But come, let us sit and eat together. I see that you are hungry, although the waters of the lake have refreshed you."

The Lady Danu waved a hand, and they looked in the direction in which she pointed. There, a short distance away, were a number of large stones that were set deeply into the hill so that only their surface showed, and in the middle of these was a large circular stone, also set deeply in the ground, so that the entire arrangement appeared to be a round stone pavement surrounded by a dozen round stepping stones.

The Lady seated herself on one of the smaller stones and invited the others to do the same, and when they were all seated, with the Wigglepoxes all sitting together, she began another song.

It was a song of thanksgiving, and its sweetness filled their minds with a profound sense of gratitude for all that was.

As the song ended, Lily gave a squeal of delight, for up the hill, on all sides, were coming scores of little people. There were gnomes and leprechauns and sprites and fairies, and folk of every sort, many the size of little Rose, but some at least a foot tall, and some as tiny as dandelion seeds when they fly in the breeze. Most dressed in green or brown or red, but some of the fairies were dressed in gossamer of gold or silver or white.

Colleen and Frederick gaped wide-eyed at the sight. Up and over the hilltop they came, hundreds of them, gathering around the table and darting here and there in the air.

Soon the whole hilltop was filled, and when everyone was quiet, the Lady Danu spoke.

"I see that we are all here," she said, and then she looked at Colleen and Frederick.

"These are the remnants of the little people who have fled the Sleeping Wood and come to me for protection. So few, so few!" she sighed.

"My songs and the waters of the Lake keep them safe and hidden here where the eyes of the Court Witch and the Goblin King cannot yet see. But look! All around us, the great Sleep has taken hold. Here alone, and in a few hardy trees where the little people yet dwell, is there yet wakefulness," she said.

"Do you mean that these are the only people left in the whole world who are free from the power of the Witch, besides those few with Cian?" asked Colleen.

"Cian!" she said with surprise. "So, you have met him? That is good. I have not spoken with him for some time, although I hear that he is well. But, no, these are not *all*. As I said, there are a few others, like Mrs. Wigglepox and her daughters, who fight on," replied the Lady.

"Is the Witch that powerful?" asked Frederick. "Isn't there anyone who can fight her?"

The Lady smiled at him and said, "Oh, yes, Frederick. Everyone can fight her. But her greatest power, unless you should meet her yourself, is this Sleep that she has cast across the land. It is not only a drowsiness of the body, but of the heart as well. Once, the spirits of the trees here were lively and strong and true, but she has lulled them into forgetfulness and inactivity, and they have nearly all truly fallen asleep. Intertwined within the Spell, she spreads the fear of the Gray Man, and this gives it strength. She can be fought, though. We all here fight against her spells. We sing, and our song is something that she has no power over, nor can she overcome the light in the Lake, and she fears it, lest it one day overflow its banks, flow into the forest, and awaken it. She knows then that the spirits that dwell there would awaken, and their wrath would be great!"

"*Spirits*?" asked Colleen. "Are there actually ghosts or something living in the woods?"

"I will tell you the *Tale of Beginnings,*" said the Lady, "But first, we must eat together."

She waved her hand over the round stone pavement before them and, with a flash, there appeared dozens of dishes spread out before them. Some were tiny, just the right size for the little people and others were large enough for the children. All were filled with fruits and vegetables and breads and muffins of all sorts. Glasses and pitchers of many colors and shapes were there as well, and delicious smells rose from steaming pots and bowls. A cheer went up from the little people, and they all came forward, helping each other load their tiny plates with every sort of good thing.

"Help yourselves, my young friends," said the Lady, and Colleen and Frederick gladly took plates and filled them with every sort of dainty that was there.

"*Today we feast in the midst of a sleeping world*," sang the Lady, "*and tonight we rest with the restfulness of the Waters of Light. But, tomorrow we begin a new thing.*"

Colleen had never tasted such delicious food before, nor drunk such sumptuous drinks. There was nothing that tasted bad, even in the slightest, although all was different. She ate her fill and felt completely satisfied, although not stuffed, as did all the little people that had come for the feast.

But she noticed that Frederick only nibbled at his food.

"What's wrong, Frederick?" she asked. "Don't you like the food?"

He paused and said, "Well, it's not *bad*, exactly. It's just that my throat kind of hurts when I swallow it."

He turned to look at her, and she noticed that the gray color and black spider veins were now creeping across his neck.

"Are you all right?" she asked.

He nodded, pulling his cloak closer about him. But Colleen felt a growing concern for him. His mood was all wrong for this happy place, and while everyone else danced about or lay in the sunshine, Frederick kept his hood pulled over his face, and kept glancing toward the shadows of the trees.

Mrs. Wigglepox talked happily to the other little people, and Lily and Rose ran here and there on the hill with the many little children who had come. Pure delight was in their eyes to find so many of their own people alive and living so well in the care of the Lady Danu.

Colleen and Frederick talked with many of the little people, who were quite curious about them, for most of them had never seen a human before, and they were amazed at their size. Many of the children of the little people came up to them shyly and asked permission to touch them, just to be sure they were real. And when

Colleen offered to lift some of them in the air, they were delighted, and laughed as she gently lifted them up and held them high.

Then a shining pixie flew to Colleen and introduced herself.

“My name is Alephria,” she said.

“Pleased to meet you,” she replied.

The pixie curtsied in the air, sparkled, twirled about laughing, and then vanished.

Colleen looked about, wondering where she had gone, but the Lady turned around and gazed out over the lake. The others followed her gaze, and there, right in the lake's center, a bright pink twinkle appeared, and Alephria's high laugh rang out over the waters. Again, she vanished and reappeared right on top of Frederick's head.

For a moment, he was startled, but then managed a laugh that sounded more like a snort.

“You can disappear!” he said.

“It is because the Witch has no power here,” she said with glee. “See!”

She vanished again, then reappeared, and all of the other pixies began to flit about the shores of the lake.

“I am Meadow,” said a green one and, all around Frederick's feet, flowers burst into bloom. She called to the trees around the lake, and they answered her by shaking and twirling their branches until she quieted them.

“And I'm Leleuma,” said another, who shone a bright blue.

She swept across the lake, raising a high wave that took the shape of a powerful stallion that galloped across the surface of the waters, and then sent it splashing down again, sending ripples across the surface. On the lake's shore, Badger neighed and kicked at the air with his front hooves.

Then all three of the pixies flew high above their heads, and fairy dust rained down upon them like fine gold. As it landed on them, it seemed not to settle *on* them, but *into* them.

“Strange things can happen to people who are sprinkled with fairy dust,” said the Lady Danu. “And few have had the blessing of three so notable fairies at once. Beware, my friends, for you may find yourselves awakening to your true selves after today!”

Then, a fat gnome strode forward and bowed to Colleen and Frederick and all around him. “I am Earwin,” he said. “I can hear the stories of the earth.”

And Earwin put his ear down to the ground and just listened, a look of deep satisfaction filling his face. “The land speaks to me here,” he said. “It says that no goblin's feet have soiled this place.”

He then took a handful of the earth and tossed it in the air at the feet of Colleen and Frederick.

“May the blessing of the earth be upon you,” he said. “Now quiet your heart and listen – what do you hear?”

Both of the children got down on the ground and pressed their ears to the ground. At first, they heard nothing, but then a quiet murmur came to them. It was a sound of flowing water, of stretching roots, and the odd sounds of shifting rock far below.

Frederick shut his eyes and listened deeper, further.

“I hear...” He paused, listening, and then it was as if something gripped his mind, and he heard himself saying, “I hear far, far away, the sounds of hammers and shovels and picks ringing beneath the ground in vast tunnels that stretch to untold depths and there is much sighing and many tears amid deep pits.”

He shivered and looked around, embarrassed.

They all stared at him and, after a moment, Earwin said, "Few can hear so far, Frederick. You have heard the echoes of the pits of the Goblin King far, far to the South in the midst of the sea."

For the first time since they had arrived, Colleen's heart grew heavy as she remembered her mother. She bowed her head and a tear trickled down her cheek.

The Lady knelt next to her and put her hand on her shoulder. Frederick watched with amazement as the light of the Lady seemed to flow into Colleen through that touch until she shone with the same radiance.

"There is yet hope, Colleen," she said. "There is hope for her and for all who are bound in the Witch's dungeons and pits. As long as you are here and are free, there is hope that you will rescue them."

"But what can I do?" she said. "Couldn't you free them? You seem to have power that the Court Witch can't overcome. Won't you come with us and help us?"

The Lady looked sad and said, "Alas, child, I cannot. Here there are unspoiled waters that hold hope for this world. If I should leave them, the Witch may indeed find a way to darken them, and through them to spoil other lands. I guard not only this place – this last refuge from her dominion. I guard other lands as well from all who would spoil what is good and right. I cannot leave that charge."

She paused then, looking intently at the two children. After a moment, Frederick spoke.

"Lady," he said. "It seems as though everyone here has some gift – some power within them to use against this Witch. But I have nothing. I'm just a boy. I can't sing like Colleen and I can't do anything like these marvelous pixies and such. What use am I? Especially with this..."

He threw back his cloak, and a murmur of shock and amazement ran through all the little people as they saw his arm and hand and neck, now a mottled gray-green. A searing pain shot through him, and he quickly pulled his cloak back, hiding his infected flesh from the light of the Lake.

"You too are here for a reason, Frederick. There is some great part that you must play before the end," she said. "I cannot see all ends, but I foresee that some great struggle lies before you, and in you, but beyond that, I cannot see."

Frederick looked down, feeling small and sad. And then a thought struck him.

"What about Dvalenn?" he said.

"Yes!" said Colleen. "I almost forgot about him. He's still sleeping in the cart!"

"Dvalenn sleeps hard under the Witch's spell, children. It will be no easy task to awake him. I shall take him tonight to a place where he may choose to fully wake. But for now, we shall hear the tale I spoke of!"

Excitedly the little people all gathered around the Lady and grew silent, and Colleen and Frederick seated themselves to listen as well. Oracle sat down at her feet and looked up into her lovely face.

Then the Lady began the tale. It was not a song, so much as a chant, of sorts, and its words Colleen would never forget, for they seemed to be carved into her memory by the powerful voice of the chanter.

"In times of old, 'ere worlds were born,
'Ere stars did shine, before first morn,
Songs did rise in heaven's halls,
And waters flowed from hallowed falls.
The sacred sea did rise and shine
With Wind and Light of kind divine.
The Wind did blow, the Light did blaze,
And from that Sea leapt many Waves.
With voice and praise they leaped and then
Returned into the Sea again.
But some did venture from that Sea,

Lifted by the Wind to be
Eternal voices fair and strong,
To sing forever heaven's song.
And in those halls, before that Sea,
What ages passed, what came to be,
Only rumor now can tell,
Whispers of those who know so well.
But for a cause the gates spread wide,
And the Sea gushed forth, a thunderous tide.
A River of Fire flowed from the throne
And rushed in mighty currents of foam.
Into the Deep, like brilliant falls,
Spilled forth the waters from heaven's halls.
And falling into that Chasm far,
Dispersed and spread, a mist of stars.
Yet still within that sea remained
Those who had fallen back again.
With the stars they were swept along,
And in that dew 'twas heard heaven song.
For they once again were given voice,
To sing and praise fair heaven's choice.
But those who were outside the Sea,
Watched, and the River of Fire did see.
And they were told to guide each star,
Lest they disperse into the Deep too far;
To bring them back into their course
Where the River of Fire flowed from its Source.
But one who came was strange and bold,
One who had leaped from the Sea of old.
Not back again to the River of Fire,
But to himself was his desire -
To sway the stars not to their Source,
But to a place that was his course.
And so he wove the storied lie
That all the stars, and themselves, would die
If they 'ere should ever flow
Back to the River's fiery glow.
"Not back to heaven's placid Sea!

Into the Deep, come follow me!"
And with such speech, he swayed a third
Of the hosts with his convincing word.
And so the Kingdom rent and tore,
And evil came to Time's fair shore.
But soon not only stars did shine,
For new worlds the Maker did design.
And so He made the Spheres, and then
Those spirits of fire entered in.
And finding mount or meadow or tree
Took them as their house to be.
Dwelling there and clothed therewith,
Became the stuff of legend and myth.
And other folk He then did make
And gave them power their worlds to shape.
Yet 'ere did the Dark One go
And seek to spread his dread and woe.
Yet to each world the Light gave Light
To shine however dark the Night.
And to give them hope when shadows fell
He gave the Lady of the Lake to dwell
In every world of trial and test,
To bring the Waters that give them rest.
To stay the Night that comes too soon,
And tell them of the Light Triune.

The song ended and all those that heard it sat in silence and awe, its memory echoing, as it were, in their minds and hearts, bringing strange thoughts of ages long past.

At length, the Lady spoke again. "So, do you see, children, where the spirits of the Forest come from? They are ancient – more ancient than this land – and, they came to it long, long ago 'ere even the little people were born under the Waking Tree. They are mostly sleeping now, lulled to slumber by the Court Witch."

"She must be terribly powerful," said Frederick.

"Yes, she is," said the Lady, "but her power is not all her own. She is but the vessel of one darker than herself, and it is that one's power that she wields, although she believes it not. For long ago, she gave herself over to the Great Darkness, and it entered into her. She is but its channel.

"You must be wary of her, my friends. Her magic is great, and she can do you great harm. But her tongue is her fiercest weapon, and she will seek to sway you to join her before she seeks to destroy you. She seeks to pervert all good folk, just as she has done to many of the little people."

"I simply do not understand how any of the little people could follow her," said Mrs. Wigglepox.

"You have never met her, good lady," she replied. "Although I foresee that that day will come all too soon, and you will be tried. But yes, there are those even of the little people whose hearts have been darkened through her deceits, and they walk among your people, seeming to be free, but are her secret servants."

At this, a murmur went among the little people, and they glanced around, doubt sweeping across them like a troubled wind.

"Do not fear!" said the Lady. "There are none here who have tasted of the Waters of the Lake who are under her spell, for these are the Waters of Light, filled with a virtue that breaks all spells of darkness. None who taste of them can be forced to do her bidding, although they still may *choose* to do so."

"I wonder," whispered Frederick to Colleen, "if there are any here who have *not* drunk from the Lake, or might really be on her side anyway. *They* might be here as spies."

Even as his said it, Frederick saw Oracle turn his head and look to the wood, and there he thought he saw a small group of little people slip down the hill and into the trees. He stood up and peered down the hill where they had gone, but they were nowhere to be seen.

"What is it, Frederick?" asked Mrs. Wigglepox.

“I thought I saw... well, maybe it was nothing,” he replied.

But the Lady Danu was also gazing into the forest where they had gone and looked sad. “Beware, young people. Not all hearts are pure, and even your own will be tested,” she said.

For some time, the gathering of people talked with the Lady Danu and with each other until the sun began to set low in the west and the assembly began to disperse. At last, only Colleen and Frederick and the Wigglepox family were left alone with the Lady. Even Oracle had wandered off, following a group of leprechauns that had gone off toward a large tree.

“Now,” said the Lady, “we must try to wake Dvalenn.”

She rose, and they followed her down the hill and to the wagon. She gazed down at the dwarf, who snored contentedly beneath the dusk sky.

“That's the most peaceful I've seen him,” said Frederick.

“I must take him into the Lake,” she said. “There, he must make a choice regarding his fate.”

She lifted him from the wagon and held him effortlessly like a child, then walked back into the lake until the water was up to her waist.

Looking down at the sleeping dwarf, she said, “Hear me, Dvalenn. Your long night is ending. I give you a choice. You may choose to stay forever in your troubled sleep, or awake to the light, and come to the end of your days.”

Dvalenn's eyes remained closed, but in a weak voice he croaked, “Waken me, my Lady. I cannot bear this dark night of my senses any longer. Waken me, oh Lady! Waken me!”

“Then first, you must wash away the Spell in these waters, for their light will drive away the dark night of sleepiness,” she replied.

"Dwarves don't care much for water, Lady. I might die beneath these waters," he said.

"Yes, so you shall. Still, you must if you wish to fully awake," she replied.

He was silent for a moment and then said, "Then take me."

She nodded to him and carried him into the deep water. The waves of the Lake began to rise, and as they went in deeper, three times the waves swept over their heads, and on the last wave they heard the Lady say, "Rest friends. I shall see you again soon." Then the water completely covered them, and they were lost from view.

When Dvalenn and the Lady did not return that night, Colleen and the Wigglepox family slept by the shores of the Lake. Frederick, however, climbed into the wagon and curled up in the hay.

"I wonder where they went," said Colleen to Mrs. Wigglepox.

"Well, she said that this is not the only land that she cares for," she replied. "I think that the goblins are her great enemy, and wherever they seek to spread their dark domain, she is there to oppose them. Perhaps she took Dvalenn to a different land. I wonder if we will ever see him again."

That night, the sky was brilliantly clear, with so many stars that Colleen lay on her back in the sweet smelling grass, just gazing upward for long hours. The lake glowed with a white-blue light that often drew her eyes into its depths, and both lake and sky somehow seemed equally deep and compelling, each filled with mystery and wonder, and holding secrets that she could only imagine.

* * *

But Frederick lay wrapped in his cloak, and muttered to himself, "The stars are strange here. I don't see any of the constellations."

He gazed into the unfamiliar sky for some hours, thinking of all that had happened to him. Not so long ago, he would have called anyone who believed in goblins and dwarves and little people foolish – something his father had passed along to him. To believe in superstitions was beneath the educated person, his father had said.

Frederick snorted. *How ironic*, he thought. *Now I'm becoming a superstition.*

Would his family know him when he got home? Would they still accept him as their son with this Goblin Phage coursing through his veins, changing him into something unrecognizable – something inhuman?

He held his infected hand up to the stars. His knuckles were bulging, and his fingernails were growing long and pointed. He made a fist, then spread his fingers wide. There was an odd sensation of physical strength in that hand that he had never felt before. Something about it had a whispering appeal – a subtle temptation seemed to be rising within him to embrace this thing that was changing him. But it also felt *alien*, not entirely his own – as if some part of him were slowly coming into contact with, or was becoming, something totally foreign to his own humanness.

After some time, he fell asleep and dreamed that he was in a great battle. Goblins surrounded him, biting him again and again, and as hard as he tried, he could not run away, for his feet had turned into goblin feet. He wallowed in some sticky muck that threatened to pull him down into its reeking depths. But just beyond the muck was a shining lake, and a voice kept calling to him to try harder and run to the lake, to dive in and escape from the goblins.

He woke once, covered in sweat, and found that the left side of his face felt hot and burned. He pulled his hood up to cover it, and it immediately felt cooler. Then he drifted off into a fitful slumber. But in the early hours of the morning, one more dream came to him, clear and full of purpose.

* * *

On the shore of the Lake, Colleen and the little people slept peacefully through the night, also dreaming of many things.

Chapter 4 – The Dismal Bog

For several days, Adol had found signs that someone, or something, was coming and going from Grandpa McLochlan's house, and the trail always led south, toward the Dismal Bog.

He had tried setting animal traps, but none of these were ever sprung, so on the third day, he decided it was time to do some tracking.

Taking a knife, his club, and a pack of supplies, he headed out of the house and across the farm, following the signs left by the visitor – a broken stick here, matted grass there, and occasionally some sort of dark, oily film that stank.

He reached the wall of white and gray stones that bordered the bog, sighed, and climbed up to the top and sat down. Immediately, the smell of rotted vegetation hit him, and the great field of misshapen trees and vines, hanging moss, and wisps of fog lay before him. For nearly a mile, this tangle spilled southward, and from there, a dank leech-filled stream flowed, along whose banks angry insects buzzed, and strange worms dug in the fouled banks. He wondered why this place was even called a bog – it was more of a swamp.

He had been in here on numerous occasions, but always a feeling of uneasiness accompanied such ventures. It was as though there was a *presence* here – a spirit of malice that strove against all that was free and living. It bent its will against them, but drew kindred evil to itself. Over the years, there had been many tales of thieves and robbers and lawless people hiding out in this place. Adol had twice led the authorities through its strange depths to root out escaped criminals. He turned his head to his farm and breathed deeply once, and then climbed down the wall into the bog below.

There was no clear trail apparent, but still, signs of something passing were there. What was worse, as he slowly made his way toward the center of the bog, there were small pools of a black oily skim that covered patches of the already dark waters.

For an hour, he moved silently through the twisted shadows, trudging through thick muck and only occasionally finding solid ground on which to stand. His boots were heavy with mud and rotting weeds, and his nostrils were full of the dank smell that never left the fetid air. At last, he came to the place he was seeking – a place he had been only once before – the place his son Bran had mentioned when they were on the Hill. It was here that he suspected the black creature came – a place fitting for such a thing.

Up a small incline he trudged, thankful for at least some solid ground under his feet. And yes, there were the signs of the thing's passage. In fact, there were so many obvious footprints and trampled grasses that there was no doubt – this seemed to be where it had made its lair.

Adol circled a pile of broken rock that he thought must have at one time been a wall. The huge stones were stained with ages of lichen and moss and vine growth, but there was one place in particular for which he was searching. He knew it was here somewhere, for he had seen it once before when he was a youth.

Then he found it – three blocks as tall as himself, cut as perfect cubes and inscribed with many runes, and beneath them was a hole that led down into darkness.

The memory of this place came rushing back. He had slipped down into this dark pit those many years ago. He had been hunting in the wood east of the bog, and it had been growing dark, when a deer leaped across the trail in front of him. It had been covered with sweat, its mouth was lathered with foam, and the coppery smell of fear filled the air. It was gone in an instant, but behind it, bounded a huge dog. It had to have been a dog – wolves in Ireland had supposedly disappeared half a century before. But it was close on the heels of the deer.

He had followed the chase into the bog, and the deer fell. It had been too dark for him to see clearly, but he knew the dog had killed it and dragged it away – to this very place – to this very hole in the ground.

He had lit a torch and gone into the pit, and found it to be more than a pit. A broken staircase led downward, and the most intense sense of dread that he had ever experienced flooded his soul. Yet, down he had gone until he came to a dark hall, and from there to a closed and locked stone double door. A bottom portion of one of the doors had been broken, leaving a hole large enough for the dog to drag the deer through, but too small for him to enter.

He had shoved the torch into the hole and looked in, but could see nothing but something huge and shiny – like a wall of black tiles, but nothing more.

It was beyond those doors that lay the source of that dread that was growing in his mind and soul by the second. It was not the dog – he had no fear of that. There was something else here, something beyond his experience or imagination, something that desired nothing but to *consume.* And it was famished. He could put no other words to that feeling.

He had backed away, and when he had climbed out of that pit, he had run. He had run through the bog and climbed the wall and tumbled down into the farm, breathing deeply and basking in the freedom from the oppressiveness that had pursued him out of that place.

But here he was again, over twenty years later, and he did not want to go down there again. Something terrible was down there – something, he believed, that was the cause of the bog's very existence. Something that lay trapped and hidden from long, long ago, which must never be released. And, he thought, this black-robed thing had been living down there. It had been drawn to this place, and here would be his best chance of catching it. He did not know if the creature was in its lair or not, so he moved from the hill to a grove of twisted trees where he could watch the entrance but be out of sight, and there he sat down and waited.

He did not have to wait long, for very soon, a black-cloaked figure slunk up the hill. It paused briefly at the entrance to the pit, pulled a small shiny crystal ball from its cloak, held it up to the setting sun, cackled madly, and then slunk down into the pit.

Adol was tempted to go after it then and there, or to move a great boulder over the hole and trap it, but he was not sure what lay beyond the broken door where he had been those years ago. He would bide his time. Now he knew for sure that the creature was here. Rising from his hiding place, he silently slipped away, back toward the farm.

As soon as he was well away from the hill, he picked up his pace. Back over the wall he went, breathed the good air of the farm, and then ran to Grandpa's hut. He hooked his club to his belt and went to the cellar.

There, next to one wall, was a huge, ornate mirror. Days before, he had discovered it, although how it had come to be in this cellar he could not say. He knew that it was more than simply a mirror, though, for the black creature had somehow opened a doorway *through* it to somewhere else, and had escaped capture. He would not allow that to happen again.

"*Can't leave this here*," he said to himself. "*At least now that thing won't be going anywhere that I can't follow.*"

Picking up the mirror, he carried it across the fields and back to the farmhouse. He took it down the basement, threw several old blankets over it, and then proceeded to pile things in front of it, hiding it from view.

Then back upstairs he went, and locked the cellar door, putting the key in his pocket.

"*Tomorrow the hunt begins,*" he said aloud, and went to the kitchen to make a pot of tea and think through his plans.

Hours later, in the dead of the night, Adol heard a distant scream outside, coming from the direction of Grandpa's hut. It made his skin crawl, but he smiled anyway, turned over, and fell asleep until morning.

Chapter 5 – Parting

Colleen awoke to the warm sun on her face. She sat up and looked around. Frederick was sitting in the shade under the wagon. His hood was pulled over his head. He looked up, saw her staring, and he waved his right hand at her.

"Have you been awake long?" she asked him.

"About an hour," he mumbled.

She stood and walked over to the lake and took a deep drink. It satisfied her right down to her bones and, when she was done, she cinched up her robe and put her feet in. The water was perfect, and soothed her feet like nothing she had ever felt. It seemed to sink into her somehow, satisfying and relaxing her, quieting her whole being. It was as though everything in her grew still and at ease.

"Come and join me, Frederick. Put your feet in the water," she called over her shoulder.

He considered the invitation for a moment, then shook his head.

"Colleen," said Frederick. "I had a dream last night."

Colleen left the water and walked over to him.

"I have to go, Colleen," he said sadly. "In my dream, the Lady told me so. She said that it was really important."

Colleen looked at him. She could not see his face, covered as it was with the hood.

"Look at me, Frederick," she said, but he did not raise his face.

"Frederick, are you all right?" she said.

Very slowly, he lifted his face, and with his right hand, he slid his hood back. She involuntarily gasped and stepped back, for his entire face was changed. It was gray and misshapen, his nose and ears had grown, and his hair was a mop of dark purple, almost black tangles. Quickly, he pulled the hood back and bent his head to his chest.

"She told me that my only hope was to plunge into the Lake, Colleen," he said. "She said it would burn away the Phage. But that I would have to go down deep into it if I wanted to be really healed – to dive all the way through – that I couldn't just splash around the edges and then leap out again. Only then would I come out healed. I'm scared, Colleen, really scared."

She sat down beside him and touched him on the shoulder.

"But you would be healed, right?" asked Colleen. "Why not do it? Don't you want to be healed?"

At first, he wanted to say yes, but then hesitated, and unconsciously scratched at his wounded arm. A strange reluctance came over him, as if a part of him wrestled with the idea of actually being free. Something nagged at his mind – a whisper that said he would lose out on something if he let this thing go. Why not let the Phage take its course? What *would* he become? Would he become a dark wizard with mysterious powers? The goblins supposedly possessed magic – would the Phage grant him that as well? Perhaps he would become a goblin leader. Fantasies of greatness and power whirled in his mind.

"Frederick?" said Colleen when he did not respond.

He blinked and shook his head, suddenly coming to himself. What had he been thinking? Where had those thoughts come from?

"Well, of course. Who wouldn't want to be rid of it?" he said.

He took a deep breath and continued. "But there's more. The lady said I won't be able to get back this way if I do this."

"Why not?" she said.

"I have to pass through the waters completely – all the way through the deepest and brightest part of it – only then will the Phage completely die. Only then will I be rid of it and it won't come back again, unless I allow it to. And Colleen – if I make it, I'll pass through to the other side," he replied.

"And what is on the other side?" she asked.

"Home, Colleen. Back to our world," he said.

"Home!" she whispered.

He nodded. "The Lady told me in my dream that she could send me back, and there, I was to find help."

Frederick expected Colleen to yell or cry or do something emotional, but instead, she only nodded her head and sighed.

"I'm scared too, Frederick," she said. "I don't want to go on alone, but I had a dream too. The Lady said you had to go, but that you could, perhaps, come back as soon as you did something really important."

"But maybe you could just stay here at the Lake until I get back, Colleen. It's safe here," he suggested.

"No, I can't. My mother is in danger – somehow, I know it. I've got to keep going. The Lady said I could go with you if I wanted. But I can't, Frederick, I just can't!"

She started to cry then, her tears streaming down her cheeks.

"Oh, Colleen, now don't do that." His own eyes blurred, and he hastily wiped them on his sleeve. "I'll be back, I promise, just as soon as I can. And I'll bring help if I can."

"But how? That goblin has the crystal ball, so you can't come through the mirror," said Colleen.

Just then, the Lady Danu appeared, rising out of the middle of the Lake and walking toward them. Her steps made neither splash nor ripple on its crystal blue surface, and she was carrying something long and wrapped in a golden cloth.

"Good morning, my young friends," she said, smiling. "Did you rest well?"

"Yes, Lady Danu," said Colleen, wiping her eyes.

"Perhaps you know what you must do next?" she asked.

"Yes, Lady," said Frederick. "Although I don't know how to do it."

"There is a way, dear Frederick," she said. "We will sit and talk while we eat breakfast."

She led them back up the hill to the stone slab where they had eaten the day before, and there, waiting for them, was a sumptuous meal all prepared. Many of the little people, including all of the Wigglepoxes and the gnomes, were already eating or were finishing their morning meal.

"Ah, the sleepyheads are awake at last," teased Mrs. Wigglepox when she saw them coming to the top of the rise. "We were all wondering if you were going to sleep forever. I've heard of such things, you know."

"Aye," said Humble the Gnome. "That's what happened to old Dvalenn."

"Yes," said Nemon. "And then there was that other tale of the young maiden who slept in the Wizard's castle for hundreds of years."

"I thought it was a thousand years. And what about..." began Zelo, but he was cut off when the Lady Danu laughed.

"Please, please, dear friends!" she said, smiling. "If we tell these good folk all the tales of the land, we shall be here for the rest of the year and into the next! Come now, let them eat in peace. Go and enjoy the sun and the lake for a time while I speak with them. There is little time before they depart, and some of you will be going with them."

“A grand idea!” said Rose, and they all danced away down the hill toward the lake.

The Lady watched after them until they were out of earshot, and then turned to face the children.

“Did Frederick tell you what he must do, Colleen, and why?” she asked.

Colleen looked at the ground and said sadly, “He said he has to go back home. He said that it's the only way he will be healed, and that he has something to do.”

“Indeed he does,” she replied. “I foresee that many dangers and adventures lie before him.”

She held out what she had been carrying, and Frederick took it from her and unwrapped the golden cloth. Inside was an ornate sheath for a sword and a gold and silver belt that was light as a feather. Frederick turned the sheath over and over, marveling at its intricately carved body, which was laced with gold and tiny gems.

“It's marvelous!” he said.

“But where is the sword that goes in it?” asked Colleen.

Frederick unbuckled the sword that hung at his side and handed it to Colleen. “I think you might need this,” he said, then buckled the empty sheath in its place.

Colleen took the sword without a word and fastened it around her own waist.

“But why an empty sword sheath?” asked Colleen.

The Lady held a finger to her lips and did not answer, but held out something else to Colleen. It was a white pouch with a silver drawstring that fit in the palm of her hand. Colleen took and opened it and removed its contents. Inside was a small crystal container in the shape of a pitcher, with a small, ornate lid. Even in the sunlight, they could see that it glowed with the same blue radiance of the Lake, only the glow seemed deeper somehow.

"In this container is water from the very source of the Lake, Colleen. It will cure many ills caused by the goblins and disperse every evil spell. Use it wisely and sparingly, and only at the greatest need. You will know when the time comes. Remember that it has the power to break every spell cast by the Witch and her minions, and to heal and give life."

She looked at her for a moment longer, as if considering something.

"Colleen, do you remember how the pixies, while here at the Lake, are able to call to the world around them? How Leleuma raised a stallion from the waves, and how Meadow caused the flowers to bloom? And all that the others did?" asked the Lady.

"Yes," she replied. "It was quite amazing!"

"I would like you to do something for me, Colleen. Look around. What do you see?" she asked.

"I see the sun shining on the lake. It's like a thousand pieces of light dancing in the wind," Colleen replied.

"Yes," she said. "The wind on the water is like a symphony. Every dancing ripple in the sunlight sings to me. It so reminds me of the First Day. Do you think you can sing with it?"

"Sing with it?" Colleen asked. "How would I do that?"

"Look and listen to the music all around you, child. A symphony surrounds us of all there is to see. The orchestra of nature plays unendingly. The whisper of the wind, the roar of the sea, the silence of a meadow, the songbird's harmony – yet so often, people fail to see its beauty and the truth it so clearly declares. It reflects the Maker himself, in a way. But also, in this land, there are many ancient spirits – in the trees, in the lake, in the rocks, in the mountains and meadows. As the tale that I sang to you tells, they came long, long ago when this world was young, and they are still here, although so many now slumber beneath the Spell. But you, Colleen, may be able to awaken them," she replied.

"Do you mean that I could make the water stir like Leleuma did?" she asked, amazed.

The Lady smiled. "There is more to you than you know," she said. "Was it not your song that got you here through the sleeping forest, even though the Spell is so terribly strong around this place? Come, now, listen to the music of the Lake and sing with it. Open your heart to what it says."

Colleen gazed out over the shining waters and tried hard to listen. Gradually, her mind grew quiet, and it seemed as though some great peace filled her. There were no thoughts at all in her mind, only the peace. In that moment, it seemed that all was at peace around the lake, although it was like an island in some great storm.

She sensed that all about the lake, the Spell of the Court Witch was at work, pressing its terrible weight upon the forest, causing the last vestiges of its strength to slip away into a fitful sleepiness, and a great weariness lay from horizon to horizon. But the lake stood free of it, a refuge and a fortress untouched by that weight, although the Spell strove against the lake like a raging sea against a lighthouse on a granite cliff.

Then it was as though she saw something more. It was only a glimpse, but just for a moment, she saw *deeper* than her eyes alone could see. Beyond the water, beyond the shoreline, beyond the trees, she saw... saw... But no, she could not describe it. No thought seemed fitting for it. It was something that she perceived, not with her physical senses, but with another sense, that, for a moment, awoke within her.

It was not the scores of little people that she glimpsed who lay sleeping amid fitful dreams beneath root and trunk in the dreadful night of the Spell. Nor was it the hidden spirits that dwelt in many of these things that now transfixed her, although she saw these too – those creatures of another time and place that had come to dwell within these things and made them their homes so long, long ago. No, this was even deeper than them, for it encompassed those spirits as well. It was like a song, although it was not with her ears that she was now hearing it. The forest sang it as well, and its part was deep and sad, and had sunken to a whisper, as though it longed to be released from its deepening slumber.

Now, she saw her own place in that song – the part that *she* was to sing in it. If she could just stay within that part, and seek nothing beyond it, desire no more than her given portion, and yet let none of her responsibility within it to slip, all would be well. She could see how the Spell strove against the Song and sought to dominate and control it. It was like a noise that rose to drown out the sweetness of the music so that none could hear it and would grow weary under its constant clatter.

Colleen tuned her heart to the music and began to sing. And as she sang, she saw those ancient powers stir and turn, as it were, toward her. The waves stirred on the Lake, and within them water sprites danced. The trees around the edge of the forest murmured and shook their branches, and she could see the dryads within them smiling. In the breeze, a voice whispered, blowing in mighty gusts through the grass and trees. It was a joyous wind, not a raging gale, and nothing was harmed by it.

Then she was aware of the Lady speaking to her, although her voice seemed almost distant. "Once, long ago, there were the Great Ones who were granted this gift. I believe that gift lives in you now. Yet there is even more to you than that... something..."

The Lady looked closely at Colleen, her face amazed. "There has only been one other..." she said, almost to herself. Then she continued, "Beware, Colleen, there are those who have corrupted their gifts into a desire for power and now use such gifts for their own ends."

Suddenly, the vision was gone, the wind subsided, the waves splashed back into the Lake, and all was calm. Colleen sat transfixed, keenly aware that she had just participated in something so incredibly *beyond* her, yet of which she was also a part.

After a few moments she said, "Is that what the wizards were - people with gifts that others do not have?"

"In a way," replied the Lady. "At first, they were all good and used their strengths for the bettering of the worlds and their peoples, but many were corrupted. The Court Witch is one such person. Something dreadful happened to her, and she has lost her place in the Great Song. It is a sad thing, for she was once a great singer."

She looked sorrowful for a moment and then said, "Remember, Colleen, use your gifts for good, and do not overstep your bounds. And your bounds appear to be quite large for one so young. I wonder what you will become when you are grown?"

The Lady looked curiously at her again, as if pondering some deep thing.

"But I still don't understand, Lady," replied Colleen. "Just what *is* my gift, and why do *I* have it?"

The Lady looked even more thoughtful for a moment before continuing.

"I cannot teach you all that you will need to know in one day. And you and I are not of the same kind. There are things about you that I do not know, nor ever will know. Only one of your own kind can truly teach you. All I can tell you is to keep your heart true wherever you go and whatever happens to you. That is the first step in becoming what you were made to be. Remember, child, others have been turned by the Witch and her spells, and much evil has come upon the world because of it. However, I can tell you this – to you has been granted to taste of the nature of other beings. What they sing, you can sing. You need only be near them to hear their song and learn it. Take care how you sing – you may find that strange things happen when you do. I believe this gift is awakening within you."

The Lady looked intently at both of the children for a long moment and then said, “It is time. Frederick. Are you ready?”

He gazed out across the lake and shivered. Then he looked at Colleen, remembering their plight.

“I suppose so,” he replied reluctantly. “But I really don't want to leave Colleen by herself.”

“She is *not* by herself, you silly goose,” said a small voice behind him.

They turned to see Lily standing with her hands on her hips, gazing up at him from the grass. Mrs. Wigglepox and Rose stood beside her, and behind them, Oracle grinned.

“We will be going with her,” she said.

“Well, now,” said the Lady. “Are you sure that you all wish to go with Colleen? It will be a dangerous journey, filled with hardship and loss. There is more for you to face, I think, even than the goblins and the Spell of the Witch.”

“That's why we're all going,” said Mrs. Wigglepox. “She's going to need us!”

“There will be one other who will go along as well, at least for a time, but I will speak of that later,” said the Lady.

Frederick smiled under his hood and said, “Well, I do feel much better knowing that you will have such good companions. But I promise, as soon as I am done what I have to do, I'll come back somehow if I can.”

“Come friends, gaze into my lake!” said the Lady. “Tell me what you see.” She waved her hand out over the lake, and it grew still. It was as though it went from a dancing lake surface to a perfect piece of glass.

Frederick turned to the lake and shielded his eyes with his good hand.

"Look!" he said. "There's something... something like a picture moving on the waters!"

Frederick and the Lady Danu leaned forward, as did Colleen, and the little people gathered at the edge of the lake, staring out onto its reflective surface.

"It seems to be changing," said Colleen. "Like it's shifting scenes or something."

Oracle stepped forward and began to chant, and for once, his voice and words were not garbled, but distinct and clear.

"Water of Light and fairy dust,
Into a crystal ball was thrust,
Suffused with magic from 'tween the lands,
Shaped of old by Dwarven hands.
Blessed by Elven magic bold,
Wished upon by Leople's gold.
Passed to Humans long ago,
And where it went, we do not know."

He ended his chant and stared at the mirrored lake and its shifting scenes with his big brown eyes. He looked, for the first time, deeply thoughtful rather than silly.

"Is that how it was made, Oracle?" asked Colleen. "The crystal ball, I mean?"

He turned and looked at her and said, "Colligal had it?"

"Yes, Oracle, I had it, but I did not know what it was. Now a goblin has it."

Oracle looked dismayed and turned back to stare at the waters.

The scene in the water shifted from a shining lake high in a mountain range, to an ornately carved stone pool filled with water. It shifted again, and there was a woodland lake near some large college or mansion, which somehow seemed familiar to Frederick. Again, it changed, and a shining pool shrouded in some heavy darkness in a dank cavern was pictured. Colleen shivered at the scene, and just before it changed again, she thought she had seen a pair of eyes staring out at her hungrily.

The next scene was that of a gigantic lake with an immense bridge over it. It seemed to stretch for many miles, but the bridge was crumbling and in disrepair. Again, the scene changed, and a lovely forest and wildflowers around a lake edge were pictured, and Colleen realized that it was the very place that they were sitting.

"Many doors open from this place," said the Lady. "The Witch would dearly love to seize it for herself. Frederick, you must choose one of these doors, and before the scene changes, you must step in. Are you ready to accept this task? You must find help and bring it back here."

Frederick took a deep breath and leaned closer. Again, the scene changed, and each time, there was a lake or some other body of water. Together, they watched as strange and wondrous and even frightening scenes shifted before them until there was a still lake reflecting a blue sky with white clouds. Maple and oak trees sat on the banks, their gnarled roots hanging low as if drinking from its cool waters.

Once again, the scene changed, and there was again an underground scene with a shining lake.

"That's the one," he said, and glancing once at Colleen, then at the Lady, who nodded to him.

He hesitated a moment, trembling. Then he threw back his hood and whipped the cloak over his back. His face was gray and distorted, with green blotches spreading over his cheeks and bulbous nose. He cried out in pain, and his very skin writhed as the light of the lake shone upon it. His heart pounded, and a great struggle seized his mind and body, as though his mind and passions violently fought against this mad action that he was about to undertake.

Then, something in his heart rose above his rebelling reason and burning flesh, and with one great cry, he ran toward the lake and, with all his might, dove in head first, swallowing mouthfuls as he plunged downward into the blue depths.

Colleen reached out for him for an instant, and then withdrew her hand as the vision in the lake swirled into three interlaced spirals. It seemed to her eyes that he was falling into the midst of them, down into a great depth. Then the image vanished, and only the infinite blue remained.

Frederick was gone.

Chapter 6 – The Sword in the Tree

Frederick dove into the water with one thought on his mind. "Wash it away! Wash it away and take me home!"

He fully expected the lake to burn him like fire – to sear his wounded flesh like the hot knife had done in Cian's cave. But to his utter astonishment, nothing of the kind happened. As he swallowed the cool water and felt it touch his infected skin, he felt not a fire, but both a warmth and a coolness at once sinking deep down, driving away the poison in his veins.

His face seemed to stretch and pull, as though something was peeling away from him. He looked over his shoulder, and for a moment, he saw a deformed and twisted shadow of a goblin writhing in the brightness. It reached out for him with one ghostly hand as he left it behind, then it seemed fade, vanishing into nothingness as he plunged onward into the mystical blue depths.

As he left the Goblin Phage behind, he thought he heard the Lady say – or perhaps it was an echo from his dream – *You will be free, unless you allow the goblins to bite you again – and then the Phage will return, and with a vengeance. Remember.*

Then he was falling swiftly and, in an instant, the world was a dazzling blue, and then began to shift around him. He heard the distant voice of the Lady calling after him, saying, "Take care, young Frederick, and seek the king in the sea!"

Down and down he tumbled, falling, ever falling, and then he knew that he was through, and found himself underwater – normal water, and he knew he had to get to the surface.

A vague light above him told him which way was up, but a faint glow below him spoke of light as well. He hesitated a few seconds, holding his failing breath, but fascinated by the orange whisper of light that seemed to be coming from ... what was it? A cavern? Yes, it must be. But his air was gone now, and he was sinking fast – the chain mail coat he was wearing was weighing him down. He kicked hard toward the surface again and again, gaining inches with each kick. Just when he thought his lungs would explode and he could hold his breath no more, he reached the surface and gasped, drinking in stale air that now surrounded him. He blinked and looked around. Everyone had vanished. He was alone, treading water in the middle of ... of what? A cavern?

Frederick looked about in the faint light as his eyes began to adjust. There, some distance away, there appeared to be a torch burning. He swam toward it, and found that it was not very far – perhaps only fifty feet. Still, it was a hard swim with all he was wearing, and he was quite exhausted as his feet touched bottom and he began to wade neck deep toward the shore.

Suddenly, something bumped into him. It was large, as big as himself, he thought, and it hit him, pushing him back toward the deep water, and then swam by. He hurried on toward the land, and again the thing swam around him and pushed him back. Then again, and again. He pushed forward, scared now, and desperate. Then there were two of them, bumping and jostling him, always away from shore, and he thought he felt slippery hands grabbing at his ankles, slowing his progress. He reached down to his side to draw his sword, and then remembered that he had given it to Colleen. Only the empty sheath was there. He struck at them with his fists and kicked furiously. They darted away from him, and he desperately pushed himself toward the shoreline.

Again, they came at him, this time from behind, grasping at him, pulling him, drawing him back toward the deeper water. Again and again, he kicked at them as he pushed himself through the water. But he was nearing the shore now and, with one last desperate effort, he kicked and then found he was in shallow water. He struggled to the shore and collapsed there, exhausted.

He looked out at the dark water before him and shivered. What had that been in there? He sat for several moments, breathing heavily, trying to get hold of his fear.

Then he remembered himself and he felt his face and ears. The bulging nose he'd had a few minutes before was gone, and the formerly drooping, pointed ears seemed to be his own again.

He smiled and looked at his left arm. It was his own. The black spidery veins and gray-green skin were gone, replaced by his own human flesh, and the bite marks were only faint scars.

"Well, that's to be expected, I suppose," he said aloud. "I suppose I'll always have the memory of it as well as the scars."

But he felt free, and taking a deep breath, he looked about. Not far away was what appeared to be an ancient fountain, although no water flowed in it now, and beside this was a large gnarled tree with dead branches spreading out and upward to a stone archway. It was as though the ancient tree were gripping the damp stone, forbidding it to fall. A torch was fixed to the tree in a metal bracket, its flickering light casting eerie shadows over the scene.

Over one branch was hung an old cloth that appeared to have once been red and white. He walked over and took it, shook it once, and wiped his face dry, then stuck it in his pocket without further thought.

As he walked around the strange tree, a stone bench came into view, and on this was stretched out a prone figure.

"Hello?" Frederick called.

He saw now that it was a very old man. Long white hair fell from his head, and a long white beard and mustache lay on his chest. Bushy eyebrows nearly hid his closed eyes.

"Hello?" he called. "Are you all right?"

The man did not answer.

Frederick paused for a moment. The old man's face was grim and absolutely ancient. Was he sick? Did he need help? Was he... dead?

"Hello, my good man!" Frederick called. "I say, are you all right?"

But the man still did not stir. He lay still as death. Frederick walked up to the prone form and looked down at him. He wore a tattered robe that looked as old as he was, and by his left side was a twisted walking staff.

"Sir?" said Frederick. But the man did not move.

Frederick reached out to give him a little shake, but when he did so, his hand passed through some sort of an invisible barrier and it went icy cold, or perhaps *cold* was not the word for it. It was as though his hand simply *stopped* before reaching the man's body. Stopped moving, stopped working, stopped *being*. He jerked his hand away with a cry and stepped back. Slowly, the weird feeling faded, and his hand returned to normal.

He picked up a small round pebble and tossed it at the man's chest. As soon as it got within a foot of the prone figure, it simply stopped in midair, and seemed to *float*. Then he noticed that there was a collection of things floating above the man – droplets of water, a fine mist, and dust. It was like a thin film surrounding him. But all were suspended with perfect stillness in the air about the figure, immobile and silent.

Frederick studied this for several moments, and then leaned against the tree to think. As he did so, his shoulder touched something, and he turned to see what it was. There, stuck into the tree, nearly all the way to the hilt, was a brilliant, beautiful sword. What showed of its blade was ornate and covered in runes, and its hilt was studded with gems and gold and silver. It was truly magnificent, like no sword he had ever seen. It did not appear that the sword had *pierced* the tree, but rather that the tree was, somehow, *holding* the sword.

Hesitantly, he reached out and put his hands around the handle. It was not cold to the touch as he expected, but was warm, even welcoming. He pulled. It cleanly and effortlessly slid from the tree with a singing ring of steel. It flashed with a brilliant green-white light in the darkness, momentarily blinding him. The tree seemed to shudder from deep within, and its branches, for a moment, trembled, and the fold that had held it closed.

The weapon felt perfect in his hand, balanced and true, much like the dwarf-made sword that he had given Colleen. This one was longer, however, more than three feet long, he thought, and he wondered how so large a sword felt so good in his hand. He slashed it through the air a few times, and marveled at the ease with which it obeyed him. Effortlessly he swung it around his head and the air *swooshed* with its passing. Then he remembered a portion of the dream he had the night before. It had been dark, like this. And yes, there had been a sword.

He looked at the steel in his hand, then at the sheath at his side. He slid it in, and it fit perfectly.

"Like it was made for it," he said aloud to himself. "She sent me here to get this sword. But what about this old man? He wasn't in my dream."

He turned to look at the old fellow. He still lay on the stone, surrounded by the weird dusty cocoon suspended about him. Frederick pulled the sword from its sheath again and looked at it.

"I wonder..." he said to himself, and he leveled the point at the pebble that he had thrown and jabbed at it.

As soon as the sword tip pierced the layer of floating dust, there was an audible *swishing* sound as all of the bits of dust and water fell onto the old man or on the stone on which he lay. The pebble went *plink* as it dropped to the man's chest and rolled to the ground, and the creatures in the water began to leap and splash.

But what startled Frederick the most was that the man drew a great shuddering gasp of air, his eyes flew wide open, and his chest began to heave up and down as though he had been running a great race and was catching his breath. He looked about the ceiling of the cavern, moving only his eyes at first, but then, after a moment, slowly turned his head and, seeing a figure holding a sword above him, moved with a speed that Frederick did not think possible for so old a man. Off the stone table he rolled, seizing the staff that had lain beside him, and crouched in a pose like a trained warrior, his staff held before him like a weapon. An eerie light burst from the tip of the staff, and the old man seemed to grow ominous and threatening, possessing a hidden power that seemed about to burst forth in a raging fury.

Frederick backed away, still holding the sword before him.

“Wait! I...I didn't mean to disturb you. I've come to...” stammered Frederick.

The old man relaxed slightly and then, slowly, he looked about the cavern again, yet still watching Frederick with suspicious eyes. The fellow's beard hung down to his waist, and his hair halfway down his back. Dark eyes looked out at Frederick from beneath thick, bushy white eyebrows. Then the man said something in a language that Frederick could not understand. His voice was strong, stronger than it should have been for so old a man, although Frederick thought he sounded extraordinarily tired.

“Sorry,” said Frederick, still keeping his distance and holding the sword. “I'm not sure I understand.”

The man seemed to relax slightly, but still hesitated, looking at the sword. They stood staring at one another across the stone table for a moment, and then slowly, the old man stood upright and leaned on his staff. The hidden power that had been present a moment ago faded and the imposing presence that had filled the room was replaced by an ancient wizened figure who seemed old beyond reckoning. Frederick slowly lowered his sword.

“The Lady… I mean, someone sent me,” he said. “I'm... on a mission.”

There was a sudden stirring in the water again, and Frederick glanced around. In the dim light of the torch, he could now see many faces watching them. Their hair was long and green or brown, like seaweed, and there were both men and women.

The old man saw them too and said something in his strange language. Frederick hesitated again, not knowing what to say. But the man seemed to grow weary and his face flushed. His legs gave way beneath him, and he began to fall. Frederick rushed forward and caught him, helping him to sit on the stone slab. The man said something again, leaned heavily on his staff, and hung his head down.

After a moment, he looked at Frederick, reached out and touched him on the head with his staff, shut his eyes, and murmured something.

A strange sensation shot through Frederick's mind, as if in an instant of time the old man had read his thoughts and knew all that he knew. He scrambled off the rock shelf and backed against the tree, which quivered at his touch.

But the old man only smiled weakly at him and said, "Do not be afraid, Frederick."

Chapter 7 – The Wizard

Frederick stared at the old man for a moment and then said, "What did you do to me? I can... I can understand you now."

"And I you," he replied. "Don't be afraid. I have not harmed you, nor will I. It was a simple thing to learn your language. But now, see here, I thank you. I seem to have been... been... I do not know. Nor do I know where we are now. But somehow, I think that I have been under an enchantment. And this place – where is it? It is underground, is it not?"

Then Frederick remembered why he was here, and he did not answer the old man at first. There must be a passage out of here somewhere, he thought, and knew he had to find it. He went to the tree, took the torch from its bracket, and walked around the bit of land on which he was standing. It was a small island, surrounded by water on all sides. But he could see no passages beyond the boundary of the lake, only rock walls that reached upward to a stalactite-covered ceiling.

"Yes, we are underground," said Frederick. "I am on an errand for... for a friend. I can't stay here for long."

"Please," said the old man. "Sit with me for a moment. I am weary, but there is a great deal I must know."

Frederick looked out into the water and once again could vaguely make out a dim glow coming from the underwater passageway. The faces of the lake people watched him intently.

"Are they friendly?" asked the man.

"I don't think so," replied Frederick. "They gave me a fit when I arrived."

"Please, grant an old man a moment," he said.

Frederick looked at the lake and then at the old man. He sighed and went to sit next to him.

Then, an impossible thought struck him. He knew it was impossible and absurd, but he had already seen so many impossible and absurd things in the past few days that he could not help but ask.

“Sir,” he said. “Are you a wizard?”

The old man looked sidelong at him and said, “A wizard? What makes you ask such a question?”

“Well, you look the part, you know. What with that robe and beard and bushy eyebrows and staff and how you *were* a few moments ago. And besides, I've heard quite a few stories lately about wizards. Why, the Lady Danu...”

He stopped himself, for the old man looked at him curiously at the mention of the Lady.

“You know the Lady Danu?” asked the man softly.

“Er, well... all right, then, yes. I've only met her just the other day. We spent the night at her Lake.”

“We?” said the old man.

“Well, yes, my cousin and I and ...”

The old man raised his eyebrows questioningly. Frederick somehow felt that he could trust him. He *needed* to trust him – needed someone to help him. He took a deep breath and sheathed the sword.

“Fine then,” he said. “I've been in the Land of the Little People with my cousin and we found the Lady, and I've come back to get help to fight a witch that's taken over the land. There it is, then.”

The old man sighed.

“She has taken over the whole land, then?” he asked quietly.

"Well, that's what they say, at least," replied Frederick.

The old man looked about again and fell silent for several long moments.

"The reason I ask," said Frederick, "is that I think a wizard would be, you know, *useful* if you're going to be fighting a witch. I'm supposed to be finding help. Maybe you're the one I'm supposed to take back with me."

The old man looked deeply thoughtful at this and, at length, seemed to come to some conclusion.

"Well, to answer your question, yes, I am a wizard. But last I remember, I too was fighting a witch in the Land of the Little People. We were in a fierce battle. There was a collision of powers such as the world had never known. It seemed to me that the sky itself ripped in two, and there was a terrible explosion. The last thing I remember was falling on a stone bench, then waking up here."

"Were you in the Council of Wizards?" asked Frederick, amazed.

"You seem to know quite a bit, lad," he replied.

"Well, I've learned a thing or two lately," he said. "But please, you know my name – what is yours?"

"It is no small thing to give one's true name, especially to a stranger," said the wizard. "And I am still uncertain of all this. This arch, and this tree, for instance – they are familiar and yet... *aged.* How long, I wonder, have I been here, lying on this slab of stone? And who put me here? Was it the Lady?"

"I don't know," said Frederick. "The Lady didn't mention you when she sent me. I've come to find help, though, and would welcome yours if you can give it."

The man looked about him in wonder once again, then at Frederick. He considered him for a long time and then said, "Very well. I shall tell you one of my names, and this name you may tell to others. I am Gwydion, member of the Council of Wizards."

For some reason the name sounded familiar to Frederick, although he could not recall how.

"Come now, Frederick, you must tell me more. You say that the Lady sent you and that you fight against the Witch?" said Gwydion.

"It's all really quite by accident that we got there – into the Land of the Little People, that is," he replied. "We came through the mirror in the wood."

"Mirror in the wood?" asked Gwydion. "Was it a large mirror with many shapes and runes about it?"

"Well, yes, as far as I remember. We didn't have a lot of time, and I... I lost that crystal ball, so we couldn't get back. That goblin got it. But we made it to the Lady's Lake, and she sent me back," he replied.

"All of this is very strange news to me. Is this cavern somehow connected to the Dwarven mines? Is that how she sent you here?" asked Gwydion.

"We're not in the Land of the Little People anymore," replied Frederick. "We're back in the World of Men. As to how I arrived, I leaped into the Lake and *fell* here, you might say. Or went through that lake to this one. But see that light down in the water? That must be the way out. I've got to go for it."

"I am weary," said Gwydion. "I do not know if I could swim down to that light and then back out again. Surely there is another way?"

"Not that I know of," answered Frederick. "But, I am sorry. I've got to try to make it through. I'll tell someone that you're here, if you like, and they might make it back to help."

The old man looked at the light that twinkled dimly beneath the water, then at the faces that continued to stare at them from the lake.

"I wonder if they will even let us try," he said. "But perhaps we might convince them. You have a sword, I see. Can you use it?"

Frederick slid it halfway out of its sheath. It glittered in the light of the torch that he was still holding. As he did so, the old man's eyes went wide again with amazement.

"Where did you get that sword, lad?" he asked.

Frederick glanced at the tree. "It was stuck in that tree. I pulled it out. But the Lady Danu gave me the sheath."

"May I see it?" asked Gwydion.

Slowly, Frederick pulled the sword out and hesitantly handed it to the wizard.

The wizard turned it over in his aged hands several times and said, "This grows stranger by the moment. I am almost certain that I have seen this sword before, although not in the hands of a boy. But it has come to you now. Bear it well. Again, I ask, can you use it?"

"I... I don't know," replied Frederick.

"Well, lad, let us find out. Together, we shall see if these lake people are friendly, and can face an old man with a staff and a boy with a great sword," replied Gwydion, handing it back to him. "Come, my new young friend, we will brave these waters together."

Frederick placed the torch back in its bracket, then went and stood next to Gwydion on the shore. The old man leaned on his staff.

"Let us try speaking with them," he said to Frederick, and then, in a loud voice, said, "Friends of the lake, will you let us pass? We must leave this place, and we bear you no malice."

A single figure approached them in the water and came near to the shore. She was beautiful, Frederick thought, although strange. Her hair was green as seaweed and her eyes were as dark as amber, and although he could not see it well, the lower half of her body was silvery and sleek, and he thought that he could make out a tail. When she spoke, her voice was high pitched, and sounded like running water.

“We are the guardians of the Sword, the Wizard, and the Tree,” she said.

“Are you... a mermaid?” asked Frederick.

When she did not answer, he said, “I've been sent by the Lady Danu. Please, she sent me to find help for the Land of the Little People. Please, let us pass.”

“You have taken the Sword that cannot be taken, and have awoken him who cannot be woken. You must wait for the fruit of the tree as well, and restore it to the sun,” she said.

“What? I don't know what you're talking about. I just need to go and get help and get back as quickly as possible,” he said.

Then she began to chant, and the music of her voice was spellbinding.

“When the sword within the tree
Shall once again be taken,
Then wizards once again shall rise,
And kings of old shall waken.
One of royal lineage shall come,
As prophecies once told.
And do great deeds upon the earth,
As 'twas in days of old.
The wounded tree that withered,
Its fruit shall give once more.
And what was burned shall live again,
As 'twas in days of yore.”

“Right,” said Frederick. “I don't know about any of that. But I can't wait for some dead tree to bear fruit underground. I'm coming through and going for help for my cousin and Mrs. Wigglepox and Lily and Rose and the all the rest of them."

"But you must wait for the tree to bear its fruit," said the strange lady.

Frederick looked back at the tree. The torch bathed it in orange light, and its withered branches still gripped the stone arch. But to his surprise, he saw a single blossom on one branch – a small yellow flower, bright and beautiful.

"Now I am sure that I know this tree!" said Gwydion. "It is nothing less than the tree from the courtyard of the castle in the Land of the Little People. Ever it blossomed with bright yellow blossoms such as this, and its fruit gave life and strength to all who ate it, and those who lingered under its fair branches found all weariness of life leave them and their youth renewed. But the fruits were ever seedless, and the tree was the only one of its kind. The little people named it the First Child of the Waking Tree, and planted it there as a token of friendship to the big people, as they called us. It held a special place in their prophecies. But I greatly fear now that some dread thing has happened in that land. For I am certain now that both this stone arch and this tree once were there. Yet how is it that they have come here? Come, Frederick, we must not go yet. Let us sit and watch."

Together, they returned to the stone slab and sat. To Frederick's amazement, the blossom brightened, then folded in upon itself, and a small green fruit formed and slowly grew. Soon it was larger, and bright yellow, and hung heavily upon the old branch.

"It is ripe," said Gwydion. "And I think that it is your place to pick it."

Frederick walked slowly to the fruit that now hung low before him. The old tree seemed to have shrunken further, as though it had poured the last vestiges of its life into this one fruit. It was shaped rather like a pear, although rounder, and it gave off a sweet fragrance that made his mouth water. He reached up and carefully pulled. The fruit popped from the branch. The tree shivered and seemed to sigh, and then was very still. Frederick wondered if it had died. He cupped the beautiful fruit in his hand and took it to Gwydion.

"What shall I do with it?" he asked.

"Keep it safe for now. I do not know what role this fruit shall play in days to come. But know this, Frederick, that it is not by mere chance that you have come to this cave in this hour, pulled the sword from the tree, breaking what enchantments I cannot say, and now this tree, in its final hour, has given its last fruit to you."

Frederick looked at the fruit in wonder. It fit easily in the palm of his hand and was warm to the touch, and firm. He took a handkerchief from his pocket and carefully wrapped the fruit in it and placed it in an inner pocket of the blue cloak that he still wore.

"I hope that I don't smash it," he said to Gwydion.

"Yes, take care that you do not. Nor eat it! It is given for some purpose that I cannot see," he replied.

They both looked at the ancient tree. It seemed shrunken now, and brittle, as though it were withering before their eyes.

Frederick gazed at it for a few moments, and then said, "I think we ought to go now. Look – the torch is going out."

Indeed, the light of the torch seemed to be fading with the tree, and as it did, Frederick noticed something dimly shining at the tree's base.

He walked over to it, stooped down, and began to clear away the dirt.

There, buried just below the surface, was a shining vial of clear, bright liquid.

He pulled it from the ground and held it up.

“How did this get here?” he said aloud. “This looks exactly like the one that the Lady just gave to Colleen.”

He wiped the dirt from it and stuffed it into an inner pocket of his robe, wondering what would become of it.

“Come!” said the mer-lady. “We shall escort you to the surface.”

Hesitantly, Frederick and Gwydion stepped into the water. Frederick sheathed his sword, and Gwydion gripped his staff as they waded deeper and deeper, until they took one last breath, and dove beneath the waters toward the dim light below.

Suddenly, Frederick felt strong hands grasp his wrists, and he was pulled downward. Although his vision was blurred, he could make out two mer-men swimming swiftly, pulling him down, down toward the light. Gwydion also had two pulling him, and soon they passed through a cavern entrance. But already his air was running out, and he struggled not to breathe in water.

Out of the cavern entrance, he pushed into a dim light, and under the water, he could hear the voices of the mer-people singing to them as they rose upward toward the surface.

Frederick's lungs were burning now, and his limbs did not want to move. The weight of his clothing and the sword at his side tugged at him, but the strong hands of the mer-men did not let him slip.

When he could take it no more, and his body and mind howled in agony, he burst through the surface and, choking, gasped in great gulps of air.

Then Gwydion was beside him, clinging to his staff.

The mer-men held them for only a moment, and then, in the moonlit night, said, “Farewell, sleeping wizard. At the Lady's bidding, we have guarded you for long ages. Now our task is done, and we shall return to our home in the sea. Farewell!”

Slowly, they slipped beneath the waters of the lake and disappeared into its depths.

Frederick, however, found that his strength was gone, and he began to sink again. He tried to tread water, but his clothes were soaked and weighed him down.

"Come!" said Gwydion. "We must make for the shore. See, it is not far."

But he slipped downward, and kicked frantically, struggling to regain the surface. His head rose up, and he gasped for air. He splashed, raised a hand toward the sky, and sank.

"Frederick!" yelled Gwydion, and stretched out a hand to him.

Frederick vainly tried to reach Gwydion's hand, but he was too far away. He tried to yell, but water filled his lungs, and as he sank, he saw the old man trying to swim down after him. As he lost consciousness, his last memory was of powerful hands gripping his own and a rushing sensation of being pulled upward.

Chapter 8 – The Return of Frederick

The hour was late and the moon was full. Aonghus and Bran sat by the great window of the common room in their hall, gazing out across the lake.

"Where do you suppose that stone of McPherson's really came from?" said Bran.

"Who knows? He said it been passed down in his family for longer than anyone could remember. His ancestors must have come from Ireland long ago – maybe from the area of our farm," said Aonghus. "They must have taken that rock with them when they left."

"Could be. Anyway, it's really good of him to go to Ireland with us to see the farm himself and meet Father," said Bran. "Now we just have to wait until Colleen and Frederick get here."

He gazed out over the lake, watching the full moon's light dance on the rippling waters. Strange shadows danced beneath the waves, giving the illusion of things swimming beneath the surface. Suddenly, he leaned forward and stared hard into the night.

"Aonghus... what... there's someone thrashing about in the lake... come on!"

Bran dashed from the room. Aonghus glanced out the window, then followed his brother, speeding down the stairs after him. Together, they ran out the door and sprinted like deer to the lake's edge and peered out on the water. Moonbeams fell on the rippling surface, revealing a struggling figure. For a moment, a face shone pale in the dim light, then was gone. A hand reached up, and then sank beneath the waves, but did not return. Then, a second figure broke the surface and looked around desperately.

Bran and Aonghus both moved, running into the shallows and then diving in, swimming hard to the place where the remaining figure was now treading water. He appeared to be an old man with a long white beard and hair.

“Help him!” gasped the man.

They dove down together and, twenty feet below, they saw someone sinking – a boy. Down they swam and, far below, Aonghus thought he could see something very strange – shapes – almost human shapes – swimming down, down, and entering a cavern. He looked up and saw that Bran was swimming with the boy to the surface, so he lingered a moment longer.

One of the shapes below turned and looked upward at him. He thought that surely the shadows were playing tricks on him, for there was the face of a woman – a beautiful woman – with long green hair floating all about her fair face and body – but the lower half of her body bore a silvery sheen. She paused before entering the underwater cave with her companions, waved at him, and with a flip of what appeared to be a tail, she vanished.

He blinked and looked again, but she was gone. He looked upward to the surface. Bran was already there and almost to the shore. He swam hard, upward, and saw that the old man was slowly making his way there as well.

“Are you all right, sir?” said Aonghus.

“I will be fine. Help the boy,” he said.

Bran was already dragging him onto the grass as Aonghus' feet touched bottom and he hurried to his brother's side.

“He's not breathing,” gasped Bran.

Aonghus turned the boy on his side and began to push his legs, bending them up against his chest and then straightening them again and again. Water poured out of his lungs. For a full minute, the boy did not respond, but then began to cough violently. Bran brushed his wet hair out of his face and looked at him and gasped.

“Aonghus, look! It's Frederick Buttersmouth!” he said, astonished.

"What in the world is he doing here – and in the lake?" said Aonghus. "And what were those..."

He looked back at the water, but only ripples now danced in the moonlight.

"Something was in there," said Aonghus. "Something..."

"And what's this?" said Bran, seeing the sword at his side. He unsheathed it and held it up in the moonlight.

Frederick coughed and choked, but managed to sputter out, "... my... sw...ord... found... it.... Aonghus... Colleen... needs... help."

"What do you mean, boy? Spit it out! Where is Colleen? What's wrong?" demanded Aonghus. "Is she in that lake?"

"No... not... there... a moment..." he said, and coughed violently.

"Give him a moment," said Bran.

The old man had now reached the shore, and Aonghus went to him and helped him climb up the bank. He leaned wearily on a wooden staff, breathing heavily.

"Are you all right?" asked Aonghus.

The man waved a hand and nodded, but said nothing.

Frederick continued with his coughing spasm for several minutes, and then finally said, "We think we know where she is, Aonghus! Bran – we think we found your mother!"

Aonghus seized him by the shoulders and his face grew dark and threatening, like none Frederick had ever seen before.

"If this is some sort of cruel joke, so help me..." he began.

“No!” said Frederick. “She is, or we think she is... is... in a different place. I cannot explain it. But I left Colleen there, and she is going after her.”

“I thought you said you had found our mother, Frederick. Now where is she and where is Colleen?” said Bran, impatiently.

Suddenly, these two brothers that Frederick had thought of as rather big, jolly oafs looked tall and terrible, their faces livid with expressions of anger and expectancy. In that moment, he had a sense that something *primal,* some uncontrollable power was rising up within them that would burst upon the world and lay it waste to rescue their mother and sister.

“Please, give me a moment to explain. You're going to find it all hard to believe!” he said.

“Try us,” said Aonghus through gritted teeth.

But then, Bran's face softened somewhat, and he said, “Aonghus, let's get him inside and into some dry things. He can tell us the whole thing in our room.”

Aonghus exhaled and nodded.

“Wait, Gwydion should come too,” said Frederick through another coughing fit. “I'll explain.”

The four of them made their way back to the brothers’ room and, as they went, Gwydion looked all about, observing everything he saw with great wonder. When they finally arrived, Frederick and Gwydion began to dry off.

“Where did you get those clothes?” asked Bran as he saw the blue robe and cloak, and the chain mail shirt and sword at his side, and saw that the old man was wearing an odd robe and carrying a staff.

“And this sword – it's marvelous!” said Aonghus, swinging the blade in the air so that it sang.

“Never mind all that. Tell us your tale now,” said Bran. “And you can introduce your friend as well. Please forgive us, sir, but we are most anxious to hear of our mother.”

“I am just as anxious to hear his tale,” said Gwydion. “Mine can come later.”

Frederick paused, looking at the expectant faces of the two huge brothers, and at the old wizard who had taken a seat nearby and was wringing water from his beard and hair.

“It was a mirror in your grandfather’s cellar,” he said. “It’s magic, or maybe some marvelous invention. It turns into a doorway of sorts.”

“A doorway to what?” said Bran. “What are you talking about?”

“It's like a doorway to another place – a land or world or something. And there are little...” He was going to say “little people,” but realized that this would sound too incredible, so he said, “There are people there. Bad people. And they have captured your mother. Somehow, she went through the mirror to this place, and they took her. And Colleen and I fell through it too and ended up there. We found out your mother was there and we've been looking for her. We think we know where she is, but we need help. I left Colleen there with some decent folk that we met, but she's going on without me. We've got to get back to her and help.”

“What's all this about?” demanded Aonghus. “That's rather hard to believe. Why can't you Buttersmouths be straight about things? Now let's have it. Where is Colleen, really?”

His face was stormy, and Frederick was not a little afraid of what might happen next, so he said, “Aonghus, I know I've not been very trustworthy in the past, and you have a right to think I'm lying. But I swear to you that I'm telling the truth. We went through that mirror and ended up in that strange place. You've got to believe me!”

The brothers looked hard into the face of Frederick, and, after considering him, Bran said, “I think he's telling the truth, Aonghus. I don't see any lies in his eyes.”

“Neither do I,” said Aonghus, softening. “But how could it be?”

“Aonghus, would you have believed what we've been speaking about all evening, even a day ago? Suppose this mirror also came from... from the same lost culture we've been talking about?”

Aonghus thought for a moment and then nodded.

“All right then, Frederick, let's say what you're saying is true. How did you and this fellow get into that lake? And what's all this you're wearing, and what about this sword? And how did you get back here from... there?” asked Aonghus.

“One thing at a time, please,” said Frederick.

There was a knock at the door and in came Professor McPherson.

“Aonghus... Bran... and who is this? I saw you dashing down to the lake. Is everything... *Frederick*?”

Professor McPherson's face lit up with surprise and delight at seeing Frederick, but he immediately composed himself and said, “Frederick Buttersmouth, you are soaking wet... and how did you get here so soon? And who is your guest, who is also soaking wet?”

Frederick looked at Aonghus and Bran, and Aonghus said, “It's all right, Frederick. Tell him everything.”

Chapter 9 – The Waking of Dvalenn

Colleen stood on the shore, gazing down into the depths of the lake. Frederick had disappeared, and she felt terribly alone. He had been her only connection with her own world, and the thought struck her that she was the only human being in this entire land.

Except for Mother! she thought. *Or perhaps that old hag, Mal.*

That gave her a little courage.

"Colleen," said the Lady. "Frederick has arrived back in your world. Do not be afraid. You will not be alone. Come and walk with me. I would like to show you something."

Colleen walked beside her and marked how tall and beautiful she was. Then she noticed that the Lady Danu cast no shadow, but rather illumined all that was around her. She was like no earthly woman she had ever met, and she seemed to radiate both goodness and a sort of holy fear, as if one might become *undone* by being in the presence of such a power. It was a strange mixture of awe and peace and dread to walk beside her.

When they had reached the rock where Colleen had first seen her, the Lady said, "I would like to show you something of this world, Colleen. Please, stand here on this stone and look into the Lake."

Colleen climbed onto the rock and gazed into the infinite shining blue depths. All at once, a scene appeared, and she could see what she knew was the forest – but it was green and growing, and all sorts of little people danced and played and worked among the trees. There were leprechauns, gnomes, pixies, fairies, sprites, and many others that she did not recognize. Some were knee-high to her, and others so tiny that they were like cherry blossoms floating on the wind. All were happy and productive, and they spread the Forest across their world seed by seed, planting and harvesting and grooming it into one majestic whole where they lived in peace.

"This was the Land of the Little People before the coming of the Witch," Lady Danu said.

FLASH! The scene changed, and a shining silver double door appeared in the wall of a cavern, and out stepped a blue robed elven lord with a golden crown on his head. He greeted the little people that gathered to see this strange sight, and he became their friend. The scene changed again, and there was a great castle being built in the midst of the forest, and seven great gathering houses were raised. Big people came and went, and for a brief time, all was well.

FLASH! The scene changed again, and a terrible battle was taking place. A great giant rained down blows on armies at his feet, lightning struck at the giant, whirlwinds howled, and fiery flames raged. A tall figure on a tower raised a white staff. There was a brilliant flash of blue and red, and it seemed as though the sky itself tore open, swallowing the giant. Then, as the wounded heavens seemed to close and heal, something huge came hurtling through, ripping it open once again, and crashed upon the tower where the man had been.

FLASH! Great heat and flames and lightning crashed together. The forest was blown down for miles and miles in all directions. A great section of the castle was hurled through the air, flung far away, and there was a strange collision of lights and shadows, as if the very fabric of existence were ripping apart. A great earthquake struck, sending a great piece of land hurtling into the sea. A terrible wave followed the concussion, the fallen trees were swept away, and the land was gouged down to bare rock.

FLASH! The Cataclysm passed, and a ruined castle sat in the midst of a broken and flooded land. Nothing stirred.

FLASH! Years sped before Colleen's eyes, and she watched as a desert formed. The castle of the wizards and the Witch herself were nearly forgotten, fading into legend.

FLASH! Dwarves braved the desert, and found the castle, and there settled for many a year in tunnels beneath its broken towers. There, they found a thing of great beauty – a maiden of golden-red hair fallen on the floor of a glass room and sleeping there. But they could not wake her.

FLASH! An island appeared in the sea and, with it, a ship, and on that ship was a pirate. He explored the land, crossed the desert, and found the castle, and there found the bones of the last wizard under a cairn built by the dwarves.

He took an amulet from the wizard's skeletal hand and put it around his own neck. Then, in the castle, he found the beautiful sleeping woman. He kissed her, and the amulet swung from his neck and touched her on the chin. She awoke, but she did not know her own name. But the dwarves were in their tunnels when he came, and when they returned, their sleeping lady was gone, and they searched long for her, but did not find her. At length, they left the castle in despair and returned to their houses in the forest.

FLASH! The pirate and the lady sailed the seas, finding great treasures from ancient times, and plundering the Land of the Little People of many of its gifts. But the maid was lost to the pirate and, in that time, the Witch returned. The pirate fled, leaving the world to the Witch, and lamenting his lost love. In his grief, he returned all but a few of the riches he had looted, and was not seen again.

FLASH! Goblins came, and the Great Sleep crept over the forest. Year by year, fewer and fewer trees blossomed, but fell under the dread spell, as did the little people. They and their children grew smaller and smaller through the years, and their powers diminished as well until they were small indeed.

FLASH! The lake scene changed one last time to a barren and deserted forest. No little people danced under the dead trees. Thick black waters sputtered from polluted springs, and in the midst of it, a lake of black ooze gurgled up hideous fumes that hung like smog over the whole land.

Then suddenly, Colleen found herself staring into the bright blue depths of the clear Lake again.

A tear rolled down Colleen's cheek and fell into the Lake, sending tiny ripples across its surface.

“The final vision that I saw, Lady - is that fated to happen? Will this shining Lake become a stinking black blight on this land?” she asked.

“Few things are fated, Colleen,” replied the Lady, “and this is not one of them. All that we do with the time we are given shapes the future of all things. Even the single tear that you have shed and which has fallen into this Lake, Colleen, has become a part of the Waters of Light, and will ever shape them as they flow to all the worlds.

“But if the Darkness has its way, it will not be tears of pity and mercy that are shed and shape the worlds, but tears of fear and grief and woe and bitterness that blacken hearts and minds – a black ocean of impenetrable night that hates the Light. The same darkness that inhabits the world of the goblins will make its way here in full measure, and into all the worlds, unless it is stopped.”

“But what can I do?” asked Colleen. “I'm just a little girl.”

“You can finish the task you have been given,” she replied. “Carry on to the very end. Never stop part way. And don't give in to fear or despondency. Pity the goblins and even the Witch that live in the darkness. They do not know what they are doing, and are only puppets to a greater evil. Keep your mind in her dark pits, and do not despair.”

Colleen stared a moment longer into the infinite blue, and then the Lady said to her, “Today, you will rest your body, soul, and mind by my Lake, Colleen, for today it is still free and full of light, and in that, you will find strength and peace.”

So she did, talking to scores of little people, listening to their stories, and telling them of the World of Men, and of the legends of their races that were told there. Then night came, and the sky over the lake was brilliant and clear. Colleen found a soft patch of moss and lay down on it, and there, to the song of tiny fairies, she fell into the most restful sleep she had ever known.

The next day, she woke with daisies woven into her hair, and to the voice of the Lady Danu calling her.

“Come, come!” she called. “Someone is here that you will want to meet.”

The clear blue of the Lake began to change, and rising from those depths came a bearded figure, striding as if he were climbing some great height. Upward he came until he broke the surface of the water and stepped onto the shore, and yet he was completely dry. He gazed about him, a look of bewilderment and wonder on his face.

“Dvalenn!” cried Colleen, and ran to him and gave him a hug.

Even deeper surprise flooded the dwarf's face, and he held Colleen at arm's length, gazed into her face, and said, “Do I know you? I was dreaming...”

“Oh, I forgot! You've been sleeping all this time. My name is Colleen McGunnegal. Frederick and I and some of the little people brought you here from your brother Doc's house,” she replied.

“My brother Doc's house?” asked Dvalenn, looking all about him.

“Yes. Doc... Sindri... He decided to stay and guard the...” Colleen began to say the “Gate of Anastazi,” but decided against it.

“... the house,” she finished. “He also said he was too old for such a journey. But it seems the Lady has wakened you from your long sleep!”

“Sleep?” said Dvalenn slowly. “Yes, I was asleep, wasn't I? But how long? I had such terrible dreams.”

“We're not sure, although Doc thought it was at least twenty years,” she replied.

"Twenty years!" said Dvalenn. "But how could that be? What dark magic..."

Then he paused, looking about him again and, for the first time, seemed to see the Lady.

"Lady Danu!" he said, and bowed. "Forgive my lack of greeting! The pits of the Witch make one calloused, and I have endured them for many years. I have forgotten my manners. But how did I... the last thing I remember is lying down by a tree. I was so very tired."

"The Spell overtook you, Dvalenn," said the Lady. "You gave in to its power and fell under the dread Sleep. You might have gone on in its nightmares until you were carried to the Eternal Sleep, had not Colleen and Frederick brought you here. But now, you are free!"

"Free. Am I?" He spoke the word as though it were something alien to him. "Yes, I do feel free! And I hope that I shall never sleep again!"

The dwarf danced a little jig on the shore of the shining Lake, and Colleen laughed with glee to see him so happy.

The Lady laughed as well, and her voice spread like music across the Lake.

"You are free indeed, Dvalenn. But beware, you may still fall under the Spell if you are not careful. You must be ever vigilant and watchful, for those who have been touched once by the Spell may easily be swayed by it again."

"Thank you, Lady," he said, and bowed low. As he did, he spotted a shiny pebble on the shore and picked it up. He gazed at it for a moment and then dropped it again.

"Take care, dear dwarf. You have slept long under the Spell, and your time of departure is near. When that moment comes, you must choose your path – to go to the house of your fathers within the stone, or dwell alone in the dark and lonely places beneath the earth," she said.

For some time, they spoke, with Dvalenn asking many questions about the world and what state it was in, about Colleen and how she had come to the land, and about his brothers, especially Sindri. He listened with particular interest when Colleen told him about the Crystal Cavern that his brother had made, and in which Lily had made a wish by which Badger had become a mighty war horse.

"I wish I could go see this hall of Sindri," said Dvalenn. "What a place it must be!"

They talked on, until at last the Lady Danu sighed and said, "Well, you must prepare to leave us now. I have seen to it that your wagon is well supplied with more than you will need for your journey, although I found that others have supplied you well already. And you may find other help along the way. There are still some who oppose the Witch."

"Must we go so soon, Lady?" asked Dvalenn. "I would stay here and live in the light of this Lake forever by your side."

"Ah, Dvalenn," she said, "time is so short. Colleen and these others have a great task to do, and your path lies with them for a brief time. But whenever you sit by a spring, or see the ocean, or swim in a lake, or walk among the *fountains*," and she emphasized the word *fountains*, "then remember me and the Waters of Light that have awakened you from the dread Sleep. Remember this day, Dvalenn, when the Witch's Spell would try to bring the darkness to you again. And watch over Colleen and the Wigglepox family for as long as you can."

"Yes, Lady, I will remember," he said.

"And to you, Colleen, I give these words – remember the gifts that have been given to you. An ancient bloodline runs pure in you. Be true to what you know is right and do not listen when the goblins and Witch try to persuade you to follow them."

She paused then, looking intently at Colleen and said, “I cannot see your future, Colleen – it is hidden from me. But I think that perhaps your destiny lies among many worlds.”

She stooped down to look Colleen in the eyes and placed her hands on her shoulders. Colleen gazed back into the most beautiful face she had ever seen – a face radiant with goodness and peace.

“Do not be afraid, Colleen. Only be true,” she said.

“I will try, Lady Danu,” she replied, and a tear rolled down her cheek.

Then the Lady led Colleen a little ways away from the others and said in a low voice, “Colleen, Dvalenn's time of departure is near.”

“But I thought he was going with us,” she said.

The Lady looked sad, bowed her head, and said, “Dvalenn is dying.”

“Dying!” whispered Colleen. “But you have just awakened him! And I thought that...” She lowered her voice and continued, “I thought that the Gate was leaking timelessness into this land. How could he be dying?”

“The Spell takes its toll on even the hardiest of folk – even on dwarves,” she replied. “He would have fallen into the final sleep out in those woods had you and Frederick not rescued him. Oh, his body may have gone on and on in this never, yet ever-dying world, but even timelessness does not truly preserve a person. Something much deeper must happen for *that* to take place. Now Dvalenn has a chance to make his final choices. It is true that he can choose to stay in this place and go on and on, never wholly healed of the effects of the Spell, but that would not be living as life was intended for him.”

“How long does he have, Lady?” asked Colleen, feeling very sad.

“That is not for me to know. I can only see a shadow falling upon him. But I do not know when it will overtake him completely,” she replied.

"Does he know?" asked Colleen.

"He feels it within himself, but he fights against it. He is not yet ready to depart. There will be a struggle before his time here with us is over," said the Lady. "But come now, wipe your eyes and let us go back to the others."

Together, they walked back, and the Lady Danu said, "I foresee that we will meet again, friends. Fare you well! Stay to the course you have set and you will reach your destination."

Colleen, Oracle, Dvalenn, and the Wigglepox family walked to the wagon, and Colleen hitched up Badger. She then climbed into the driver's seat and took the reins.

Hundreds of little people gathered to see them off, all of them looking somber. They waved and followed the wagon to the forest's edge and, as they entered the sleepy wood again, Colleen looked back and saw the Lady standing on the waters, her hand raised in farewell.

Chapter 10 – The Southbound Road

Soon they were on the southbound road, and once again, the weight of the Spell was upon them. Colleen felt it at once as they left the protective power of the Lady Danu behind, and Dvalenn seemed to hunch his shoulders under its oppressive presence.

"I had forgotten this weight that I bore," said Dvalenn, "and I am loath to feel it again. I wish we could go back to the Lady."

Colleen did not say anything, but instead began to sing quietly. Immediately, their spirits all lifted, and the heaviness around them lessened. She urged Badger on faster, knowing that the Spell was strongest around the lake, and the sooner they put some distance between them and it, the safer they would be. She sang as they rode on, and Oracle hummed happily along.

When she finally felt it was safe, she stopped singing, looked over at Dvalenn, and said, "Dvalenn, tell me about yourself. Your brother, Doc, said that you had disappeared many years ago. What happened?"

"Ah, that is a long tale. Too long, I think. But I'll tell you what. If you tell me your tale, I'll tell you mine," he replied. "And I'd like to hear the tale of these Wigglepoxes as well, and of this Oracle fellow who says so little."

"Fair enough," said Colleen, and she began to recount the tale of how she and Frederick had accidentally come to the Land of the Little People, and of all that had transpired since then. On she talked for a good hour as they continued down the old south road until finally, she had finished and said, "So here we are, traveling together to free our families from the Witch."

"An amazing tale!" said Dvalenn. "Truly amazing! I wish I could have met this Frederick. He seems a brave lad. But here now, I will begin my tale with telling you why I am even going with you on this journey.

"Of course it was because of the Lady. She took me to a strange place, Colleen. It was a place where I awoke from my long sleep, and she made me face myself."

"That seems to happen a lot here," said Colleen.

"She made me look into my own heart and mind and soul and face exactly what I had become, and then she had me choose. Choose to serve the Witch, or myself, or to return to who I really am – the person I was made to be. She then said that it would be a choice that I would face every day. She said that I needed to go with you because she saw that my time was short, and that with what time I had left, I needed to help you."

He looked down at the ground for a moment, and then continued. "Did Doc tell you about the seven of us? We were all Doctors of Stone, you know, and each of us had a house that we governed here. It was our assignment from the High King of the Dwarves. We were to come here and build and manage these great meeting houses for the other races."

"Yes, Doc mentioned something about that," replied Colleen.

"Well, we did that for a time, until the Witch came. Then there were rumors of trouble in other worlds too – the Lands of the Goblins and Trolls and Giants and Orogim all had strange reports coming from them. Then a terrible thing happened. We heard news that the trolls had invaded the world of the dwarves by surprise and had stolen the Great Stone – the heart of our world, and had taken it through the Gate of Anastazi to their own land. We seven brothers began to prepare armor and weapons in our houses as a defense should the trolls come here. The War of the Trolls was a dreadful one, and many lives were lost.

"But then the war with the Witch and the goblins came, and the Black Orogim were revealed. There was chaos everywhere in all the worlds. Giants turned evil, and there was a civil war among them. Wizards rose and fell, as did and many great heroes.

"In the end, Anastazi the Great shut the gates and was never heard from again. I suppose there were folk from all the races that were trapped in the various worlds, just as we were trapped here. And somehow, the Witch got trapped here too."

He paused for a moment and then continued. "Did Doc tell you about the beautiful sleeping maiden that we found in the castle?"

"Yes, he did mention her, and a pirate," she replied. "And I saw the maiden in the Lake. The Lady showed her to me, although I could not see her face. Our path takes us to that castle, you know."

"Yes. If we make it that far, I will show you where we found her. But at any rate, when the Witch returned (she had been gone for a long time after the War of the Wizards), that's when the Sleep began to creep across the forest.

"Now comes a part of the story that I do not relish telling, but I think you should know. I was out alone one day – a foolish thing to do when there are witches about. But I had begun to grow confident that the Witch would never catch me and that her creeping spell did not affect me, for I was young and strong and was a Doctor of Stone, and wielded power over rock and earth.

"It was then that I met her. Or I suppose it was her in a guise – as the beautiful maiden that we had rescued and who had disappeared with the pirate. I thought our maiden had returned, and I rejoiced and wanted to go and call my brothers. But she forestalled me, and bid me listen to her tale.

"We sat in the cool of the day and she told me of many travels she had made, and said she had met this so-called witch, and that she was not a witch at all, and undeserving of the attacks upon her. In fact, it had been the little people who had begun the war against her, beginning with Lugh himself, and he had wished a terrible plague upon the good goblin peoples that horribly disfigured them. And nearly the whole of the leprechauns had followed after him, and through their evil wishes, were destroying whole worlds. They were even involved in the civil war among the giants.

"She said that the witch was actually a good sorceress from the World of Men, who was trying to stop the madness of the little people, and especially the leprechauns, and the only way she found to do so was to put them all to sleep temporarily – a harmless spell that would stop their evil and not harm them.

"She also said that she had discovered great caverns of gems, and veins of gold that were untouched by the greedy leprechauns, who would have it all for their pots of evil wishing. These would be given to us if we would help her.

"Through her arts, she showed me a vision of these things, and I longed to see such marvelous places with my own eyes, and mine their gems of power. Slowly, I began to believe her lies.

"She bid me not tell my brothers, for she wished to tell them herself, and she gave me a map to follow to where these great mines could be had. This I followed, and indeed, I found the caverns as she had said. And there I met the Witch again. She was cloaked in black, and bid me take all I wanted – for these gems were gems of great power, and would give me power over the wicked little people who strove to corrupt the worlds.

"I took the gems and hoarded them, although this was unlawful. We were forbidden from taking anything from any world without the permission of the king of that land. But the Witch said that there was no king in this land, for the Elders of the Little People had corrupted themselves and abdicated their authority.

"The more I mined, the more I felt my power grow, but in truth, the more I was deceived. Soon, I was living only for the gems, and when I had mined all of them, I sought for others. Long I dug and gained more and more for myself, always encouraged on by the Witch.

"When the gems and gold and silver were gone from those mines, I took to gathering lesser stones, for my hunger for these things was never satisfied.

"When even the lesser stones were all hoarded, I hoarded yet more. Every stone I desired, and I fell to the place where I even gathered worthless pebbles if nothing more could be had.

"At long last, I fell into the black dust of my mines and, seeing the emptiness around me, I wept, for I hungered for yet more, but there was no more. My mines were played out, and I was left with nothing. I returned to my vast treasuries, and lo, they were empty, for the Witch and her goblins had stolen away my long years of labor.

"Then the goblins came and took me to the pits, and there I slaved in their mines for many years. I went mad there, and even considered consuming their filthy ooze, so great was my desire for… for anything! When finally I came to my senses, I said to myself, 'My brothers live in good houses, and here I sit in the dust. I will escape and go home.'

"So, on a moonless night, I used the last vestige of my rock craft and slipped away. I hid among the cargo of a ship, and eluded the goblins in the terrible crossing of the sea, then slipped ashore at night. I crossed the desert – how, I cannot remember – then came through the Great Hills and returned to the forest that I had left so long ago.

"But I found the Spell had grown strong, for the Witch had used all the gems of power that I had dug and made her own power stronger with them.

"I grew weary, but pressed on, but when I came to my old house, it lay in ruins. I ran blindly through the forest, seeking my brothers, but every house was destitute. Only Doc's house was left to return to, but I was too weary, and the Spell pressed upon me. I lay down in a ravine against a tree and fell into the dreadful Sleep. I will not speak of what I dreamed."

"That's where we found you, Dvalenn!" said Colleen.

"And for that I am ever in your debt. I would still be in that torment if it were not for you," he replied. "And in repayment to you and the debt I owe this whole land, I will go with you as far as I may."

The wagon bumped, and they came to a place on the old road where the stones were raised up above the ground and no grass or weeds grew on them.

"Ah! See here!" said Dvalenn, "Would you stop for a moment?"

Colleen stopped Badger, and Dvalenn climbed down from the cart and examined the stones. He ran his fingers over them as if caressing their smooth surface and then said, "Fine, fine stone! Dwarven carved, you know. See how they are neither chipped nor worn even after all these years? These were made from good hard rock and given special blessings. I think we have come to the Northern Spoke – a seventy-mile stretch that leads straight to the castle."

Dvalenn caressed the stones once more and mumbled something about revenge, and then climbed back into the cart.

"Seventy miles!" said Colleen. "That will take days and days!"

Badger snorted, tossed his head, and danced his front hooves on the stones of the road.

"Your horse doesn't think so," said Dvalenn.

Colleen laughed and said, "Yes, I think Badger would run a hundred miles if we let him. But we would bounce right out of this cart, I think. And we need to stop and rest and eat and such. But perhaps we could give him a little rein. This road seems smooth enough, and the way seems straight through the trees."

Colleen slackened the reins and said, "Hold on, everyone. Let's go, boy!"

Badger neighed and shot forward like a bolt. The Wigglepoxes and Oracle, who were sitting in the back of the wagon, went tumbling into the hay. The leprechaun girls laughed, and Mrs. Wigglepox gave a little shriek. Dvalenn held on to the seat, and Colleen's hair flew in the wind like a golden flame.

She had never felt such power in a horse before as Badger ran faster and faster, his great head poised as if he were in a great race.

"Whoa, boy! Slow down!" she called, laughing, and the great horse reluctantly slowed to a trot.

"I wonder how your horse might do in a race?" said Dvalenn. "Seems to me, my brother, Sindri, had a horse like him once. Big thing, if I remember right, and the same color. But that was years ago, and I can't recall his name now."

They moved southward, speaking now and then about the World of Men and Dwarves and of the Little People, and Colleen was amazed at how alike and yet how different they all were.

It was not long before they came to a region where the land began to rise and fall, and the road had been cut through the hills. Dvalenn remarked on the skill with which the Dwarves had carved this region and had mined the hills as they built the road and given the riches they found to the little people in the area.

They steadily climbed upward until ahead they could see that they were coming to a great hill, and the road passed directly through a tunnel that had been carved in its side.

"This is the Tunnel of Agap the Gnome," said Dvalenn. "He was in charge of its construction. It runs for a half mile through this hill – the Great Hill of the Great Hills! We dwarves aided in its construction. You will love the masterful work that was done on it! And the stone through this region was rare indeed!"

But as they approached, they could see that they would not be able to pass through, for the entrance, although at least twenty feet high, was completely blocked by huge boulders that had been rolled in front of it.

"Goblin work!" spat Dvalenn. "They hated Agap, you know, because he thwarted them so many times. He had a power over the Spell when it came. I wonder whatever happened to him, poor thing. I do hope he escaped the Witch somehow."

They rode up to the great boulders and stopped. Dvalenn got out of the cart and walked over to them, examining them carefully.

"We might go around, through the woods," commented Colleen.

"No, I think if we can go through here, we should," he replied, and began touching the boulders, which were twice his own height.

"Ah, not bad stone," he said. "I could carve these into good building blocks."

Then he began looking about and said, "And this hill – ah, the Great Hill! Good solid stone too! See, even the pebbles by the roadside shine. Good quartz!" He stooped down, picked up a handful, examined them, and slipped them into his pocket.

"Dvalenn," said Colleen. "Oughtn't we to be doing something about his blockade if we are going to go through this tunnel?"

"What's that? Oh! Yes. Well, let me see," he replied.

Once again, he put his hands on the boulders and mumbled, "Good stone. Did you happen to bring a hammer and chisel?"

"Whatever for, Dvalenn?" asked Colleen.

"Well, just to try this stone a bit. It might be worth saving – for later, of course," he replied.

"Dvalenn!" said Colleen, a bit exasperated. "We need to move on."

Oracle had climbed into the front and was watching the dwarf carefully. He squinted his eyes and said, "Creepicouns."

Then Colleen saw them – dark little faces peeping out from the shadows around the boulders, staring at Dvalenn as he caressed the rock.

"Dvalenn! Get away from there! Come here to the wagon!" she cried, and began to back the wagon away from the tunnel entrance.

She glanced to the right and left to see which way she could take them, and decided that the right seemed more open.

Mrs. Wigglepox, who was peeping over the seat and looking at the tunnel, said, "They're cluricauns! I think they're trying to cast the Spell on Dvalenn again! The more they distract him toward what he loves the most in this world, the more it will take hold!"

Dvalenn was now trying to wedge himself through the boulders to get into the tunnel.

"Dvalenn! No! You've got to snap out of it!" shouted Colleen.

Oracle peeked over the wagon's edge, waved his cane in the air, and ducked down again. All at once, there was a trembling in the ground. Badger reared, and the boulders began to shake and move. The little faces in the dark shadows vanished with a screech and Dvalenn seemed to come to himself. But the ground continued to shake, and the boulders began to roll toward the cart and down the slope. Dvalenn dodged out of the way and barely escaped being crushed.

Colleen pulled on the right rein and yelled, "Move, Badger, move!"

The horse pulled hard, dragging the wagon off the road. The boulders bounded by, just barely missing them.

Then Colleen saw it. It was a gigantic thing – a spirit that was somehow *in* the hill – or was it the hill itself? How she saw it, she did not know, but it was there, and was waking, stretching as it were, and shaking the ground as it rose from its slumber.

It looked out of the hill at her for a moment, seemed to smile, then gazed about. A frown crossed its earthy face, and a deep moan echoed from within the tunnel, like a deep pipe organ playing its lowest note. The sound resonated deep in the ground, and spread out, echoing through the forest. For a moment, the trees around them stirred, but as the sound died, they slipped back into their slumber.

But four black-clad cluricauns that had been hiding among the boulders flew frantically about for a moment, hating the light of the sun that now shone upon them. Filled with dread, they sped away into the shadows of the woods. The tunnel seemed to sigh, and it seemed to Colleen that the guardian lay back down again and then vanished.

The rumbling ground grew still, and Colleen exclaimed, "Did you see that?"

"See what, dear?" asked Mrs. Wigglepox.

"I thought I saw something, or someone – the spirit of the hill, I suppose. I think it woke up for a moment, and then went back to sleep."

Dvalenn came walking back to the cart, his head down. "Forgive me, Colleen. I did not know what I was doing. I... I got distracted."

Colleen could see that the pockets of his trousers were quite stuffed with rocks and pebbles.

"And I had forgotten about the Guardian of the Tunnel of Agap. It once watched over all travelers who came this way. But it seems mostly asleep now. Even it seems to have fallen under the Spell," he said.

"But it woke for a moment," said Colleen. "This world is full of all sorts of creatures that one can't see outright, isn't it? That's what I saw back at the Lake – trees and rocks and streams and hills, all the homes of beings just beyond our sight."

"Oh, yes," said Dvalenn. "Isn't it that way in your world?"

"I don't know about that," she replied. "I suppose some people might think so. At least I've heard stories like that. But if they are there, I've never seen them."

"Well, at any rate, I think the tunnel is safe now. It looks as though the cluricauns have fled. Shall we give it a try?" asked Dvalenn.

"All right," said Colleen, "but it looks very dark."

"Ah, it is true that from the outside, the Tunnel of Agap can seem dark and fearful. But once you enter into it fully, it is quite bright and cheery. You'll see," he replied.

"Dvalenn," said Colleen, "shouldn't you empty your pockets of all those stones?"

Dvalenn looked down and blushed. "Oh, well, one never knows when a good stone will be needed. Might as well hang onto them for now."

Colleen looked at him doubtfully, but said nothing. Oracle shook his head sadly and returned to the back of the wagon with the Wigglepox family.

She maneuvered the wagon back on the road and they set off, passing into the wide mouth of the dark tunnel. For a moment, they were shrouded in darkness, as though the light from outside could not penetrate into this place. But an instant later, they could see a steady glow growing before them. It was warm and inviting, and with every step that they took, it grew in both warmth and intensity.

The interior of the tunnel was perfectly round, and ornately carved with many pictures of all the races, all of them happy and joyful – friends sitting under trees, lovers walking hand in hand, families dining together, fathers holding their children, and many other scenes of love and friendship. Here again was a place where Colleen felt the power of the Spell lifting the further in they went.

"Prepare yourself, Colleen," said Dvalenn. "This tunnel has a special power about it that makes you see yourself as you really are."

Indeed, as they slowly made their way along, to Colleen's mind came many memories of her still young life – her mother and father, her brothers and sisters, and friends. Mostly fond memories, but also tinged with sad memories of how she had hurt someone's feelings or spoken or thought badly of someone. These memories, good and bad, seemed to rise sharply in her mind, and she decided that should she see the people she had hurt in any way again, she would make it right. But the feelings and thoughts of deep fondness and love for her family and the people of her community swept in like a wave, and she thought to herself, *That's how one ought to feel and think about everyone.*

She looked over at the Wigglepox family and saw that each of them was deep in thought, and that a tiny tear trickled down Mrs. Wigglepox's cheek.

Dvalenn also was deep in thought, a pained expression on his bearded face. He too was remembering his past, and somehow deeply examining himself.

What memories, she thought, *would a dwarf who had lived for thousands of years have to face going through this magical tunnel?*

His hand slipped into his pocket, and he seemed to be grasping the stones stuffed in there.

"This is beautiful," Colleen said after some minutes. "Did you and your brothers carve the whole thing – every scene, I mean?"

Dvalenn seemed to shake himself and said, "What's that? Oh! Yes. Well, Agap directed the whole thing and considered this tunnel one of his grandest achievements. It was the work of many, many years. He wished to make it a reminder to everyone who passed this way just what was most important in life."

"And what is that?" asked Colleen.

“I suppose each of us has to decide that,” replied Dvalenn as he fingered the stones in his pocket.

They rode on in silence, although Colleen wondered why the dwarf seemed so glum in such a beautiful place.

They emerged on the other side to see that the land and the road steadily fell toward a great valley below, and far, far to the south at the horizon was a thin line of tan.

“Behold, the southernmost stretch of the Sleepy Wood. Beyond the edge of these hills lie the Burning Sands,” said Dvalenn.

“Why don't we rest here and have a bite to eat,” suggested Colleen.

“A grand idea,” said Mrs. Wigglepox.

They untied Badger and let him wander a bit, then looked in the wagon to see what they could make a meal of.

“Mushrooms!” declared Dvalenn with glee. “I've not eaten mushrooms in... in... I can't even remember how long it's been!”

“From your brother Doc's own stores,” said Colleen.

Dvalenn picked one from the sack and popped it in his mouth, savoring its exquisite flavor.

“And we shall have some of Cian's roots,” said Mrs. Wigglepox.

After she had laid these out for them, she saw another sack that the Lady Danu must have given them. It was a dark red sack, and when she opened it, she found three sacks, each filled with water, and a bag of assorted nuts. There was also a note written on a roll of pure white parchment in a delicate hand that read, “*This water is from my own spring, and has my blessing. Even a little will quench great thirst.*”

So they sat together at the mouth of the Tunnel of Agap and ate a small meal and sipped some of Doc's draft, having decided to save the water from the Lady for the trip through the desert.

As they were preparing to leave, Badger, who had been grazing in a small patch of grass, whinnied and bolted directly toward Colleen, charging full speed.

"Badger? Badger, stop!" she yelled, but the horse charged forward, the whites of his eyes showing, his golden hooves pounding the ground furiously.

"Badger, what's wrong?" she yelled again.

Colleen and Dvalenn and the Wigglepox family ducked down as the great horse thundered right up to them, and then, with a great leap, jumped right over their heads and landed behind them.

They spun around just in time to see Badger slam into a goblin that had been sneaking up behind Colleen. It had a club in its hand, and it now screamed and went rolling backward into Agap's Tunnel.

It vanished behind the veil of darkness that cloaked the tunnel's interior, but inside they heard the goblin gasp, hiss, and then begin to shout, "No... no! It's not my fault! He did it, not me! No, *NO!*"

Its screams faded into silence as it ran blindly into the depths of the tunnel.

"What happened?" asked Colleen, shaken.

"Goblins don't like the Tunnel of Agap. They call it the Tunnel of Judgment. It makes them see just what they really are," replied Dvalenn. "Good thing Badger was keeping watch."

"Yes!" said Colleen, and she got up and soothed Badger, who was pacing back and forth in front of the tunnel, snorting and blowing.

"Good boy," she said to him, and hugged his neck.

"We had better post a watch from now on," said Dvalenn. "It's too easy to forget that this land is controlled by the goblins and their Witch. I suspect that the great bellow that the hill spirit gave attracted this goblin's attention. There might be more on their way, so we'd best be off, and quick."

While the others packed up, Colleen hitched up Badger, and they started down the slope toward the valley. But they were on their way for only a moment when Rose screamed.

Colleen turned, only to see dark shadows leaping through the woods on either side of the road and drawing closer.

"He-ya!" yelled Colleen and whipped the reins. "Run, Badger!"

Badger ran, but even as he did, a black shape leaped from the trees and grabbed hold of the rear of the wagon. Its feet flew off the ground as Badger ran faster and faster, and it held on for dear life.

Its hood flew back, revealing a hideous gray-green face with a long pointed nose. Yellow and brown jagged teeth filled its mouth, and it pulled itself forward and came face to face with little Rose, bearing its teeth in wicked grin.

Colleen glanced over her shoulder just in time to see Mrs. Wigglepox jump in the air, allowing the wind to carry her to the back of the wagon. She jumped again and landed square on the nose of the goblin, and with courage that amazed Colleen, she kicked the creature right in its great yellow eye with her pointed green shoe.

The goblin let go of the cart and grabbed its pained eye, and both it and Mrs. Wigglepox went tumbling backward off the wagon.

"Mother!" screamed Rose.

Colleen knew instantly what she had to do. She reined in Badger and brought them to a halt, just in time to see Mrs. Wigglepox run from the road and into the woods. The little woman dodged left, then right, but the enraged goblin was right on her heels, and now several of the other goblins had caught up and surrounded her. Both Lily and Rose screamed and began to cry.

Colleen grabbed her walking stick and leaped down from the wagon. She hit the pins that held Badger to the cart, releasing him, jumped up into the saddle, wheeled him around, and charged back at the pack of goblins, yelling like a banshee.

The goblins spun about to face her, and Mrs. Wigglepox dashed behind a tree and vanished beneath the leaves.

Colleen drove through the goblins, howling and swinging her staff, sending them running. But there were seven of them now, and although Badger was frightening as he neighed and stamped and reared, the goblins were sly, and circled around her and behind trees where the great horse could not kick them. Soon they were all around her, laughing their hideous laughs, and began to tighten their circle. Badger pranced in place, ready to fight, but Colleen was growing increasingly scared. She knew that they would take her eventually, but she had to give the others time to escape.

"Dvalenn!" she shouted. "Get the others and run for it!"

Dvalenn did not answer, but instead came leaping from behind a tree, and with a sound *crack*, knocked one of the goblins in the head with a hefty stick. Down the goblin went, but instantly two of them were on top of him. One of them got it in the ribs, but the other tackled him and the two went sprawling.

One of the other goblins took advantage of the distraction and, jumping onto Badger's back, grabbed Colleen, and sent her tumbling to the ground.

She screamed and kicked and managed to get to her feet. She swung her staff about her madly and called "Badger!"

But three of the goblins had seized his reins and were tying him to a tree. He neighed and kicked and pulled and thrashed his great head, but the bridle held fast.

Now four goblins circled about her, and she glanced to one side and saw Dvalenn lying unconscious on the ground, although three goblins lay there groaning as well.

Then she remembered the words of the Lady Danu. Reaching out with something beyond mere thought, she sensed the slumbering beings all around her – in the trees, and the giant in the hill. She reached out to them and felt their latent power – felt it begin to flow into her.

There was a sudden whipping of wind in the trees, and the deep moan of the tunnel, but in that moment, the goblins jumped. She was hit from behind, and the last thing she saw as she fell was the little form of Mrs. Wigglepox tugging desperately on the tied reins of Badger.

Chapter 11 – The Professor, the Wizard and the Sword

Frederick took a deep breath to steady himself. Would anyone believe him? *Could* anyone in their right mind believe what he was about to say? The eyes of Professor McPherson, Aonghus, and Bran were fixed on him as he began to tell his tale.

"First, let me introduce my... friend here," he said. "This is Gwydion. He is... well, I suppose he comes into my tale last of all."

Gwydion smiled and said, "Indeed, only in the last hour. But please, tell your tale from the beginning."

"Well, it all started when Colleen and I snuck away from the ship just before it sailed," he began.

Professor McPherson held up a hand and said, "Wait, Frederick. The other McGunnegals should hear this too if it involves Colleen. Is she here or still back in Ireland?"

Frederick swallowed hard and said, "Neither."

The professor raised an eyebrow and said, "Then where is she?"

He gulped again and said, "She's ... in a different land."

McPherson looked hard at him and said, "Do you mean she boarded the wrong ship and sailed, perhaps, to France or Spain?"

"No, sir," replied Frederick. "We didn't board a ship at all." He looked about uncomfortably and said, "We fell through a mirror into a different land... a whole different world."

The professor looked questioningly at Aonghus and Bran and then said, "Frederick..."

But then he paused and saw the sword that was propped against the wall. He walked quickly over to it, picked it up, and examined its blade and hilt.

"Frederick, where did you get this?" he said.

"It was in a cave under the lake out there. It was guarded by..." he began, but was cut off by Professor McPherson.

"Hush!" he said, and went to the door, opened it a crack, and peered out.

He then looked at Gwydion for a moment, hesitating.

"I trust him," said Frederick. "He was there when I found the sword."

McPherson raised his eyebrows in surprise.

"Under the lake?" he said.

Frederick nodded.

"It is true," said Gwydion.

Professor McPherson paused, thinking, then took the sword, wrapped it in a blanket from the bed, and said, "All of you, come with me, quietly."

The five of them silently left the room, and Professor McPherson led them through the Common Room, down the stairs, and back across the yard to his office. He shut the door behind them and locked it.

He then shut his windows and pulled the curtains shut. Only the light of one lamp illuminated the room, giving it a rather eerie appearance with all the strange objects that lined the wall, and the many books.

Gwydion looked about the room with great interest. But the professor then sat down at his desk, unrolled the sword, and laid it out before him. “Please sit down,” he said, indicating two seats in front of his desk and several to one side. “Now, Frederick, begin again. Where did you get this sword? No, actually, begin at the beginning, from the time you left the ship. Do not leave out any details,” he said.

Frederick told the whole tale, beginning with their leaving the ship, falling through the mirror, of the Little People, the goblins, of finding Dvalenn, and meeting Doc, and seeing the Gate of Anastazi the Great, of the pixies, of Mal and Cian, and fighting the goblin in Mal’s cave. He told them that he had nearly become a goblin, but had been healed, and showed them the two scars on his arm. Then he told of the cluricauns, and then of the Lady Danu and how incredible she was, and how she was the one who had sent him back to bring help.

They all listened with great interest, at times looking at one another with questioning eyes, and now and then they stopped him, asking questions or having him repeat what he had said, so extraordinary was his tale.

“And then I was in that cave, and *that* is where I found Gwydion lying on a slab of stone, and there was this sword and those mer-people, and I was nearly drowned, and would have been if it hadn't been for Aonghus and Bran here. And oh, there was the strangest tree...”

Suddenly, he remembered the fruit in his cloak pocket, and he carefully pulled it out, unwrapped it, and examined it.

“It blossomed and grew this fruit,” he said.

It was unharmed by the whole experience, and he placed it carefully on the professor's desk, allowing them all to see its bright form and smell its fragrance.

“Then the tree seemed to die. We left the cave, helped by the mer-people, and that's when Aonghus and Bran found us floundering about in the lake,” he said.

The whole story had lasted for nearly two hours. All the while, the professor had listened intently, occasionally fingering the sword. Then he stared at Frederick for a long time.

"It's all true, Professor," said Frederick flatly. "Whether you believe it or not, it's all true."

He was silent again for a long time, staring at the sword and thinking.

At last, he hesitantly spoke and said, "That is an incredible story, Frederick. No one in their right mind would ever believe you."

A look of distress washed across Frederick's face, and he began to protest, but the professor held up a hand.

"But perhaps I am not in my right mind," he said.

"You believe me then?" asked Frederick, looking hopeful.

The professor smiled a half smile and then continued. "I have something to tell you. It is a secret I would only share with my own son."

He glanced at the others, and noticed that Gwydion was watching him, his deep eyes intent under his bushy eyebrows.

"Something important is happening here, my friends. This meeting tonight is no mere chance, I think," said McPherson.

He paused, then continued, "And here is Gwydion – I know the name! It is an ancient name. But if it is true, how is it that you came to be in this cavern under the lake?"

"My own tale is long," replied Gwydion, "and I do not yet know many things. As to how I came to be in the cave, or how long I was there, I do not know. The mer-people hinted that it had been long ages, although how that could be, I cannot say. What is the year?"

"It is the year of our Lord, 1846," replied the professor.

“More mysteries,” said Gwydion. “I do not understand what that year means. My last recollection was that it was the nine hundred and eighty second year after the opening of the Gates.”

“The opening of what gates?” asked Aonghus.

“The Gates of Anastazi the Great, of course,” said Gwydion.

They stared at him blankly, and he realized that they did not know what he was speaking of. Then Frederick spoke.

“That's the gate that I told you about, under Sindri the Dwarf's house,” he said.

“Yes, and it was not there when I was last in that land,” replied the wizard.

“Wait, wait,” said the professor. “There are too many stories to tell here.”

He smiled at them then and said, “Let me show you just one thing – something that will likely keep you awake and thinking.”

He then placed the white brick that he had shown them before on the table and one of their own stones that they had left with him beside it, and then laid the sword beside these two.

There, on all three, were the same strange letters and runes and symbols of the language.

“What does it mean, Professor?” asked Bran.

“Obviously, all three come from the same culture. The same people who built on your farm are the same people who made this sword, and some time, long ago, my ancestors knew those people and passed this stone down through the generations. The family stories that surround it are quite incredible as well.”

Frederick was staring down at the sword, a look of wonder on his face.

“What's wrong, Frederick?” asked the professor.

“Gwydion, was there a wizard's castle in the World of Men?” asked Frederick.

“Why, yes, there was. But it was destroyed not long ago... Or was it very long ago?” said Gwydion thoughtfully.

Frederick's mind whirled. Could it be that the wizard's castle in the World of Men had been built... on the McGunnegal farm?

But before he could express the thought, Gwydion spoke.

“Professor, tell me, where did this white brick come from? What do your family stories say?”

Professor McPherson looked at each of them for a long moment and then said, “It came on the last ship... the last ship from Atlantis.”

Chapter 12 – Captured!

Colleen woke with a headache. She was lying in the wagon next to Dvalenn, and she found that her hands and feet were tied, and she had a gag tied over her mouth. Dvalenn was likewise bound, and he was staring at her with a concerned look. Oracle was nowhere to be seen, nor were the Wigglepoxes.

The wagon was bumping along at a slow pace, and Colleen could hear harsh goblin voices arguing.

"It's your turn to pull it, Grip. I'm tired," said one voice.

"Shut up and do the deed, Bof," said another, who must have been Grip.

"Don't tell me to shut up!" yelled Bof.

"Both of you shut up, or I'll have your tongues. Now all four of you pull!" said another.

Colleen surmised that there were four goblins pulling the wagon, and she wondered what had happened to Badger. Had Mrs. Wigglepox freed him in time? She hoped that they had not harmed him!

And what about Lily and Rose and Oracle? She lifted her head and glanced about the wagon but could not see much. At least the two leprechaun children were nowhere in sight.

The goblins went on arguing with one another, but the wagon slowly rolled on.

All at once, there was a tiny whisper into her ear. It was Lily. "Colleen!" she said. "I'm hiding under the straw by your head, so don't roll over. I think Mother got Badger loose. She climbed up his harness and sat between his ears and... Oh, what a sight! Oracle said to hide, so we did, but not before we saw Badger kick two or three of the goblins real good. They didn't get back up after that, but then the others pulled out swords, and Mother made Badger run into the Tunnel of Agap, where they wouldn't follow. You can bet she went for help, or is following from a distance. We're not sure what happened to Oracle. I don't think we should untie you just yet. Wait until tonight and then we'll get you loose. Don't nod, just remember that we'll get you loose first chance we get."

They rolled on and on, and the goblins grumbled on and on as well, occasionally having yelling matches. Once a fight broke out over who was going to walk in the shade, and Grip, the head goblin, had to break it up.

"Next time there's any of that, I'll rip your cloak off and tie you up in the sun!" he said, and after that, the arguments settled down a bit.

The sun began to set and the stars came out, and the goblins quickened their pace. Long into the night, they rolled on until the goblins began to grumble again about needing a break, and after a few more minutes, Grip reluctantly agreed.

"We stop here for four hours rest, no more!" he growled. "Make a camp!"

Colleen was desperately thirsty now, and as the wagon came to a stop, she tried to peer around to see if their packs had been discarded. Fortunately, they had not, but she did not dare to ask for anything.

But as if in response to her thoughts, Grip looked over the edge of the wagon and snarled.

"Make sure the prisoners are still tied securely," he yelled. "And give 'em a drink. They'll need it in the desert."

The goblins all laughed their hideous laughs.

"What shall we give 'em? Maybe some gribic?" asked another.

Again, they all roared with laughter, and Grip said, "They couldn't take it. Just give 'em a mouthful of whatever they brought."

One of the goblins began to rummage through their packs and found the water sacks that the Lady Danu had given to them. He squeezed one of them once and jumped into the wagon. He then went to Dvalenn, yanked the gag from his mouth, and splashed it on his face. Dvalenn sputtered, and the goblin laughed, then poured more of it into his mouth.

Dvalenn swallowed the water and sighed. The goblin then kicked him hard and turned to Colleen. She stared up at the creature with scared eyes, thinking that it would also deal her a blow. A tear rolled down her cheek.

To her utmost surprise, the goblin knelt down, gently removed her gag, lifted her head, and gave her a drink. She drank long, and the goblin allowed her to drink her fill. It then loosened her gag and replaced it, and likewise checked her bound hands and feet, made them more comfortable for her, and turned to go. It paused for a moment as if thinking, then pulled back its dark hood and looked at her.

"Nous!" she muttered through her gag, which was really no gag at all, now that the goblin had loosened it.

The goblin glanced up to be sure the others were not watching, put a finger to its lips, turned to Dvalenn, kicked him again, and jammed his gag back in place. It then put the water sack back, hissed at Dvalenn, looked at Colleen, then leaped from the wagon and went back to setting up camp with the other goblins.

Colleen shut her eyes and breathed a sigh of relief, hardly daring to believe what had just happened. Then she lifted her head and looked around, but could not see or hear any goblins close by. Turning slightly, she looked at Dvalenn. His right eye was swollen shut, and there was dried blood on his forehead.

"Are you all right?" she whispered through her gag.

The dwarf grunted and nodded.

"Dvalenn, don't worry. We still have a chance. Lily and Rose are with us and are free, and Mrs. Wigglepox has Badger. I'm sure she went for help. But I am worried about Oracle. I don't see him in the wagon," she whispered. "But did you see what that goblin did?"

Dvalenn rolled his one visible eye and grunted again.

Colleen lay back just in time, for she heard the voice of Nous say, "What ya wanna do with these ones for the night? I'm not gonna watch 'em."

Grip hissed, then barked, "You'll do what you're told, especially after deserting your own troop! You'll be in for it with the Witch when we get back, unless you shut up and follow orders."

"I told ya I never left 'em," lied Nous. "They lefted me. Musta thought I was dead."

"Well, you can just guard the prisoners now and be happy about it," said Grip.

Nous hissed, but Grip said, "And give me any trouble and *we* just might leave you for dead too, if you get my drift."

The other goblins laughed at this and Nous slunk back to the wagon, climbed up, and sat hunched on the seat and began to talk to himself.

"They left me for dead," he hissed under his breath, "but this one didn't." And he looked down at Colleen. "But *that* one," he said, raising a bony finger and pointing it at Dvalenn, "*that* one gave me a whack in the side. Haaa, now it's my turn to pay it back!"

He made a threatening gesture toward Dvalenn, then turned his back on him and went on mumbling something that Colleen could not make out.

"Now, this big leprechaun!" And he hissed more loudly. "That one will fetch a pretty price!"

Nous grew silent for a time, and Colleen could make out bits of the conversations that the other goblins were having.

"What about this rebellion down in the pits?" asked one of them.

"No such thing," said another. "The King and the Witch wouldn't allow it."

"I hear that there's big trouble," said a third. "They say there's a Sorceress that's risen up and fights against the Witch."

"Bosh!" said another that Colleen recognized as Grip. "No one's ever contended against the Witch and survived. Even those evil Wizards way back. They're all dead, and she's still here."

"But there have been losses, they say," said another. "Escapes."

"Where would they escape to?" said another voice. "They're all in the middle of the sea."

"Nobody knows," said the other. "But they've been disappearing all the same."

The conversation went on, shifting from news of this rebellion to stories of finding and capturing little people.

After some time, the noise of the goblins grew silent, and Nous climbed down from the bench, quietly rummaged around in the food sack, and pulled out some of Doc's mushrooms and a sack of water.

He then went to Colleen, bent low next to her ear, and said, "The not-Pwca-killer must promise not to speak or try to escape."

Nous' body and breath stank and nearly made her retch, but Colleen nodded her head. He then pulled down her gag and untied her hands. He then pulled back his hood, sniffed the mushrooms, wrinkled his nose, and handed them to her, along with the water. She gratefully took the food and water, took a bite, and then pointed to Dvalenn.

Nous hissed and whispered, "Not that one!"

Colleen leaned closer to the goblin and whispered, "Please, Nous, he was only trying to protect me. Please let me give him something."

Nous thought about this for a moment, a strange expression on his face as if he were trying to figure something out.

"*Quick!*" he hissed at her, then climbed back to the seat and turned his back, watching the camp.

"Thank you, Nous," she whispered, then scooted over to Dvalenn and untied his gag.

He was already awake and had been watching, but she held a finger to her lips, fed him a few mushrooms, and gave him more water. She then ate one more herself and took a drink.

Then re-tying Dvalenn's gag much looser than it had been, she shifted back to her own place. She remembered the crystal jar of water that the Lady had given her. She checked all of her pockets. It was missing.

"Oh no," she whispered.

She knew there was nothing she could do at the moment, so she tugged on Nous' black cloak. He hissed and turned. "Thank you, Nous," she whispered. "You are a friend."

A confused expression crossed his face for a moment, replaced by the harsh one that was generally there.

"Nous, what about the big leprechaun?" she said quietly. "Where is he?"

Nous grinned wickedly and nodded toward the front of the wagon. Colleen peeked over the edge and saw, to her horror, that Oracle was tied, hands and feet, to one of the wagon poles. He hung there limply, like some animal caught in a hunt, being carried home like a trophy.

"Nous!" she said, "You've got to let him loose! Put him back here with us. What if he dies, hanging there like that? I don't guess the Witch would be happy about that, would she?"

Nous pursed his gray lips and spat over the edge of the wagon. "Let it die," he said. "It's lost its mind anyway."

He climbed down into the wagon, retied Colleen's hands, although not too tightly, and put her gag loosely back in place. He then climbed back up on the wagon seat, curled up, and seemed to fall asleep.

Colleen shut her eyes, worrying about Oracle, worrying about where they were being taken, but also wondering about the goblins. Nous had actually been *kind* to her, in a way, although not to the others. What did that mean?

She woke some hours later to noisy shouts of goblin voices as they broke camp, and Grip stalked about, making sure all was in order.

"Check their bindings, Nous," he croaked.

Nous crawled down into the wagon and tugged on their ropes. Seeming satisfied, he glanced once at Colleen, hissed at Dvalenn, and climbed down from the wagon. There was a thud and a groan, then a good deal of laughter from the goblin band and Colleen could only imagine that they had done something cruel to Oracle.

It was still dark as they headed off again, with Grip once again sitting on the driver's seat and the four goblins pulling the wagon.

They slowly bumped along for several hours before the goblins began complaining again, and one of them yelled at Grip.

"Why can't those prisoners pull this thing? There they are lying in a soft bed of hay while we work and sweat down here. I say we let them pull it, and we ride up there," it said.

Grip grinned a wicked grin and shouted, "Halt the wagon! Let's see just what these prisoners can do."

The wagon stopped, and Nous was the first one into the wagon. He quickly untied Colleen, and removed her gag, then proceeded to do the same with Dvalenn.

"Out with you two!" he barked and gave Dvalenn a kick.

The dwarf groaned and slowly sat up, rubbing his wrists and feet where his bindings had given him rope burn. With Colleen's help, he slowly stood, wobbled, and then fell back in the hay.

"Up, I said!" shouted Nous, and would have slapped him, but Colleen looked hard at him, and instead, he grabbed Dvalenn by the shirt and hefted him up and over the side of the wagon, dropping him to the ground. The dwarf fell and rolled, and all the goblins laughed. Colleen jumped down after him and helped him to his feet.

"He can't pull the wagon in this condition!" she said to the goblins. "He can hardly stand up!"

They barked and hooted their harsh laughs, and Grip said, "Then perhaps you, little one, would like to pull the wagon yourself?"

Dvalenn struggled to his feet and said, "Never you mind, Colleen. I'm all right."

Then he slowly walked around the wagon and took hold of one of the poles.

Colleen followed him. Now they could clearly see the plight of poor Oracle. He was indeed tied like a pig to a spit, and his eyes were squinted shut as if in pain.

"Please let him go," said Colleen turning to whom she thought must be Grip. "He could help us pull, after all."

The goblins howled and leered again, and all jumped into the wagon.

"Why not?" said Grip. "Go on, then, untie him yourself."

Colleen went over to the leprechaun and began to struggle with the bindings. They were terribly tight, and she could not get the knots undone.

Dvalenn dropped his pole and helped her, and together they managed to free Oracle and lower him to the ground.

He lay there for a moment, breathing heavily, then opened his old eyes.

"We have to pull the wagon, Oracle," whispered Colleen. "Can you walk?"

Oracle slowly sat up, rubbing his legs and arms.

He looked up at Grip seated in the driver's seat and grinned. But there was no mischief or malice in the smile. It was simply a grin.

"He's insane!" cackled Grip. "Now get him up and have at it. Tie a rope around him. He'll be out in front."

One of the goblins tied the ends of a rope to rings on either pole, then threw the middle of the rope at Oracle.

"Pull, slaves!" yelled Grip.

"I'll bet you ten to one they can't even get it started," jeered one goblin.

"Maybe we should beat them with the whip. They'd pull then!" hissed another.

"Pull!" yelled Grip. "Pull like your life depends on it – because it does!"

Colleen and Dvalenn pulled on the wagon poles, but the wagon only rocked a little, and did not move. Oracle, weak as he was, added nothing to their effort, and without his cane, he even had trouble walking.

“Pull, I said!” screamed Grip.

Colleen looked over at Dvalenn, and he looked back at her with his one visible eye.

“I'm not a dwarf for nothing,” he whispered through the laughter of the goblins. “And dwarves made this road. Let's see what we can do with it.”

He began to sing a dwarvish song – a song of rock and labor and pulling and pushing of stone. It was a simple tune, and Colleen began to hum along, her sweet voice adding to his old dwarvish one.

Oracle looked back at the dwarf and nodded his approval and strained forward against his ropes.

Dvalenn sang, Colleen hummed, and they all pulled, and somehow the wagon slowly began to move. Oracle reached into his cloak for a moment, shut his eyes, and Colleen thought that for a moment there was a flash, like the briefest rainbow had come and gone. A moment later, a breeze began to blow. Leaves swirled in the air in front of them, and the forest debris was blown from their path.

The goblins took no notice of this and laughed loudly, hooting and slapping their thighs as the wagon rolled along.

The more they sang, the easier their burden seemed to be, and once they got going, although it was a heavy load, they found that they could do it. It was, after all, a wagon created by a leprechaun wish in a most extraordinary place.

But after some time of this, the goblins realized that something was not quite right, and one of them said, “Wait a minute. How is it that little thing and those old grumpers there can pull this big old wagon? And I don't like that singin' that they're doin'. And how is it that there's a wind up ahead and, we never feels it? Tell 'em to shut it up, Grip.”

“You want to pull with 'em, Hapless? Go on, you can join 'em if you want,” said Grip.

Hapless started to reply when another of the goblins riding in the cart said "Hey... hey! I smell somethin' funny here. It smells like... like... like little people!"

He began to dig about in the hay as though some frantic fit had taken hold of him.

This got the attention of all of the goblins, and they all began sniffing about. Colleen knew that Lily and Rose were still hiding under the seat and beneath the hay, and that she had to do something right then and there to distract them.

"Dvalenn, Oracle, we've got to run for it, now!" she whispered.

"I'm no good at it!" replied Dvalenn.

"Well, do something!" she yelled, and dropped her pole and took off at a sprint.

Dvalenn grabbed Oracle and dove under the wagon and out of sight, and found that there was a storage cubbyhole that they had not seen before, which he quickly opened, unceremoniously shoved Oracle in, then crawled in after him, shutting the door behind them. Colleen saw him do this, and sped away as fast as she could.

All five of the goblins leaped from the wagon and Grip cried, "After them!" and took off after Colleen, not seeing Dvalenn or Oracle anywhere.

But Colleen was fast, and as she raced down the road, she began to outdistance the goblins. This actually worried her, because she realized that she was running away from the wagon where all of their supplies were, and she wanted to lead the goblins far enough away so that Lily and Rose would have time to get out and escape. So she slowed down and pretended to tire, allowing the goblins to gain on her a bit.

At this, they shouted and howled, and called out, "Come back here, you little beast, and we'll show you what we do with escaped prisoners!"

"You'll never catch me!" she yelled, and ran on down the road.

Back at the wagon, Dvalenn cracked open the baggage compartment, saw and heard nothing, and slipped out, looking about the dark wood.

"Now you just stay put, Oracle," he said, shutting the door and leaving him in the compartment.

Suddenly, in the trees, a great dark shape moved. Dvalenn froze, knowing that it was much too big to be a goblin. He knew that there were other creatures in these woods at night, and as the great black shape drew near, he steeled himself and prepared for the worst. He knew he had to face it to give the little people children time to escape.

"Lily! Rose! Get ready to run!" he yelled.

The leprechaun girls climbed to the edge of the wagon, their faces tense with fear as it drew nearer and nearer. Then a huge shape emerged, and out of the woods trotted Badger, his great black mane waving in the breeze and Mrs. Wigglepox riding between his ears.

"Bless my soul," said Dvalenn. "I nearly died of fright. But my, I'm mighty glad to see you."

"We've been following you all night long," said Mrs. Wigglepox. "And when we saw the wagon stop again and heard the commotion, we snuck up a little closer. Then we saw Colleen run and the goblins go chasing after her."

"We've got to get Badger hooked up to this wagon and go after them," said Dvalenn. "Good thing I grabbed these pins."

He reached into an inside pocket and pulled out the pins that held Badger's saddle to the cart poles. Mrs. Wigglepox maneuvered Badger into place and Dvalenn hooked him up.

"I've gotten pretty good at horse-ear riding," said Mrs. Wigglepox. "And Badger is a real joy to ride. Quite a gentleman, but fierce in a fight. Where is Oracle?"

"Oh!" said Dvalenn, and quickly opened the compartment and helped him out.

"You best ride in the back," said Dvalenn. "I bet you could use a rest and a stretch."

He helped Oracle in and the old leprechaun lay down in the hay and shut his eyes.

Off they went down the road as fast as they dared in the dark, with all four of them sitting on the seat. It was a harrowing ride, but soon they began to wonder why they had not caught up to Colleen and the goblins yet. Surely they could not outrun Badger, so great a horse, and tireless.

They rode on, but saw nothing, and finally Dvalenn brought the wagon to a halt and said, "Begging your pardon, Wigglepoxes, but I think we must have passed them by, or the goblins have gotten Colleen and taken her away through the woods to one of their hideouts. Surely we would have caught them by now."

"I've been thinking the same thing, Dvalenn," said Mrs. Wigglepox. "But I'm not sure what to do about it. We can't just sit here, and we can't go back. We've just got to go on. The forest isn't safe at night."

"I suppose you're right, miss," replied Dvalenn. "Still, I wish we could see better in this dark. It's a good thing this old road is still around. At least it knows the way."

Dvalenn's eyes widened and he straightened in his seat.

"Why didn't I think of it before?" he said, and climbed down out of the wagon.

The little people watched as he brushed the leaves away from the stones of the road, laid his ear against them, and shut his eyes.

“Mother,” said Rose, “is Dvalenn listening to the stones the way Doc did?”

“I believe so, dearie,” she replied. “But let's be quiet now and see what happens.”

Dvalenn lay on the ground for a long time, and then slowly rose and said, “They've been this way, all right, and they're not that far ahead of us. But the stones go silent just ahead of where they are. Let's get going.”

He climbed back into the wagon and off they went, once again flying down the road as quickly as they dared.

Colleen raced on. She had been running for at least half an hour now, and she could tell that the goblins were tiring, for she had slowed considerably since they had first begun this race. She thought about Dvalenn and Oracle and Rose and Lily back at the wagon, and she glanced back to be sure that all five goblins were still after her. They were. She only hoped and prayed that Mrs. Wigglepox would come with help before the goblins tired of their chase and returned to the cart.

She slowed down again, making sure the goblins were staying with her. She was not tired yet, although she felt the oppressive weight of the Spell still bearing down upon her and upon the whole forest. Still, she was sure that if she just kept a song in her heart and often on her lips, its weight would be bearable and she could run on, even with a pack of goblins on her heels.

A moment later, one of the goblins, through labored breath, yelled, “I say we shoot it, Grip, before it gets away!”

“And I say you're an idiot, Bof,” panted Grip. “You know the order – no big people get shot – they get taken to the ship and to the Witch herself.”

“Bosh with orders!” heaved Bof. “This one's too fast. We could just wound it and knock it senseless, then take it to her.”

"And what if we do kill it?" said Grip. "Word gets back to her and then we're all done for."

"Who's to know, Grip? Just one arrow and if we kill it, who's to know?" said another goblin.

Suddenly, there was a twang of a bowstring. Colleen heard it and dodged aside just in time to hear an arrow *zing* past her ear.

"You foul idiot!" screamed Grip. "Put that thing away. You're a lousy shot anyway, Bof."

"I've had just about enough of you, Grip," yelled Bof.

Cries of anger and sounds fighting from the goblins reached Colleen's ears, but began to fade as she ran on. She turned to see the shadows of two goblins rolling about on the road and the other three dancing about them and shouting for one or the other.

Then a club was in the hand of one of them and the other took a hard blow on the head, then another, and it lay still in the road. Colleen stopped and dashed behind a tree to see what would happen. She was glad for the rest, but fearful of what might come.

"So much for the mighty Grip!" said the victor, which was obviously Bof. "I'm in charge now! Throw him in the trees over there and cover him up with leaves."

Two of the others grabbed the limp body of Grip and unceremoniously tossed him in the trees and piled leaves over him.

"What we do now?" said the third goblin, and Colleen recognized the voice as that of Nous.

"We go back to that wagon, that's what," said Bof.

"What about the girl?" asked Nous.

"Forget her. The stalkers will do her in anyway," said Bof.

Nous stood very still for a moment and then said, “How abouts one of us goes after the girl and the others go for the cart? Then we meets up tomorrow night at the big tree down by the desert?”

“The big tree?” said Bof.

Colleen thought that Nous was speaking much too loudly now, and the thought struck her that he was letting her in on their plans.

Good old Nous, she thought. *I think he's actually trying to help me.*

“Yea, Bof,” said Nous. “You know, the one at the desert's edge about a half day's march from here. It's hidden just a ways off to the side of the road. Use to be some old nutter there 'til he moved closer to that evil lake.”

“Shut up, Nous. Now listen to me. We're going to need all four of us now to pull that cart. So you just come right along with us, hear?” said Bof.

“What about Grip?” said Nous. “Is he dead?”

“Never you mind him. If he's not dead, he will be when the stalkers find him,” sneered Bof.

Nous stared at the mound that was Grip for a moment, trying to think of something that just wouldn't quite rise to the surface of his mind. He seemed to wrestle with something within himself, wagging his body back and forth.

“Nous!” shouted Bof, who had already begun walking up the road with the other two goblins.

Nous looked after them, then back at the mound again, and then down the road where Colleen had disappeared. He scratched his head, then turned and walked slowly behind the other goblins. Bof seemed satisfied with this and quickened his pace back to the cart. But Nous stopped again, glanced over his shoulder, and then dashed into the trees and disappeared into the shadows.

The sound of the three goblins faded into the night until Colleen could no longer see or hear them. She listened a moment more, then slipped from her hiding place, wondering about Grip. What were these *stalkers* that they had been speaking of? If Grip was alive, she just couldn't leave him to be eaten by... by who knew what.

Staying in the shadows at the edge of the forest, she silently made her way to the mound that was Grip, knelt down beside him, and brushed the leaves away. In the dim light, she could see that something dark and shiny stained his ugly face. But she could also see that his chest was slowly rising and falling. He was still alive. She pushed back the black hood and propped up his head. A long gash spilled the dark blood from his forehead. He was hideous, with a long pointy nose, which appeared to be broken, and large bat-like ears. His black tongue lolled from his filthy mouth, and his body stank.

She swallowed hard, found some moss at the base of a tree, and began to staunch the flow of blood from the wound.

"Why?"

The voice behind her made her jump. She spun around, startled and scared, and out from behind a tree came the shape of a goblin.

"Why?" it said again.

"Nous!" said Colleen. "Nous, you scared me!"

"Why does the Colleen help us?" Nous asked.

"You called me by my name, Nous. Thank you for not calling me *it*," she replied. "And I help because you're supposed to do to other people what you want them to do for you."

Nous drew closer and crouched down beside her, looking into her face, then down at Grip, and then at Colleen again. His face was just as ugly as Grip's, and he stank just as bad. But somehow, in his eyes, Colleen could see a question rising, or something that was confusing this goblin so deeply that he was forgetting that he was in the service of the Witch, forgetting his wicked upbringing, and forgetting that he could easily pounce and overpower her.

"We need to get Grip some help, Nous," said Colleen. "And what are these *stalkers*?"

But before he could answer, there was the sound of a *CRACK* behind them as if something had broken. They both spun around, and there, coming through the trees, was a set of red eyes.

Nous whipped a club from his belt and hissed.

"Run!" he said. "The Colleen must run!"

The creature bolted forward out of the shadows, and Nous and Colleen both dove to one side as its great bulk leaped into the moonlight, landing on all fours in front of Grip's fallen body. It was gray and hairy, and its head appeared to be a mixture of wolf and bat, but it was the size of a huge bear. It lifted its head to the sky and bellowed a howl that was like nothing Colleen had heard on earth, and it was answered in the distance by another. The creature sniffed the body of Grip, licked dark fangs with its tongue, lifted its head, and howled again. As more answering calls came, it turned to face Colleen and Nous, lines of saliva running from its gaping mouth.

Then Colleen heard another sound – the sound of hooves and a wagon, approaching fast. She then did something that totally surprised the creature. With speed that made Nous goggle, she sprinted forward and yelled, "Nous, grab Grip and drag him to the side of the road! Do it now!"

Then she was leaping through the air and landed on the back of the unprepared beast. She dug her fists hard into the creature's fur as it reared up and shook, trying to throw her off. It howled and growled and screamed its unholy cries, and now the answering calls were closer. Too close.

Nous grabbed Grip by a foot and pulled him roughly from the woods and to the side of the road. The sound of the approaching horse grew louder, and as the beast ran itself backward toward a large tree in an attempt to crush her, she jumped from its back, rolled, and dashed after Nous. Running into the road, she could see Badger galloping toward her with Dvalenn at the reins.

"Dvalenn! Badger! Here!" she yelled frantically.

Dvalenn pulled the wagon to a stop.

"Best get in," he said urgently.

The stalker, momentarily dazed by having slammed itself into the tree, was angry now, and seeing them, it charged.

"Into the wagon, Nous, but Grip first," she commanded.

Nous obeyed, and together they heaved Grip over the side and jumped in just as the creature charged out of the woods and came face to face with Badger. The great horse reared, threatening to upset the wagon, but then he came down hard with his mighty hooves on the head of the creature. It bellowed furiously and crashed to the side of the road. Colleen climbed to the front seat, grabbed the reins from Dvalenn, and said, "Run, Badger, run!"

He neighed and took off, just as two more stalkers came bounding from the woods.

"Run, boy, like you've never run before!" she cried.

Dvalenn went tumbling backward into the wagon, and Colleen nearly joined him, such was the strength and speed with which he surged forward.

"What's this!" cried Dvalenn, as he rolled right over top of Grip and into Nous.

The goblin hissed at the dwarf, and Dvalenn seized Colleen's walking stick, which lay within arm's reach. Nous raised his club, which he still had, and the two would have come to blows had Colleen not yelled, "Dvalenn! Nous! Stop! Now you just climb back up here, Dvalenn, and leave Nous back there with Grip!"

Nous hissed again and kept his club raised, but Dvalenn pulled himself back to the front of the wagon, still holding her walking stick, and climbed into the seat. He eyed the goblin suspiciously.

"Are you telling me that you have befriended goblins?" asked Dvalenn.

"Just hold on and I'll explain later!" she said.

He looked back again at the goblins, and at the stalkers that were now in pursuit.

"Well, those beasts are still behind us, and we nearly ran down three goblins on the road a ways back, and ... *look out*!" he shouted.

There in front of them in the road, another beast had appeared. It was smaller than the two that were chasing them, but it blocked their way.

Colleen could see no way around. Great trees hemmed them in on both sides, and there was no way to stop.

"Jump, Badger!" she yelled and, with a mighty leap, Badger jumped, flying over the head of the creature and pulling the wagon's front wheels off the ground.

As the wagon came down, it did so right on top of the beast, and it howled and went tumbling, just barely missing the spinning wheels, but taking a hard whack on the head and back. The two stalkers in pursuit jumped over its rolling form and continued their chase, and were managing to gain ground now.

"They are coming! Perhaps if we feed them?" hissed Nous, and he pointed at Grip.

"No, Nous, we're not feeding Grip to the stalkers. Just hold on tight. It's going to be a wild ride!"

"Hee-yaaa!" cried Colleen, flicking the reins. "Faster, boy!"

Now sweat poured from the great stallion's body and he gleamed jet black in the moonlight as he thundered on, his shining horseshoes like streaking whirls of gold in the night.

“They still come,” came Nous' hiss. “They are creatures of the Witch, and they run with her whip at their back!”

“Dvalenn, what can we do?” she asked desperately.

Then the voice of Oracle came from the back of the wagon.

“Night hates Light,” he said.

“Then I hope Badger can run until morning,” said Dvalenn.

But Oracle was rummaging about in the back of the wagon, digging in the hay. At first, he found his cane, and said, “Ah ha!” with great glee. Then he found Frederick's sword and set it aside. He found the vial of water that the Lady Danu had given to Colleen. This he stuffed inside his cloak and kept rummaging. Finally, he found what he was looking for - a water sack with the water from the Lady. He dragged the sack to the back of the wagon, grinning at Nous as the astonished goblin watched. But the sack was nearly as large as he was, and Colleen, looking over her shoulder, could see that he could not handle it alone.

“Take the reins, Dvalenn,” she said, and climbed back to help Oracle.

“What are you doing?” yelled Dvalenn.

“Just drive!” she shouted.

The stalkers were gaining ground. She helped Oracle open the sack of water. The beasts drew nearer... nearer. Then Oracle jumped on the sack, and a spray of water droplets rained on the first creature. It howled in protest and dropped to the ground, pawing at its face where the blessed water had splashed it. The second one, with a sudden surge of speed, leaped forward and grabbed hold of the rear of the cart, its great black claws clinging as they raced on. It opened its fetid maw and lunged forward, but Colleen pushed Oracle off the sack, picked it up, and dumped it down the creature's huge throat. The stalker swallowed, and its eyes bulged huge. A weird whimper escaped its throat, and it fell backward from the cart and went into spasms.

She stared as it disappeared in the distance behind them, then she sat down heavily and sighed, shaking.

"I think we're safe now, Dvalenn," she said. "But let's keep going, just in case."

Nous was staring at Colleen, almost with a look of admiration on his face.

"The Colleen and the Leprechaun saved us again," he said.

"Well, I'm sure you would have done the same for me. But let's have a look at Grip and see how he's doing," she replied.

She took a piece of cloth and, wetting it with water from another sack, reached over to clean the wound on Grip's head.

Nous hissed, and she froze.

"Whatever is wrong, Nous?" she asked.

"Does the Colleen wish to kill him?" he asked.

"Of course not!" she replied. "His wound needs to be cleaned."

"Not with that!" growled Nous. "Did the Colleen see what it did to the stalkers?"

"Goblins are not stalkers," she replied.

"But still Witch's people," he replied. "Water from the evil Lady kills all the Witch's people. She said so."

"You can't believe what a witch says," said Colleen. "I don't think that those blessed waters would kill anyone."

Nous snorted. "Goblins hate the Lady and her waters. Too bright! And it burns us, it does. It burns all the Witch's people."

"Well, maybe it would burn the bad right out of you if you soaked in it long enough," she replied.

"Deep fried goblin, that's what I'd be," he said.

Colleen laughed, and she realized that the goblin had actually made a joke. Was he actually befriending her? She was more convinced than ever that there was a spark of good somewhere inside them, and an idea was beginning to form in her mind.

"Please, Nous, we need to clean the wound. Let me try just a little," she said.

First, she wiped away the dark blood from his face with a dry end of the cloth, and then with the damp end, began to dab at the wound. Grip groaned hoarsely, and Nous watched with wide eyes as Colleen carefully cleaned the gash. It was a dreadful wound – deep and long, extending from the top of his forehead down to his eye, and it was still bleeding quite badly. To their astonishment, as Colleen cleaned it, the bleeding began to stop, and all along the cut, Grip's skin had turned from the rough, mottled gray-green to smooth, lavender-purple.

"Scarred!" said Nous. "See, it burns! Only baby goblins have such ugly scars, but we fix them."

"Your babies have lavender-colored skin?" asked Colleen.

"Yesss! Poor things. Cursed! But as soon as they're born, we dip 'em in the Ooze, and that fixes them right up, it does," he replied.

Then he glanced at Colleen and said, "In fact, they look a bit like you. I could fix you up a bit with the Ooze, and you wouldn't be so ugly."

Colleen almost wanted to laugh, but instead, she asked, “You dip your babies in an ooze? Whatever for?”

“To get rid of the scars, yes,” said Nous. “Grip will want to bathe in the Ooze too, to get rid of that scar.”

Colleen was not sure what to make of this, but the wound on Grip's head had stopped bleeding now, and she felt that at least he would not bleed to death.

“Would you watch him for me, Nous? I'd like to talk to Dvalenn for a bit,” said Colleen.

Nous lay down in the hay next to Grip and Oracle planted himself on the other side of the wounded goblin, watching him intently.

Colleen climbed back into the seat and took the reins. Mrs. Wigglepox, who had been holding on to the seat for dear life, sat more easily now next to her.

“Mrs. Wigglepox, I have an idea... what do you know about the Waters of Light and this goblin Ooze?”

“The Waters of Light?” replied Mrs. Wigglepox. “Well, it's said that they flow from the Source – from the Fountain of Heaven, it's called. No one's really sure where it is – except maybe the Lady – and that the Light that's in them is that same Light that shone when all things were first made. I think that's why the Witch's folk can't stand it. They've turned away from that Light to follow the Darkness.”

“What is the Darkness?” she asked.

Dvalenn glanced back at the goblins and leaned close to whisper to Colleen.

“It's said that the goblins worship it. There was a time when even the goblins were good. But something happened to them – something terrible that changed them from creatures of great beauty and talent to what they are today. The Witch might have been involved in it somehow, or maybe Mor-Fae, Anastazi the Great's daughter - although no one seems to know exactly how. But the goblins were the Keepers of the Fountain. It was from their world that the Lady first came and began to spread the Waters of Light to all the worlds after the Gates of Anastazi were opened. It was a glorious time!"

"Yes," said Mrs. Wigglepox. "But when the Darkness came, there was a terrible struggle. The Lady was involved in it, and she strove against that Darkness. But there was betrayal among the goblins, and the Source was cut off, or lost, and the Ooze took its place in their world, or so it's said."

"But what is this Ooze?" asked Colleen.

"No one knows for sure," she replied. "Some say it is the filth of the Darkness that entered the world of the goblins. Some say it is something from the goblins themselves, and some say both are true. But whatever it is, the goblins seem to delight in it."

"Nous said they bathe their children in it after they are born," replied Colleen. "He said that they are scarred when they are born, and look rather human and that the Ooze heals them."

"That I didn't know," said Dvalenn.

"But when I washed Grip's wound with the water that the Lady gave us, it looked like it changed his skin, and Nous said it was a scar like their babies bore. I wonder if maybe it's the other way around," said Colleen.

"What do you mean?" asked Dvalenn.

"I mean, what if it's this Ooze that scars them? What would happen if they stayed away from it and bathed their babies in the Waters of Light?" she said.

"One can only guess," said Mrs. Wigglepox. "But they say that the Light in the Lake is torture and fire to them."

“But it isn't,” said Colleen. “It's wonderful and beautiful and refreshes you.”

“Yes,” replied Mrs. Wigglepox. “Being immersed in those Waters makes one feel clean and warm through and through. I don't understand why the goblins and the Witch would hate it so, but they both hate and fear it. It is the Light within that they loathe.”

Colleen felt a tap on her back. It was Oracle, and in his hand was the vial of water.

“Thank you, Oracle!” she said, taking it from him.

She gazed at it for a few moments, wondering what this pure water would do – water from the very source of the Lake, the Lady had said. She put it back into her cloak pocket, and on they rode through the Great Hills, quietly pondering these things that seemed so strange.

Chapter 13 – Sailing Plans

The next morning, word came to all of the McGunnegals that they were to meet with Professor McPherson in his office right after breakfast. As they sat eating, Aonghus looked about the room for Frederick, but didn't see him anywhere.

"What's it all about, Aong?" asked Abbe. "I heard a rumor that you and Bran and someone else were in Professor McPherson's office late last night."

Aonghus leaned forward across the table and whispered, "It's big news, Ab. But I can't say anything just yet. You'll see when we get there."

They finished their breakfast as quick as they could and then headed out the door. There were whispers among the other students as they passed, but their sharp ears could hear many of them.

"They're going to be expelled before they get started," said one blonde-haired girl to another.

"That's right," she replied. "The biggest one, Aonghus, tried to drown a boy in the lake last night, I hear. And the police have been called."

"No, no," said another girl. "He didn't try to drown him – they were all swimming and the fool boy got himself in trouble and Bran saved him from drowning."

"I hear that an old man drowned in there last night," whispered another.

"That's right," said another, "and that Bran fellow was the one that drowned him!"

How could it be, thought Aonghus, *that so many rumors had begun already?* No wonder his parents had always told them not to believe everything people said, and that idle chatter led to trouble.

They made their way to the professor's office and Aonghus knocked on the door.

“Come!” said a voice.

Frederick was seated in front of the professor's desk and was looking at a map. He was wearing the same blue robe that he'd had on the prior night when they pulled him from the lake.

“Frederick!” said Bib in surprise. “How... where is Colleen? And why are you dressed in such ridiculous clothes?”

“A moment, please, ladies,” said the professor. “Now all of you, take a seat.”

Then they noticed an old man in the room with them. He was examining various artifacts sitting on the shelves about the room. The boys noted that he was no longer dressed in his old robe, but was wearing an outfit that a school professor would wear.

“Good morning, Gwydion,” said Aonghus. “You're dressed... differently today.”

“The good professor's idea,” he replied, smiling. He looked much more rested than he had the night before.

The professor had arranged chairs around his desk, and each of the children took a seat.

“Is Colleen all right?” asked Abbe as she sat down. She looked back and forth between the professor and Frederick, her eyes questioning.

“When I left her, she was fine,” answered Frederick.

“You mean you got an early ship, and you left without her? How is she going to get over here now? Why, of all the irresponsible...” began Bib, but Aonghus cut in.

“Easy, Bib. It's not like that. Just listen,” he said.

"First, ladies, let me introduce someone to you. This is Gwydion. He has just arrived with Frederick," said the professor.

"Pleased to make your acquaintance," said Gwydion.

"And you, sir," they replied.

"Now let me begin with this," said the professor, and he lifted the sword that Frederick had retrieved from the cave and placed it on the desk on top of the map.

Its golden-silver blade shimmered in the sunlight that fell through the window, and its gem-studded hilt sparkled. They stared at it for a moment, while the professor took their broken rocks from the bag and placed them one by one next to the sword.

"This sword must have been made by the same people who lived on our land!" said Abbe. "But what does that have to do with Colleen?"

"Ladies," said Aonghus, "there was something down in Grandpa McLochlan's basement – a mirror."

He paused, not quite sure how to express what he was about to say, then blurted it out.

"Colleen fell through it," he said.

"Oh my!" said Bib. "Did she cut herself? Is she all right? Did Dad take her to the hospital?"

"No, you don't understand," said Frederick. "The mirror is a doorway to... to other places. She and I both fell through it – it's like a portal or something. We ended up in a different land somewhere. It's a magic mirror!"

Bib stared at him and then replied sarcastically, "And I'm the queen of England. Now tell the truth, you, or I'll... I'll..."

"He's telling you the truth, Bib," cut in the professor.

Bib's mouth worked, but no words came out.

"It's true, Sis," said Bran. "We believe him. But she's in trouble, and we've got to get to her."

"Or maybe Frederick left her behind and made up this whole story as a big joke. Sounds like something a Buttersmouth would do, you know," she replied.

"Listen," said Aonghus. "We pulled Frederick and Gwydion here out of the lake last night. There was something in there – something... a lot of somethings... alive... they were... I think they were mer-people! And he had this sword, and he was dressed like he is now."

Bib crossed her arms and sat back, looking doubtful. But Henny slid off her chair, walked over to Frederick, and stared up into his face.

She looked at him for a long moment and said, "Frederick, tell me where Colleen is. Tell me the truth."

Frederick looked down at her and said, "She is in the Land of the Little People, Henny. When I left her, she was with the Lady Danu. I promised her I would come back and bring help if I could. I know it's terribly hard to believe. I wouldn't believe it myself. But I made a promise to her, and I intend to keep it."

Henny continued to stare up at him for a time, and then said, "I believe you. But why did you go there?"

"It was an accident. We both fell through the mirror. That little crystal ball is the key to making the mirror work, and we lost it. A goblin has it now, back in Ireland. She's trapped there unless we find another doorway to that world. And we've got to get that crystal ball back from that goblin." He blurted it all out with a feeling of desperation.

Henny went back to her seat, crawled up, and sat down.

Aonghus turned to his brother and sisters and said, "That fixes it for me. Henny has that funny way of seeing things. She can tell when people are lying, and they just can't seem to lie when talking to her."

"That's true, Bib," said Abbe. "Maybe there's something to this whole thing."

"Still..." said Bib, not wanting to believe this incredible story.

"But you were in the *lake?* And with this old chap?" asked Abbe. "What's that all about?"

"Well, Frederick," said McPherson. "I think it is time for you to tell your tale one more time."

Frederick looked at the girls. Bib still wore an unsure expression on her face, but they all leaned forward, ready to listen. So, once again, he told the tale, beginning with their slipping away from the ship and ending with the events of the night before. When he was done, they simply stared at him and at Gwydion in wonder, until Professor McPherson said, "So, it would seem that we need to either catch that goblin or find another doorway to this Land of the Little People."

"Begging your pardon, professor," said Bib, "but magical doorways are in short supply, or at least they are in Ireland. I say we sail back home and see what's really happening there. And what's all this about a goblin?"

"Bib, remember that black-robed man – or thing – that was seen the night that Mom disappeared?" asked Aonghus.

"Yes," she replied.

"We think it came through that mirror. And maybe... maybe Mom went through the other way... maybe she fell through the same way that Colleen and Frederick did," he replied.

"But I thought that crystal ball was supposed to activate it?" she said.

"Oh no," said Henny.

"What's wrong, Sprite?" asked Aonghus.

"I was at Grandpa's that day with Mom," she said. "He was sitting in his chair like always when Mom went down the cellar. But there was something round and smooth in his hand. I asked him what it was, and he told me it was a secret. He handed it to me, and I looked real hard at it. 'Don't tell anyone about it!' he said. Then he took it back and told me to run along home, so I did."

She looked scared, and her eyes began to tear up.

"I did it, didn't I? I opened the door by accident somehow. It's my fault that Mom disappeared. I must have turned it on, and she fell in, and that bad goblin came out. What if there are more goblins in there with her, Aonghus?"

"Now don't you go blaming yourself, little one. Even if you did turn on that mirror and Mom got in there somehow, you didn't do anything wrong. We don't know how it all happened, or why, but there's a reason for things, you'll see."

Henny sniffed, wiped her eyes on her sleeve, and then brightened. "So Mom and Colleen are in the same place? Maybe we could rescue them both!"

"Brilliant!" said Bran. "What's the plan, Professor? Do we sail back to Ireland and tell Dad, and get on the trail of that goblin thing?"

They all looked expectantly at the professor, and he looked back at each of them.

"That would be one option," he said. "But there is another possibility."

"And that is?" said Bib.

He sat down behind his desk, glanced at Frederick, and then said, "Let me tell you a story. Many years ago, I was a sailor and explorer. I have, since my youth, been fascinated with ancient cultures and relics and such, and I have taken every opportunity possible to go to exotic places around the world where there has been even a rumor of some lost civilization.

"I did this because, as you know, there had been certain artifacts handed down through my family line, along with family stories and legends, which spoke of a time when the world was quite different from today, and of great civilizations that arose, thrived, and were destroyed.

"It was my passion to uncover these mysteries and to find out all that I could about these ancient peoples and where they had gone.

"Why, I ask myself, are there so many legends and stories of giants and ogres and elves and heroes in the ancient past? Are they just fanciful stories made up by mothers to keep their children from disobeying them? Or was there something really there long ago?

"Once I was sailing in the area known as the Bermuda Triangle. Perhaps you have heard of it?"

The McGunnegals passed a knowing look among themselves.

"Yes, sir," said Aonghus. "Captain Truehart spoke of it on the trip over here."

"Truehart!" said McPherson, "So, just what did that old rascal have to say?"

"Well..." replied Aonghus, "he said that he rescued you down there a long time ago. That you had a stone chest..."

The professor held up a hand and put a finger to his lips. Then he whispered, "Do you see this map?" And he cleared the desk so that they could see the map better.

"This is a copy of one of the maps that was in that stone chest, children. Do you see what it shows?" he asked.

"Well," said Bib, rising from her chair and leaning over the map. "This looks like Africa, and this is South America, and this is Europe, and North America. But this large island between them all must be a magnified view of some island out in the Atlantic Ocean. Nothing that big exists out there."

"Ah! Quite right, Bib," he replied. "I see you have studied your geography. I have also pondered that very thing. Is this some small island out there somewhere? But if so, what are these cities and fortresses marked on it? The scale seems all wrong. And do you see the writing? It is the same language that is engraved on this sword, and these stones. I believe that this, my friends, is a map of Atlantis!"

"But where did you get it? Was it on that island that Truehart mentioned?" asked Bran.

McPherson leaned across the desk and whispered to them again, his eyes wide with wonder and excitement.

"I believe that I have been to this very island, children, or a tiny remnant of it. I believe that I have set foot upon the lost island of Atlantis, and I believe that *there* is where we will find our doorway to the land where your mother and sister are."

They all looked at the professor and at one another.

"But, Professor, oughtn't we go home to Ireland first and see if we can catch this goblin? Wouldn't that be quicker?" asked Abbe.

He sat down in his chair and looked at them, then asked, "Are any of you good at tracking and hunting and such?"

"Bran is the best huntsman in all Ireland," piped up Henny.

"All right. Now, Bran – forgive me – but I know you searched for your mother after her disappearance... yes, Rufus Buttersmouth told me the story. And there was this small man – or creature – that we now believe was a goblin – that was in your grandfather's house the night of her disappearance. You tried to track this thing, didn't you?"

"Of course," replied Bran. "Dad and Aonghus and I searched for months and months. We went all over. We saw strange signs and footprints, but whatever that thing was, it was more elusive than any animal we ever encountered. It was smart – real smart."

"And do you think that if we sailed back to Ireland now and went tracking it again that we would have any better luck this time around?" asked the professor.

"Maybe," said Bran. "The trail would be fresh again."

"The trail may be weeks old by the time we get there," he replied. "And we could spend months searching, and may never find a trace of the goblin or the crystal ball. I don't think we should leave Colleen alone for that long in a strange land with unfriendly creatures all about."

"But suppose this island you spoke of can be found. What makes you think that there's a doorway there to this land where Colleen is?" asked Aonghus.

"Because I have seen it!" the professor replied, and there was a strange look in his eye – a look of wonder and joy and madness all at once.

"Did you go through it?" asked Bib.

"Alas, no!" he replied, and his face returned to its normal wise look. "No. I did not go through the door. I fled from that place for fear and wonder."

"But why?" asked Henny.

The strange look returned, and he spoke in a low voice. "Because of the one who still sits on the throne in that dreadful place! When I was shipwrecked those many years ago, my ship was dashed on uncharted rocks somewhere in the middle of the Triangle. My crew was lost to the sea, and I nearly so, but Providence spared me and I clung to a broken piece of the ship and was washed through the jagged spears that surrounded that island and swept onto a broken and rocky shore.

"There, I stumbled inland, moving through that dark night and seeing only glimpses of the land around me through the flashes of lightning. At last, I came to what I thought was a cave, and crawled in to wait out the storm. All my strength was gone, and I could see nothing. I collapsed on a rough and broken floor and did not awake until the next day with the rising of the sun.

"Now, my memory of what happened next is vague, for that place is beyond all remembering. But I remember bones – many bones. And the door! The shining door that gripped my soul! That, at least, is blazoned on my mind, and I shall never forget that silver portal that shone like the moon! But something happened to me. I... I touched something, and a terrifying vision gripped me. It drove me to madness, and I fled from that place. I found the piece of the ship that I had been saved by, and pushed it out, away from that island, past the jagged teeth that surrounded it, and into the open sea.

"I remember watching as that pinnacle of rock faded in a strange fog and vanished, and as it did, I felt within my grip a stone chest. Somehow, I had picked it up in the cave, but how or why, I do not know.

"For many days, I floated, clutching that chest, until I was rescued by a ship – the very one that our good Captain Truehart was a deckhand on."

Professor McPherson shut his eyes and sighed a great sigh.

"Professor," said Frederick, "please, may I ask you a question?"

He opened his eyes, and he was himself again. "Certainly, son," he said.

"Well, I was just wondering – that door – was it really big – like twenty or more feet high? And was it a double door? And was the light a shining silvery light that kind of took hold of you when you saw it – like you just had to go to it and touch it or something?" he asked.

"Yes, Frederick, it was. It was very much like what you described in the Land of the Little People. And *that*, my friends, is why I believe it will take us there. I believe that perhaps those two doors are one and the same," he replied.

"But all the stories that we heard said that there was someone named Anastazi the Great who made those doors, and that he had disappeared long ago and had locked them," said Frederick.

"Ah, friends," said Gwydion quietly. "This is a strange tale. I know... or knew... Anastazi the Great. He did indeed create the Gates. But the Gate to the World of Men was not on this Island of Atlantis, last I knew. But the palace of the son of Anastazi was there. And there was a rumor that he had built something – perhaps a door or portal of some sort – but a terror came to his land after he had built it, and his kingdom was destroyed. The whole island vanished from this world, and we could not find it again. But if that door *has* been found again, it may be that it does indeed lead to the place we seek."

"But where *was* the Gate to the World of Men that Anastazi made?" asked Frederick.

"Ah, it still seems strange to me, all this talk of *was*, when to me it seems like just yesterday that all this happened. How long have I been bewitched, I wonder? But where *was* it, you ask? Why, it was on the Emerald Isle. It was within a great hill, inside the walls of the Wizard's Castle. But who can say where that now is. If Anastazi locked the gates, then none can open them. He alone bore their key, and he never revealed their secret to anyone, save perhaps his son and daughter, and they are lost long ago, it would seem."

"Gwydion," said Abbe excitedly, "there *is* a big hill on our farm back home. It's a strange place. It does seem magical at times, and it's inside the wall of rock that surrounds our farm. Do you think that it could be... could it be where this Gate of Anastazi is?"

Gwydion looked thoughtful and said, "I would have to see it to be sure. But if the gate is locked, then without the key, it would do us no good."

"But aren't you supposed to be a wizard?" she replied. "Could you do some spell or something to open it up?"

He smiled at her and said, "You do not understand. I am or was a wizard in my own right. But Anastazi was, or perhaps is, an Elven Lord extraordinaire. There has never been his equal. None could stand before him in either contest or battle, and what he shaped, none could undo or destroy. And what he locked, none could open."

"Doc said the Gate in the Land of the Little People was *leaking.* He thought it had been damaged in the Cataclysm," said Frederick.

"The Cataclysm?" said Gwydion.

"It's a long story," replied Frederick. "But it apparently blew things up and down and inside-out in that land."

Suddenly, a thought struck him.

"Gwydion... maybe it blew you right out of that world and back into the World of Men, along with that arch and that tree down under the lake. Wouldn't *that* be something?"

"It would indeed," replied Gwydion. "This tale grows stranger every moment. I would dearly love to go to your farm and see all that has befallen the land there. It was said that the portal, or whatever it was that Atlantis built on his island, had a secret to opening it that only he knew. If only we could find him, or his tomb, then we might be able to discover that secret."

After a long pause, Aonghus spoke. "We seem to have three choices, then," he said. "First, we can return to Ireland and hunt for the goblin in hopes of getting the crystal ball back. Second, we can return to Ireland and start digging up hills, looking for a long lost door. Or third, we can sail for Bermuda in search of some long lost island that the good professor here accidentally found decades ago. None seem good to me."

"Ireland," said Bib. "It only makes sense. There, we can do two things at once."

"But the Lady Danu told me to seek the king in the sea!" urged Frederick. "Surely this is what she meant – we're to set sail and find this island!"

"I say we vote on it," said Bran.

"Right," said Abbe.

"Yes," said Gwydion. "We must all agree. My heart is too troubled by all these things to see clearly which path is best, although I think the Emerald Isle – *Ireland,* did you call it? That seems best to me, at least at first. Is it far from here?"

"Only a day away, or two at the most," said McPherson.

"I want to go home and see Dad," said Henny.

"Where Colleen is concerned, we should talk to Dad," said Aonghus.

"Well, then, it is decided," said the professor. "We sail to Ireland first, but as soon as we see what may be there, I counsel that at least some of us go on to search for the lost Island in the Triangle."

"To Ireland, then," said Bran. "And I will hunt the goblin."

Frederick looked glum. "To Ireland, then," he said, but in his heart, he knew that he must set sail soon and find this island – and hopefully there find the king in the sea that the Lady had spoken of.

Chapter 14 - The Desert's Edge

The dawn broke in the east without further incident. Badger had pulled them through the remainder of the night, and seemed tireless even as they rode over the last low hill, broke from the forest, and gazed upon an incredible sight. A vast desert stretched out before them, a sea of brown sand that ran from horizon to horizon. The road ran straight into hot sands and disappeared.

“There's a place to hide here,” said Nous.

“Yes,” said Colleen. “I heard you saying that to Bof back there.”

“No, not there,” he said. “Goblins don't go there. It's a cursed place. No, there's a place of the *Ooze* nearby. That's where we can rest and be refreshed.”

“Nous, what is a place of the Ooze?” asked Colleen, a hint of concern in her voice.

“Nous will show you!” he said.

He climbed from the wagon and began to walk quickly along the desert's edge. They followed him for a short way and came to a black pool.

An oily looking skim covered its dark surface and, from time to time, acrid bubbles burst, releasing rotten-smelling gases. There was one absolutely gigantic tree beside it, but it was twisted and black and dead. It looked as though it had died a long, agonizing death in the presence of the dark pool. For some distance from the Ooze, the smaller trees were similarly bent as if writhing in silent agony and longing to be set free.

Oracle stared over the edge of the wagon at the great black tree and tears filled his eyes. He grasped his cane, climbed over the edge, and slid down the wheel to the ground. He slowly made his way around the dank pool to the twisted tree.

Setting his cane down, he placed both hands on its enormous roots and shut his eyes. His head and shoulders sagged as if some great weight of grief bore down upon him, and they could see him shaking, silently weeping for the dead tree.

"Do you see this pool and that tree?" said Mrs. Wigglepox angrily to everyone. "That was once a Sentinel Tree – one of the Great Trees planted by the Fairy Folk. Do you see? This is what the Witch has in mind for my world. She would turn every spring and pool into a source of death for everything that lives."

Then she turned to Lily and Rose and said, "Look hard, children, and see the work of the Witch. If she is not defeated, *that* will be the fate of the whole forest, even our Wigglepox Tree."

They stared in horror at the grotesque sight for a moment before Dvalenn broke the silence.

"Now you know where the goblins get their smell from," he said aloud, and he turned his head away in disgust.

But Nous threw off his black robe, revealing a skinny, gray-mottled body with a tattered cloth around his waist. He splashed gleefully into the pool and submerged in it up to his neck.

He called to them and said, "Come, come, join me in the Ooze! It will take away your ugliness! See! It makes us feel alive!"

He seemed rather giddy as he splashed about for several minutes, and then he crawled up out of the slimy pool, bent down, and, to their horror, took a long drink from it. It looked to Colleen as if small black worms or leeches clung to his body. But Nous did not seem to notice, and slipped his ragged black robe back on.

"Ahhh! Now we are refreshed!" he hissed. "Nous thinks the dwarf should take a dip, and the Colleen too, and the little people! Ahhh! You would feel much better, especially with the evil sun rising. And Grip will want to drink of it!"

He grinned a wicked grin and then flipped his hood up to cover his face.

"No thank you, Nous. And I think that Grip will have to do with just plain water," replied Colleen. "But I would like to see this other place that you mentioned to Bof. Some sort of hideout or something?"

"Hhhhhhh!" hissed Nous. "It is here! But not so nice as the Ooze. It is a bad place. Very evil."

Nous led them around the pool of Ooze, and Oracle slowly followed, glancing back more than once at the dead Sentinel tree.

Badger hurried past the sickly pool and, not far away, they came to another great tree, bigger than any they had seen before and, at the base, a clear spring of water flowed and made its way into the forest.

Mrs. Wigglepox exclaimed, "It is the mate to the dead Sentinel Tree back there! They always grow in pairs not far from each other. Let me speak to it!"

Colleen carefully put her on the ground, and she walked to the base of the mammoth tree.

Mrs. Wigglepox cupped her hands against it and said something that they could not hear, and immediately, the tree responded. There was a groaning and creaking that sounded not a little angry, and Mrs. Wigglepox backed away.

She glanced back at the others and said, "The tree will not allow the goblins near. It says they murdered its mate, and it will crush them if they approach."

"See! See!" exclaimed Nous. "It is an evil thing!"

Colleen said, "Please, Mrs. Wigglepox, tell the tree that I will vouch for these goblins. If they do any harm, the tree may do to me whatever it wishes. We need to rest before we enter the desert, and there are dangers in the forest right behind us."

Mrs. Wigglepox again cupped her hands against the tree, and again, it creaked and groaned, and this time, shook its branches threateningly.

"I will not go in that tree anyway," said Nous. "Trees swallow goblins and eat them. I've seen it myself. That's why we spread the Ooze on them – to tame them and make it safe for us."

"Please, Nous, we must rest, and we must stay together," pleaded Colleen.

But he was emphatic and would not go near the Sentinel Tree.

"Grip and I will stay by the Ooze today in the shadows of the black tree," he said, and he proceeded to roughly pick up Grip, throw him over one shoulder, and climb out of the wagon.

He then walked back toward the dark pool.

"And what if the other goblins come?" shouted Colleen.

Nous ignored her and kept walking.

"Should we stop him?" asked Colleen.

"Let him go," said Dvalenn. "You see, the goblins are corrupt deep inside and prefer their dark pools to anything that is good and wholesome, even if it would truly help them. And you can see that the forest itself fights against them."

Colleen felt pity for the goblins. She wondered how they had gotten to this wretched state in the first place.

But when Nous and Grip disappeared from sight behind the trees, Mrs. Wigglepox again spoke to the tree. It groaned further, a sorrowful moaning sound this time, but did not open.

"It says it is tired – so tired. It has fought so long. It longs for release. And it does not want to be a host for goblin friends," said Mrs. Wigglepox.

Colleen walked up to the tree, and it seemed to shudder.

"Please," she said, "we need your help. We will try to help you too if you will let us."

Then Oracle walked over to the tree and seated himself on one of its roots. He patted the root and sighed heavily, then looked up into its great branches that spread outward toward the sky. The tree stood silent for a time, and then a door creaked open for them. In they all went, and Badger easily pulled the whole wagon inside. Just as slowly as it had opened, the tree began to close, but openings appeared above, allowing rays of light to shine down on them far from above.

"Mrs. Wigglepox," said Colleen. "How is it that this tree is not sleeping like the others in the forest? There don't seem to be any little people to keep it awake."

"Sentinel Trees have great hearts," she replied, "and this one fights on even without its fairies. But I fear for it. Look at the base of the tree."

They all looked down, and there they could see that a bit of rot had set in.

"What's happening to it?" asked Colleen.

"I would guess that it has grown bitter at the loss of its mate," she replied. "Bitterness is like that, you know. It sinks into your roots and turns you rotten. Did you see how reluctant this tree was to let us in? I fear that this Sentinel will pass the remainder of its days lashing out at goblins and eventually even at others who would befriend it, then die alone, allowing no one to enter its heart and heal it."

"How sad," said Colleen. "Can you help it while you're here?"

"I will try," she said. "And Lily and Rose can help as well."

She beckoned for Colleen to bend low and then whispered, "And I am beginning to wonder more and more about our friend Oracle, here."

Oracle was walking about the base of the tree, examining the rot that had set in and shaking his head, touching the tree here and there and mumbling something they could not make out.

"So am I," whispered Colleen.

"He is rather extraordinary," said Mrs. Wigglepox, "and keeps on doing things that I've not seen a leprechaun do in many an age. But he acts so silly most of the time. I don't understand him."

She considered him a moment longer and then said, "Well, it's been a long day and we must try to help this poor tree."

Colleen put the children down, and they and Mrs. Wigglepox walked over to a hole in the wall and entered. Oracle also paused before a larger door, looked back at Colleen and Dvalenn, and then disappeared inside the tree. The tree moaned once and then was silent.

It had been another exhausting day in every way. As Colleen lay still, thinking of all that had happened and wondering what other strange things they might encounter, she glanced over at the old dwarf. She was about to ask him a question, but saw that he had already fallen asleep and had begun to snore.

"Tomorrow, we brave the Burning Sands," she said to herself, and drifted off to sleep.

Chapter 15 – The Announcement

The next day, during breakfast at the Ismere School, Professor McPherson rose from his usual table and called the students to attention.

"Good morning, students!" he began cheerfully. "I hope you are all enjoying your last few free days before classes begin. This year, we are going to be doing some things a bit differently."

There were glances around the room, and the students grew extra quiet.

"This year," he continued, "there will be a series of extended field trips as part of your studies. As usual, each of you will be visiting a neighboring country, but this time, some of these trips will last for several weeks rather than the usual three or four days."

At this, there were a number of expressions such as "Oh!" and "Yes!" and "No!"

"Some of you will be traveling to France, Ireland, Norway, Denmark, Germany, and to some select islands. During these trips, you will be studying your particular Focus in light of a different culture, under the guidance of a sponsor."

This remark brought nothing but groans.

"Indeed, the very first group of students will be leaving tomorrow, and I shall be their sponsor. You and your parents will each be notified of the time of your trip. Best wishes to you all in the coming semester."

As soon as he had finished speaking, he left the room. Immediately, the room broke out with scores of discussions about where they might be going and what they might study while there.

The McGunnegals and Frederick, who were all seated together, leaned in close.

“So that's how he's going to do it. We couldn't just head off somewhere across the ocean without some good reason,” said Bran.

“Do you think he'll really make us study along the way?” asked Abbe.

“Let's hope so,” said Bib. “I don't want to get behind on my studies.”

“You would say that,” said Aonghus.

“But won't it be grand?” said Frederick. “I mean, sailing! Real sailing! Don't you just love the sea, with its vastness and mystery?”

“I suppose so,” said Aonghus, “although I'd never thought of being a sailor.”

“I have,” said Frederick.

“Well, I guess we'd better get things packed then. And I think you'll be needing some different clothes,” said Aonghus.

“The professor has already taken care of that. I've got a whole new wardrobe. But I will be taking those things I found in the Land of ... well, you know where.” Frederick said the last in a whisper, not wishing to draw attention.

“Where did you put the sword?” whispered Bran.

“The professor has it,” replied Frederick. “After all, it would look rather odd for a student to carry a sword around the campus.”

“Right,” said Aonghus.

“Is the professor going to tell Dad that we're going on a field trip?” asked Henny.

“Oh, that's taken care of too,” said Frederick. “He mentioned to me that my mother has been notified that I arrived early and am fine and that I will be immediately leaving for Bermuda and neighboring islands, with a short stop in Ireland. A letter is also being sent to your father. Of course, we will be seeing him anyway.

"There are field trips mentioned in the school agreement that he was given, of course, and it does mention that some may be cultural field trips to neighboring countries. And this will just be a rather extended field trip. Don't worry, the professor will make sure everything is in order."

They spent the remainder of the morning getting their things ready to go, and saying farewell to their new friends. When afternoon came, they gathered together on the shore of the lake and gazed down into its clear depths.

"Do you see that dark rock wall, way down there?" said Frederick, pointing to a dark patch toward the middle of the lake.

They all gazed down into the water, but it was quite difficult to see anything since a breeze was blowing and the surface of the lake was shimmering in the sunlight.

"I don't see anything," said Abbe.

"Well, it's there," said Frederick. "I'm sure that's the spot. If you swim down about thirty feet, you go under a ledge, and there's an underwater passage. Follow that in for about ten feet and it rises up and into the cave where I found... it. And that tree is down there too, and so are *they*."

"This is so hard to believe," said Bib.

"But I saw them too, Bib," said Aonghus. "They were... beautiful, but otherworldly, you might say. And they had *green hair!*"

"If it came from anyone else, big brother, I'd say they were a bit loony," she replied.

But before he could respond, there was a voice from behind.

"So, the Irish are off on a little field trip, eh?"

They turned to see Ed Choke, Slick, Bigs, and Fred, along with six very sour-looking characters behind them, who obviously were not students at the school.

“Hello, Ed,” said Aonghus. “No hard feelings, I hope.”

“Better tell your little sisters to beat it, boy. And you too, Buttersmouth,” said Ed.

Aonghus' face grew stormy as he looked at the ten boys who had wicked grins on their faces.

“Go ahead, Abbe, Bib, Henny – and you too, Frederick. Go on back to the commons. We'll be there shortly,” he said.

“Aonghus...” began Bib, but he silenced her with an upraised hand.

The girls slipped away, but Frederick remained.

“Frederick?” said Bran. “Are you sure you want to be a part of this?”

Frederick did not answer, but looked stonily at Ed.

“Right then,” said Bran, grinning broadly. “Frederick, how many of them do you want to put in the lake?”

“I say we let him have 'em all,” said Aonghus with a sudden laugh, seeing the look on Frederick's face. “He looks mad enough to take them by himself!”

Before any punches could be thrown, there was a strange sound coming from the nearby woods. They all turned, and out of the trees came a herd of deer – about a dozen of them, headed by a huge buck with an impressive rack of antlers. They came charging directly at the group of boys and, as they came, the great buck lowered his head and sped forward.

"Look out!" yelled one of the boys, and the group scattered, some running this way and some that. Ed Choke ran directly into the lake and dove in as the buck followed him into chest-deep water.

Aonghus and Bran stood totally still, and Aonghus' strong grip on Frederick's shoulder kept him frozen in place.

The herd thundered around and past them, chasing the group of boys as they scattered, until they had all run from the lake shore. In the end, only Ed Choke remained, treading water as the great stag pranced back and forth in the shallows, daring him to approach.

Casually, Abbe walked from the woods, with Bib and Henny behind her, then down to the shore where the stag was. It snorted once at Ed, then trotted over to Abbe.

She wrapped her arms around its neck in a hug and said, "Thank you, good stag."

It tossed its great head once, then trotted away, calling to its herd, which returned to him, and they all returned to the woods.

"You're a bunch of freaks!" yelled Ed from the lake. "Devils! That's what you are!"

"Come on, Ed, get out of the water. There are things in there worse than deer," called Bran.

Ed looked hesitantly down at the water and quickly began to swim ashore. Aonghus waded out to meet him, and offered his hand to help. But Ed refused it. Aonghus only shook his head sadly as they both waded ashore.

Ed looked at the six of them, and as he turned and ran from the shore, he shouted, "There's something mighty weird about you all, and I aim to find out what it is."

"Ah, well," said Aonghus. "Some people are just nasty, I suppose."

"Say, ladies, that was some trick," said Bran. "How did you get those deer to do that?"

"Henny spotted them in the wood where we went to hide and watch," said Bib, "and Abbe just ran over to that big stag, gave it a hug, and pointed out Ed Choke to it. We could see that those boys were ready to start something bad. Then the whole herd went running from the wood and right at them. It was amazing! Henny and I just stayed out of the way."

"I knew you were good with animals, Abbe," said Aonghus, "but that's pretty amazing!"

Abbe blushed and said, "Thanks. I'm not sure just how it happened. It just did, that's all."

"Come on, let's get back to the Commons. I'm sure Choke and his buddies are spreading rumors already."

They headed back, washed, and went to dinner, then retired early, having everything packed and ready to go. Frederick stayed with Aonghus and Bran, but they could not sleep, and the three of them talked long into the night, wondering what the next day might bring.

Chapter 16 – The Field Trip

Morning came, and the McGunnegals and Frederick were up with the sun. They met in the Commons, where they found the professor. Gwydion was nowhere to be seen.

“All packed and ready to go?” said Professor McPherson.

“All set, sir,” replied Aonghus.

“Good, the ship is at the docks downtown not far from here. Gwydion is waiting for us. He and I took a carriage there early this morning. I've arranged for all of the supplies for our voyage,” he replied.

After a good breakfast, they all gathered their belongings and followed the professor outside. There, they found two cars waiting for them.

“Marvelous!” said Bib excitedly. “Are we to ride in these steam cars to the docks?”

“Yes,” said the professor. “This one is mine,” he said, indicating a fancy black car that puffed gray steam, “which I've just had serviced this morning, and this one belongs to my friend, Rodger Wilcocks.”

A tall thin man with graying hair, wearing a red cap and brown trousers, tipped his hat to them.

“Pleased to make your acquaintance,” he said.

Rodger's car also puffed steam, but was larger than the professor's vehicle, able to seat six with a cargo area in the rear.

“Load up your bags onto Rodger's car, and you boys ride with him. Ladies, I believe there is just enough room for the three of you in my vehicle. Come now, let's be off,” said the professor.

In a few moments, they were ready, and with a toot of horns and clouds of steam, they rolled away toward the docks.

"Sir, how did you acquire a steam-powered car? I've only seen them a few times, but I've heard all sorts of rumors about them back home," said Bib.

"Ah, I have a friend who is an inventor. This one was an older model of his. He has created a much better one, so to help finance his projects, I purchased this one from him. Rodger is his partner. They hope to start a business selling them one day," he replied. "We shall be taking this car along with us on our journey. Who can say where we may need to travel?"

"Wonderful!" she replied. "Do you think I might have a go at driving it? I mean, if we find a good open space where I wouldn't hit anything?" she asked.

Professor McPherson laughed and said, "Of course, my dear. You shall all give it a try as soon as we are able, although that may not be for some time."

For the rest of the journey, Bib and Professor McPherson chatted on about autos and ships and building things, and where the world might be going with all the new inventions that were coming about.

The professor was amazed at Bib's insights into so many fields of science that he said, "Bib, I do believe that you are destined to be an inventor one day. How about making your Focus *Science and the Exploration of the Natural World* when we return to school?"

"Well, I really do like making things and tinkering and just plain thinking. I don't have the weird talents that my brothers and sisters have," she replied.

"What do you mean by *weird talents*, Bib?" he asked.

"Well, I mean, take Abbe here, for example. You might as well say that she can talk to animals," said Bib.

"No, it's not like that," piped up Abbe. "They just seem to know what I want them to do, and they know I won't harm them, and they do it."

"And then there's Henny," continued Bib. "She can see and hear things that nobody else can. It's like she's got eagle eyes or something. And she's got this *really* strange ability to play hide and seek, and *nobody* has *ever* been able to find her. She also has a way of keeping people honest. You just can't lie to her or fool her. She has a way of seeing right through you."

Henny's cheeks blushed with embarrassment.

"And what about your brothers?" asked the professor, growing more curious all the time.

"Oh, Aonghus is just about busting with muscles. I've never seen anything or anybody as strong as him, except maybe Dad. And Bran – he can shoot an arrow through a bull's-eye from a mile away or catch an arrow right out of the air. And those two can run like horses."

"And what of your sister Colleen?" he asked.

"Well, she inherited Mom's voice. It's... I know it sounds funny... but it's *magical*. Stuff just seemed to happen when Mom sang. And Colleen seems to have that same talent. Dad used to say that Mom could sing the stars right out of the sky if she tried," replied Bib. "But me, I just think a lot."

"Don't let Bib fool you, Professor," said Abbe. "There's never been a puzzle that she hasn't been able to solve. She says she can see the solution to things in her mind like it's a picture in front of her. Plus, she makes the boys practically swoon with that smile of hers."

"Oh, hush!" said Bib.

"Don't sell yourself short, Bib," said the professor. "Each person has hidden talents that they only discover when they are needed. They may lie hidden for years and years. And besides that, having a keen mind is a rare gift."

They rode on in silence for some time, and the girls' thoughts turned to their mother. Could it be that Colleen and Frederick had actually found out where she was?

But soon the trip drew to an end, and the docks came into sight. The two cars puffed up alongside the wharf where a rather beleaguered-looking small ship was docked. It had old tarps hanging over its rails and bow, giving it an almost haunted appearance. Two tall masts jutted skyward from which yellowing sails hung limply. The group of them got out of the cars and stared at the old ship.

"Is this the ship we're sailing in?" asked Frederick.

"Yes," replied Professor McPherson. "She's seen many voyages."

"But where is the crew?" asked Bib.

"The crew? Oh, didn't I tell you? *You* are going to be the crew of this ship," he replied.

"We are?" said Aonghus.

"Yes! Well, you and a few others. I could only find three lads on such short notice, but we are only sailing to Ireland, at least for the moment, but our ship is small and needs only a few experienced crewmen and a half dozen others who are willing to listen and learn. I shall be your captain," he said. "Now, let's get your things aboard."

They all wondered if the professor was playing a joke on them, but as they gathered up their belongings and walked across the gangplank, they could only see three sailors going about the ship, getting her ready to sail. Professor McPherson carried a heavy bag and something wrapped in a blanket as they walked aboard.

"I think he's actually serious," whispered Bran to Aonghus. "This is madness!"

"Oh, don't worry, Bran," said the professor, overhearing. "You will all do just fine. It will be a short trip."

"What's your ship's name, Professor?" asked Henny.

"She's called the *Unknown*, my dear. I named her that because so many times we have sailed there together, off into the unknown," he replied. "She was built as a prototype of the bigger clipper ships we see today, and she's just as fast."

He led them across the deck, which was littered with old barrels and ropes and tarps and various other items, leaving only a small path for them to walk.

Frederick looked about at all of the junk and aged appearance of everything and secretly wondered if the old ship would even make such a short voyage. But the professor beamed with pride as he led them down through a hatch into the hull of the ship.

They descended a flight of stairs through a passage whose walls were draped with what appeared to be old blankets and quilts and curtains.

"Wait here one moment while I put these things in my cabin," he said.

He went through a door at the end of the hall, and re-emerged empty handed, trailed by Gwydion.

The old man was dressed in modern clothes rather than his old robe that they had seen him in before, and he sported a maroon coat with tails over a white shirt, and light brown britches with black shoes. In place of his tall staff, he leaned on a gentleman's cane, and his long beard and hair were both tied in ponytails.

"Hello, children," he said with a grin, revealing full set of white teeth.

"Hello, Mr. Gwydion," said Henny. "You look different today."

"And you look just the same as I remember from yesterday," he replied, and patted her on the head.

"Come along then," said the professor and he opened a door on the right. "Here are your quarters."

"This cabin is for the ladies," he said.

They all went in to find a fair-sized room with two sets of bunks against the walls and a small table with four chairs around it. An oil lamp hung from a gold chain that was attached to the ceiling, shedding a warm light about the room, and the walls were adorned with old tapestries of lighthouses and sea cliffs and other seaside landscapes.

"It's actually quite cozy," said Abbe. "I think we'll be quite comfortable."

They each picked a bunk – Abbe and Bib taking the lower ones and Henny climbing up into an upper one and grinning broadly.

"And now for the gentleman's quarters," said the professor.

He led them across the hall to a similar room that had somewhat larger bunks, which Aonghus and Bran were glad of.

"I might actually fit in this one," said Aonghus, stretching out on one of the lower beds.

Frederick selected an upper bunk and put his bag up on it.

"Now the galley is the next door on the right, and the mess hall is directly across from it on the left. You'll have plenty of time to see those rooms later. Gwydion will be staying with me in my cabin on the spare bunk, and the rest of the crew will be in the large crew quarters through that last door.

"But we must be off very soon. I have a good deal of teaching to do for you all, and there's no time to waste," said the professor. "Come along now, to the upper deck for your first lesson."

They marched up on the deck to see Rodger carefully driving the professor's car across two wide planks onto the ship.

"In all my days!" said Gwydion in surprise. "What wizardry is this? A horseless carriage?"

"Oh, it's not wizardry," said Bib to the old man. "It's technology."

"Technology! I have not heard of that. Is it akin to alchemy?" he asked.

"Yes, you could say that, although today, we would call that *chemistry,*" she replied.

"Well, Bib, you and I must have a discussion regarding this *technology* and *chemistry,* and we shall compare them to wizardry and alchemy. Truly the world has changed!"

Rodger had now maneuvered the car onto the ship, and they walked over to it to steady it while the planks were removed.

Gwydion walked about it with a look of amazement. "*Technology,*" he whispered. "It is a *device*, is it not? I sense heat and steam coming from its belly."

"Indeed," said the professor. "It is a *machine*. The knowledge of mankind is advancing quickly, and we build more and more complex machines as our understanding of the world grows. This machine is run with steam power. A fire heats water and produces steam, and that steam is used to turn an engine inside, which turns the wheels and *voila!* You have a horseless carriage."

"Indeed, I have awakened into a strange and wondrous world," whispered Gwydion.

The old man examined the car, and Professor McPherson explained some of its parts further.

"Where's he been, off on an island somewhere?" whispered Rodger to Bran with a smirk.

Bran breathed a little laugh and shrugged.

"You might say that. You know how old folks are with technology," he whispered back.

Rodger smiled and nodded.

"Well, very good, then," said the professor, concluding his explanation to Gwydion. "Let's get the car secured in the lower hold. Over here there's a large hatch for stowing the cargo."

He led them over to a brass ring that was set in a raised section of the floor of the deck, and, moving aside a bundle of old rope and a few barrels, they could see a large doorframe about ten feet square with brass hinges opposite the ring.

He unbolted two large sliding bolts that locked the door down, and untied a rope and hook from one of the masts that was attached to a pulley up above. He attached the hook to the brass ring and then pulled the rope tight.

"It generally takes two or three of us to lift this door, but Bib says that Aonghus is quite a strapping fellow. How about taking care of it for us, and tie it off once you have the door open. Bran, you stand ready to give your brother a hand. Bib and Rodger and I will maneuver the car into place. Gwydion would you like to sit in the passenger's seat? Everyone else, please clear a path for us."

Gwydion carefully climbed into the seat that McPherson indicated and looked at the dashboard, pedals, and knobs.

"Amazing!" he said, listening to the steam engine sputtering.

"Everything in the hold must be secured and tied down, or when we hit rough seas, it will shift or fall and break open. That goes for your personal belongings in your cabins as well, and everything in the galley and mess hall, and on deck. That is why you see so many ropes lying about. We shall need them to lash down our cargo, our belongings, and perhaps, even ourselves at times," said Professor McPherson.

Aonghus took the rope that was now hooked to the ring in the deck from the professor and pulled. The huge trap door in the deck lifted open silently, revealing a wooden ramp that extended down into the bowels of the ship. Aonghus tied off the rope to the mast and watched as Bib, now behind the wheel of the car, was listening intently to Professor McPherson's instructions on the use of the accelerator, brake, and steering. Gwydion listened carefully, taking note of everything. In a few minutes, a path had been cleared, and Bib maneuvered the car in front of the ramp, and then the professor showed her how to turn it off.

“Give us a little push, would you, Aonghus? Not too hard now,” said the professor.

Aonghus got behind the car, and pushed the car forward so that its front wheels were on the ramp.

“Now ease off the brake just slightly, Bib, and let her roll on down to the bottom of the cargo hold,” said Professor McPherson.

Bib did so, and slowly the car rolled down the ramp into the hold.

Aonghus walked behind, his hand still on the bar that ran around the rear of the car.

Suddenly, the brake on the car slipped, and it began to roll without restraint down the ramp. Gwydion's eyes went wide, and he gripped the dashboard in front of him.

But Aonghus pulled hard, slowing the car, and brought it to a stop at the bottom of the ramp.

“Well!” said the professor. “I shall have a look at that brake before we use the car again! Thank you, Aonghus.”

“Yes, thank you, Aonghus!” said Gwydion.

“Bravo, Bib!” said Bran. “I didn't know you could drive a car.”

“Neither did I,” she said, smiling.

Gwydion said nothing, but looked in wonder again at the horseless carriage. At length, they climbed back up the ramp and onto the deck of the ship.

"Now, Rodger, would you take care of securing the car for me, please, and oversee the loading of the rest of our supplies?" asked Professor McPherson. "I would like to take our young students to the Green Tree Inn for a brief lunch, and then we shall set sail."

"Certainly, sir," replied Rodger, and he went down into the cargo hold and began to secure the car with ropes to rings mounted in the walls.

"Come now, students, we shall have an early lunch and then be on our way," said the professor. "Gwydion, would you care to join us as well?"

"Indeed," he replied.

McPherson led them off the ship and down the wharf past a number of tall sailing ships to a friendly looking inn that had a large green sign hanging above the door that said, "*The Green Tree Inn – Welcome.*"

The professor opened the door, and the girls filed in first, and the others were about to follow when a voice from down the wharf called out, "Frederick Buttersmouth, is that you?"

Frederick stopped and looked, and walking toward them was the large form of Baroness Helga Von Faust. She had dark circles under her eyes, and she looked tired.

"What a surprise," she said in her thick German accent, "and oh, I see that the McGunnegal children are with you as well. And Professor McPherson! We have just arrived, and your father is unloading his things. But what are you doing here at the Green Tree?"

"Uh..." began Frederick, but Professor McPherson interrupted.

"Ah, Baroness, how nice to see you again," he said cordially. "As you can see, I am treating these students to lunch at the Inn. Would you and Rufus like to join us?"

"No, no," she replied wearily. "I did not sleep a wink on the trip back. I hate sailing, and always get sick. How could anyone be a sailor? I feel as though I will fall asleep on my feet. But what is this? You rode all the way from the school to bring these children to the Green Tree Inn for lunch?" she asked, a hint of suspicion in her voice.

"Well, here we are," replied the professor, "and we are also doing some educational work as well. Today, I shall be teaching each of them a bit about sailing. I have my ship docked just up the wharf there, and we shall be casting off just as soon as we have eaten our lunch."

He pointed to where the ship was, and they could see Rodger and a few other men loading barrels and crates aboard.

"Ah, your... *ship*... yes, I remember seeing it when we first met. Still floating, is it? Well, do not take it too far," she laughed, "or you might be giving these children swimming lessons!"

She laughed with her deep harsh laugh and turned to go, but then spotted Gwydion and stopped.

"And who might this be?" she asked.

"Ah," said McPherson. "This is my friend Gwydion. He is visiting and will be setting sail with us."

Helga looked the old man up and down and sniffed.

"Well, have fun, Frederick. Stay within sight of land, just in case! I shall tell your father that you are here in town, although I doubt he will have time to see you. He is going to the train station to take some sto.... well... *items* for inspection at the museum."

"I have notified Mabel," said Professor McPherson, "that we will be going on an extended field trip today. A letter is waiting for Rufus at their home as well. Please extend my greeting to him when you see him again. Good day."

* * *

Helga watched them as they turned and went into the inn. She rubbed her chin, thinking. Strange that even before the school semester had begun, they were heading off somewhere.

"What are those McGunnegals up to, I wonder," she muttered under her breath.

Then an idea struck her. She wandered up toward the professor's ship and watched as the men finished loading the last few crates of supplies down into the cargo hold. She looked at the seagulls for a moment, then turned and pretended to be strolling away, but was actually listening carefully to their conversation.

"There's one more big one at the butcher's shop," said Rodger to one of the men. "We'll take my car and load it in, then bring it back."

The three men piled into Rodger's car, and he started it up. It *poofed* out a head of steam as they rolled away toward the butcher.

Helga casually strolled up the gangplank.

"Just a quick look around," she said to herself.

She wrinkled her nose at the litter of debris about the deck, then slipped down the stairs below deck.

Poking her head into each of the rooms, she saw the crew quarters, the galley, and the mess hall, and then went to the end of the hall and opened that last door. It was the Captain's cabin. She slipped in and shut the door, peering about the lamp-lit room at the same drab tapestries that had decorated the other rooms. But then something caught her eye. There was a bulging bag of something next to a desk in the middle of the room. She opened it, and there inside were the stones that she and Rufus had given Mabel to take with her back to Wales.

"Those McGunnegal rats have stolen the stones and given them to McPherson!" she hissed.

Grabbing the heavy bag, she made her way back down the hall and up the stairs to the upper deck and was going to leave when she saw Rodger and the other men drive up the wharf and park the car next to the ship. She was near the open cargo hold, so she quickly slid down the ramp, nearly tumbling head over heels. The sight of the car in the cargo hold surprised her, making her even more curious about their journey, but she could hear the men walking up the plank and talking, and knew that she must not be seen, especially with the bag of stones.

"This one go in the cargo hold too, Rodger?" asked one of the men.

"Yep, just set it down there behind the car and lash it down. That will be the last of it," he replied.

Helga looked about frantically, and then squeezed behind a stack of crates, peering through a crack between them. The two men brought down a large box, placed it behind the car, and proceeded to tie it down with ropes. Then they walked back up the ramp, and Helga heard Rodger say, "That's it, men. Thanks for the help. Oh! One last thing, give me a hand with this."

She thought that they were going to bring one more thing down, so she stayed in her hiding place, waiting. All of a sudden, the sunlight shining down into the cargo hold grew dimmer and dimmer, and with an audible *WHUMP,* the heavy trap door fell shut, and she found herself in absolute darkness. The dull slide and click of two bolts being thrown quickly followed. Shock and surprise flooded over her, and she squeezed out of her hiding place, and tried to make her way back to the ramp.

“Wait, you idiots!” she yelled. But in the darkness, she tripped over one of the ropes that tied down a crate, gave her head a good knock, and was out cold.

* * *

Back in the Green Tree Inn, the McGunnegals, Frederick, Gwydion, and Professor McPherson finished their lunch and headed out the door and back toward the ship. The three sailors, having had their own lunch, joined them.

Rodger was sitting in his car waiting for them, and as they approached he said, “She's fully stocked, Professor. The kitchen is loaded with at least a week's worth of supplies, so you shouldn't have to dip into the stores in the cargo hold for quite a while.”

“Thank you so much, Rodger,” replied Professor McPherson. “I am in your debt once again.”

“No, no,” he replied. “Glad to help. You kids enjoy your trip. Gwydion, nice to make your acquaintance.”

They all said farewell, and then walked across the gangplank, where the professor began to give some instructions while the three sailors looked on, amused smirks on their faces.

“Well, now, since you're all new to sailing, let's go over some basic rules,” he said.

He went over basic safety rules of the ship, often stopping and asking them to repeat these back to him.

“Now, the first day or so, we may stay in sight of land, just so you all can get your sea legs on and learn your part as the crew. Now, who's best with heights and has the best eyes?” he asked.

Henny raised her hand. “I love to climb trees and look about, Professor,” she said.

“Well, lass, do you see that crow's nest way up on the top of the main mast?”

He pointed, and they all looked up to see a platform with rails around it.

“No way, Henny,” said Aonghus. “You are *not* going to climb up there.”

“But I can do it!” said Henny.

“I'm sure you can, little one,” he replied. “But it's too high. If you fell...”

“Oh, she would not fall, Aonghus.” interrupted the professor. “There is a special place there to tie in. Even on your way up, there is a rope to secure you.”

“I would have to see that for myself,” he replied.

“Fair enough. You're a good brother, Aonghus. Now, the next job is to keep the decks clean.”

They all looked about the deck at the mess, and several of the sailors laughed.

“Aye, you Irish swabbies will have your hands full cleaning this beaut!” called one of them, and they laughed louder.

“Professor,” said Abbe, “one can hardly *see* the deck, much less keep it clean.”

He laughed and said, “Ah, you shall see what I mean soon enough.”

“Then, there is the pilot. The pilot must know how to follow the sun and the moon and the stars, and be familiar with the currents and landmarks along the shoreline. There are many maps to study and become familiar with. This is a job for someone who can learn and remember things quickly.”

"That would be Bib," said Bran.

"We also need some stout lads to secure the rigging, let down and hoist up the sails, do a good bit of climbing on the masts, and know how to tie the right knots for each rope."

"Sounds like a job for the boys," said Bib.

"And we also need a captain – that would be me, of course – and a first mate and a cook."

"Ah, I know a thing or two about cooking," said Gwydion.

"Excellent," said the professor.

"However, I would like each of you to try out each job, and learn how to do it well. As we sail, I shall be holding lectures on various subjects so that your schooling truly goes on for the next two days until we reach Ireland."

"I thought we were sailing to Ireland to rescue Colleen and Mother," said Abbe.

"Ah, true, true," replied the professor. "But even when you are on your way to do important things, you mustn't neglect other aspects of your life. We have a day or two before we arrive. We might as well redeem the time and do something useful."

"Now," he continued. "Knot tying..."

Soon the professor had them all practicing various knots with lengths of rope, tying lines to masts, posts, anchors, and securing two lines together. Gwydion demonstrated a few knots that even the professor didn't know, and they watched as he tied a complex triple slip knot that he said his kin had used on their ships.

The professor was soon satisfied that they had mastered these, and quite impressed that they did so very quickly.

“Well, then, let's be off! Our next lesson will be with the sails,” he said.

He described to them how to let down the sails just enough to move them slowly from the docks and out into the channel, and Aonghus and Bran were the first to climb the masts, followed by one of the crewmen named Jake.

When they reached the top, Jake said, “By the looks of it, you Irishmen haven’t done much sailing. See here, what’s this here professor doing with you lot? Three crewmen and a split dozen of kids to sail the seas? Not that you two are kids, mind you, but it seems odd enough. And who are you, anyway?”

“We’re students at the professor’s school. He’s taking us on a field trip of sorts and we’re learning how to sail while we go,” replied Aonghus.

“Well, the old man says that Ireland may not be our last stop. He pays well enough, mind you, but if he wants to venture out into the Atlantic, he best find more than the ten of us to man his ship, I can tell you that,” said Jake.

Aonghus and Bran said nothing, but watched below as the girls and Frederick untethered the ship from the wharf and pulled in the gangplank. Then, with Jake giving instructions, they loosened the sail ties, allowing them to drop halfway, then climbed down again.

The ship slowly began to move, and Professor McPherson and Henny took the ship's wheel and guided it into the deeper water, while Gwydion stood on the upper deck and watched with great interest.

“Let down the sails,” called the professor after a time. “Be sure you tie them securely! We don’t need our sails to be footloose!”

Aonghus started to climb the rope ladder up the mast again, but found that Frederick had beaten him to it and was already ten feet above him. Frederick grinned down at him and climbed on.

Aonghus glanced over at the professor, who was also grinning, looking positively proud at the sight of Frederick.

"Are you sure you know the ropes, Frederick?" he called.

"Yes, sir!" he called back. "I never forget something once I hear it!"

Indeed, Frederick easily climbed out onto the mast, let down the sails, and secured them.

* * *

The sails caught the wind and billowed out, and the little ship shot forward. But Frederick was expecting this, and was holding tightly to the mast. With the wind in his hair and the smell of the sea all about him, he felt as if he had been set free. He smiled broadly, and looked about as they sailed swiftly away from Wales. Then he climbed up into the crow's nest, found the anchor rope, tied himself in, and sat down on a low stool that was part of the whole setup. Seagulls danced about him as the land rushed away and the open sea greeted them. He felt free – freer than he had ever felt before. And there was another feeling as well. It was as if the sea *called* to him – as though he *needed* to sail out into the great blue waters. Some destiny lay out there, but what it was, he did not know. He was only glad to be sailing toward it at last.

Then all of the adventures of the last few days rushed back to his mind. The Lady Danu had said that a great task lay before him, and that he was to seek the king in the sea. He wished that they were now sailing toward Bermuda. Would he ever get there now? He hoped so. But as the smell of the sea grew and the wind whipped his raven-colored hair about, he leaned forward on the rail and gazed outward, letting his mind wander out across the great expanse of blue that lay before him.

Chapter 17 – The Tomb

Adol McGunnegal sat very still in his hiding place amid the tall reeds in the bog. Three days had passed since he had seen the black creature, but there had been signs that it was moving about, doing what, he did not know.

Its trails crisscrossed the length and breadth of the vast bog, and he had a growing sense that something very bad was happening in this place. For one thing, strange sounds had risen up from its heart last night, and he had seen odd lights that would wink on and off, then disappear entirely. He had also learned from a neighbor, old man Gernie, that there was a rumor among the nearby farms that odd things had begun to happen. Shadows had been seen dancing in the fields under the moon, and dark shapes in the sky. A general feeling of uneasiness was settling over the area.

Some town folk were blaming the McGunnegals. They said that they had seen queer things running across their farm at night, and Gernie claimed that he had seen a ghost in the old McGunnegal graveyard while he was out walking his dog. Mothers had started to close the shutters at sundown, and good folk locked their doors until the morning's rays shone in the east. Children crawled into bed with their parents as bad dreams woke them, and there was word that the potato blight was spreading far and wide. There was something ill at work in all this, or so Adol surmised. This black creature was at the heart of it, he knew, but catching it was proving to be tricky, and it seemed to be able to vanish into the mists at will.

He suspected that it knew that he was tracking it, and it was being careful. The more time he spent in the bog, the more he felt that he too was being watched and stalked. The nameless *presence* that he felt here weighed upon him continuously, and he had a sense that smaller, although still malevolent, eyes watched from the twisted roots and boughs of ancient trees and stumps and holes in the rocks. He did not dare to go into the bog at night. Even now, the day was drawing to a close, so he rose from his place and stealthily stole down the now familiar path back to the farm.

Behind him, a black hooded shape rose from the deepening shadows and began to slink along, tree to tree, watching him depart. But Adol was an extraordinary tracker and woodsman, and it was not long before he sensed that something was indeed following him, keeping its distance, and biding its time.

When he reached the wall and climbed over and into greener pastures, it paused, waiting, and then it too climbed slowly upward and peered over the edge. When it did not see Adol, it slowly, slyly, inched its way upward, trying to get a better look, and stayed in the shadows that the trees cast on the top of the wall.

All at once, Adol's huge form sprang upward, right in the face of the creature. The big man lunged at it, but it leaped upward in the air like a startled cat, screaming a hideous cry of surprise and fear and rage, and Adol missed it by an inch. Off the wall it sprang, back into the bog, and Adol was over and after it in a flash, his big club in his massive fist. Down trail after trail, he pursued it, and as the minutes passed, the sun began to set behind the western horizon, and the shadows grew long and ominous. Onward he chased it, running through thick tangles of trees and across wet ground. Although the black creature was smaller and quicker than Adol, a rage now pounded in Adol's heart, and nothing would stop his pursuit.

Suddenly, a great boulder loomed before him, and the creature dove into a small cave beneath it. It was an old animal den, he knew, but he bellowed a great cry and, with a tremendous *heave*, he rolled the rock away. The black creature lay huddled on the barren earth, and hissed at him in fear. He leaped forward, but again it dove away, and ran down a side trail, heading for the center of the bog.

Now a mist had begun to rise, and Adol could just see the black shape as it weaved and bobbed in its mad flight. A light twinkled to his left, distracting him for a moment, and in that instant, the creature vanished beneath the haze.

He ran to where he had last seen it, but only swirls in the gathering fog showed any sign that it had been there. Adol furrowed his eyebrows, set his jaw, and walked forward. The darkness was deepening now, and as he made his way in what he thought to be the right direction, he thought that he heard a sound like little padded feet following along beside him, now on his left, and now on his right. Something shapeless flitted through the air by his ear, and he waved it away – a bat. He sighed with relief.

Mustn't let my mind play tricks on me, he thought.

Gathering his wits, he looked at the last light of the fading sky in the west, turned north, and hurried onward.

"*Nearly caught it!*" he whispered aloud to himself in frustration.

Through the old trees he went, and their branches seemed to hang low and grab at his clothes and scratch his face. He had lost all trails now, for the mist was as thick as pea soup about him, and only his keen sense of direction kept him from turning about and wandering aimlessly. Rustles and scratching and weird sounds like something pulling out of the mud could be heard from time to time, and once he thought he saw a black shape rise before him and then vanish away as he lifted his club against it.

Such a queer place – an evil place! he thought as he made his way onward.

Although his heart was bold, and the shadows and sounds in the mist did not make him afraid, still he wished his sons were with him. Best to deal with such dank places in the light of day and with good company.

All at once, the Wall rose before him. He was far to the west of the normal place he would have crossed it, but he climbed up and to the top, and looked out over the old graveyard of his ancestors. Behind him, the bog spread outward, a great white, shrouded sea with many twisted branches of dark treetops poking through like so many reaching fingers. Strange sounds began to echo in the mists – croaks and chirps and something that sounded like a high-pitched laugh. Only a slight mist curled its way among the graves on the other side of the wall. After glancing one last time southward, he dropped down and into the lighter air of his farm.

The great mounds that were the graves of the McGunnegals-past now surrounded him, and he felt no animosity from them, but something was different on this night. Was it his imagination – or did he sense a *restlessness* in the air, a sense that something was amiss?

As he passed by the largest of the mounds – the grave of Geer, son of Laar McGunnegal, he paused. The earth had been disturbed. He bent low in the dim light and looked. There, dug into the hill, was a tunnel of sorts. Adol ground his teeth and snarled. That black creature dared even to defile the graves of his ancestors! Anger rose up in him. He could not let this go until morning.

From a small pouch at his side, he pulled out an oiled cloth, wrapped it about a branch that he found nearby, and with his tinderbox, lit it as a torch. Placing his club in his belt, he held the torch in the entrance of the tunnel and looked within. It was a thin passage, barely wide enough for him to squeeze through if he lay flat, but beyond this low entry way, it appeared to broaden considerably, and he could dimly see a wall of sorts some ways in. At this wall, the floor of the passage seemed to change from brown earth to gray stone.

Now curiosity began to replace his anger, and despite some misgivings and a moment's hesitation, he pushed the torch into the hole, lay on his belly, and wriggled into the passageway.

It was a tight fit, and dusty, and the close air and loose earth threatened to choke him. Nevertheless, he pushed forward and, in a few moments, lay at the entrance to a square room about ten feet wide, on the floor of which was a single slab of gray stone about six feet wide and four inches thick, and on this was engraved a great rising sun over a plain. The slab lay shifted, revealing a crack or hole about an inch wide, with a dark hollow space beneath it.

Is this the tomb of Geer? he wondered.

The black creature had obviously tried to move the slab, but the room was too small to slide it to the side completely, and the slab was heavy.

Good, then it has not defiled my ancestor's grave, he thought.

Adol tried to maneuver it back in its place, to cover the gap, but here, with only his shoulders in the room, and the rest of his body still in the tunnel, he could find no leverage. Pulling himself fully into the chamber and sitting on the slab, he looked about. The masonry on the wall that he had entered through was broken. The creature had no doubt managed to find a loose stone, and once it pushed that one inward, the others easily moved as well, although they were good-sized blocks, at least a foot square. He knew he had to act quickly, for the room was filling with smoke from his torch.

Moving to the other side of the room, he put his back to the wall and his feet against the slab and gave a slight push to maneuver it back into place. However, the heavy stone did not yield. He pushed harder, then harder, and all at once, with a *bang,* it slid sideways and hit the opposite wall. Adol growled in frustration. Sometimes, he did not know his own strength. Now a gap of at least two feet lay exposed, but he was more curious than ever. With great care, he held the torch above the opening and peered down, thinking that he would see the bones of Geer.

But there were no bones to be seen. Rather, a white stairway led downward, how far, he could not tell. He lifted his torch, thinking. These grave mounds had been a matter of family legend and bedtime stories for generations and generations, and here he was inside one of them. He could not resist the urge to explore this further, so he squeezed through the opening and slid down to the steps into the darkness below.

Chapter 18 – The Hammer of Geer

Adol followed a long marble staircase that led downward for a long way to a white tunnel whose ceiling towered far above his head. Many, many years must have passed since this crypt's construction, for the marble was calcified, and stalactites hung in places from the ceiling, and their mated stalagmites rose from the floor to meet them.

The hall ended at a tall door made of a single slab of stone that nearly reached the ceiling. Inscribed on this was the same symbol of a rising sun over a plain that he had seen on the covering to the staircase, and around its stone frame were carved many strange runes.

There was also a large handprint carved in the door – much too large to fit a human hand – easily eight inches across and twice that in height – and within that hand, a smaller one, although still large, as though one were overlaid upon the other – a hand within a hand. Adol placed his palm in the smaller of the two carved prints and, to his complete surprise, there was a hiss of stale air and the door swung out. The smell of a chamber shut up for long ages met him.

He stepped back, not for fear, but in wonder, for the flicker of his torch caught a bright glint of something within. For a moment, he considered shutting the door and leaving the grave of his ancestor in peace, but he had come too far now and curiosity gripped him. Slowly, reverently, he stepped through the door and held his torch high. The sight inside made his eyes grow wide and his mouth drop open, for shelves of vessels and goblets and chests lined a large stone room, and in the center, on a raised dais of three large steps, sat a great white sarcophagus.

Adol looked in amazement at the adornments all about him. Never in all his wildest dreams did he imagine that such a thing lay beneath his farm, buried with Geer McGunnegal for untold generations past. To an archaeologist, this would be invaluable. It would tell stories of ancient Ireland never before told. Yet, even as he saw it, he knew that he would not take any of it, not unless others threatened to rob this place. He would save these graves from the plundering of modern men. At least for now, the mysteries here would remain at rest, and the treasure house of Geer, son of Laar, the first McGunnegal, would remain a family secret.

With these thoughts, he ascended the large stone steps to the dais where the sarcophagus lay. It was huge – twelve feet long and six feet wide, and easily four feet tall. It was polished and smooth, except for a bright yellow golden sun rising over a field of green stones that were inlaid in its surface.

What surprised him even more, however, was that sitting atop this marvelous and gigantic coffin, was an amazing hammer. It had two heads wrought of a strange bright metal. There was no dent or flaw in the perfect mallet, its head was a foot wide from end to end, and each head was at least three inches broad. Its ornate shaft was deepest black, and its handle wrapped with a scarlet red material dimpled with golden studs. A large and equally ornate belt lay circled about it, trimmed with silver and gold and the same black material. Adol reached out a hand to touch it, so beautiful and compelling was its workmanship, but he withdrew it quickly.

How many centuries, he wondered, had this hammer and belt laid here on this grave? Had it been a parting gift from the son of Geer? Surely, it had been Geer's own hammer – a mighty war hammer by the looks of it, or perhaps a symbol of power, or of some office.

Suddenly, a sound to his right, a soft *hiss*, interrupted his thoughts. He turned quickly, and there was the black hooded creature peering up at him. Adol roared in anger. How *dare* that filthy thing enter this sacred burial chamber?

With speed and reflexes that surprised even him, Adol snatched up the hammer and threw it at the beast. It flew through the air, humming as it tumbled swiftly toward the place where the black shape had been. However, the creature had been quicker, and it was gone before the weapon left his hand. Nevertheless, the hammer flew, striking the stone pavement outside the door and splitting it in two. To Adol's absolute and total astonishment, it flew back to his hand, and he caught it effortlessly.

He stared at the weapon for only a moment, considering, and then scooped up the belt and ran after the black creature. When he squeezed out of the stairway, and back into the upper chamber, however, it was gone, and he knew he could not catch it now, nor would it return here soon. Frustrated and angry, he returned to the grave of Geer, carrying the belt and hammer.

It was strange, he thought, how *right* it felt in his big hand. It was heavy, to be sure, but not too heavy for his great strength. How had it *returned* to him?

He sat the hammer carefully on the step and examined the belt in the light of his torch. It was of marvelous artistry, flawless, and had a hook of sorts on the side where he realized the hammer attached by its handle.

Suddenly, he realized that his torch was burning low, so he made a decision. He would keep the hammer and belt, at least until morning. He picked up the hammer once again, left the burial chamber of Geer, pulled the great door shut, climbed the stairs, squeezed through the opening, and this time positioned the stone slab over the stairway evenly so that not even a crack showed.

His torch burned out, so slowly he felt his way to the dirt tunnel and squeezed through it, pushing his prizes carefully before him, trying not to soil them. In a few moments, he was through and breathed deeply of the clean air.

Holding up the hammer to the rising moon, he said, "I shall call you Geer, after your last owner. May you serve me well in the days ahead, and may I bear you well."

Then holding up the belt in his other hand, he said, "And you I shall call Laar, who once held his son Geer."

Removing his old belt, he fastened Laar about his waist. It fit him well, although how, he did not know, for it appeared to be very large when he first picked it up in the tomb. Then he found how the hammer clipped onto it, and, fastening it in its place, he headed back to the farmhouse.

* * *

Beyond the wall, a pair of greedy eyes watched as the big man walked slowly away. They blinked, and then disappeared into the mist.

Chapter 19 – Mirror Mirror

Adol was tired from his chase of the black creature, and the night was getting on now. Still, he took his time, walking slowly in the cool night air, thinking of the strange things that were happening. He was glad to be under a clear starry sky, and his spirit lifted somewhat as he drew near his home. But as he gained sight of the farm, he knew that something was amiss. Everything was too still. Even the crickets were silent. Then he noticed it – the back door of the house was sitting ajar.

He quickly ran the length of the field to the house and silently slipped into the kitchen. The cellar door had been forced open, and he could hear a good deal of scuffling and shifting. Something was down there.

Then he remembered. The mirror – it was after the mirror. Somehow, it had found out where he had hidden it.

Quickly, he lit an oil lamp and held it in his left hand, then took Geer in his right. He slipped through the cellar door and quietly closed it behind him, hoping that the creature would not be able to hear him through all the noise it was making. Then he rushed down the stairs and to the back of the basement.

He was very nearly too late, for there was the creature standing before the mirror. Its hood was thrown back, and for the first time Adol beheld its grotesque head and face as it stared at its own reflection. It looked like a deformed little man with over-sized ears and a bulbous nose. Its skin was a blotchy gray-green, and what remained of its hair hung in long dark strands down its bony face. Large yellow eyes stared at him through its reflection for only an instant, and then it swiftly held up the crystal ball.

The image in the mirror swirled into mist and then changed to a dark forest. The creature grinned wickedly, revealing brown and yellow teeth and fangs, and leaped, passing right through the mirror and into the forest beyond, and then ran. This time, however, Adol moved just as quickly, and with a great cry he dove headlong at the mirror, and just before the scene began to swirl, he was passing through it, and he found himself tumbling into a bed of leaves. He jumped to his feet, seeing the creature dashing away through the wood, and instantly he was after it.

To his surprise, it turned and ran around a huge tree. Adol pursued, and the creature, with amazing speed, sped back to the mirror, holding up the crystal ball as it ran.

"No!" he bellowed, as the black thing dove back through and into his basement.

The scene in the portal swirled, and as Adol reached it, only his own reflection greeted him. For a moment, he had the urge to strike the mirror with Geer, but, realizing that it was his only way home, he stopped, hung his head, and sank to his knees.

"What have I done?" he said aloud, realizing his mistake.

The creature was wily and full of tricks. He should have been more careful. Even as he reproached himself, he heard a snapping of sticks and a low snarl behind him, and he turned.

Coming through the trees, he saw a horror that he had never encountered before, and he knew why the black little creature had turned and run the other way. Adol gripped the hammer and braced himself as a huge shaggy beast the size of a great bear, but looking more like an unearthly wolf, growled, bent its head low, and showed its massive teeth. He readied himself for its lunge, but even as he did, two more of the creatures came leaping from the darkness and began to circle around him.

Before the first one could attack, Adol remembered what Geer had done in the tomb. With a sudden movement, he hurled the hammer at the foremost beast, striking it straight between the eyes. It howled and dropped to the ground and lay motionless. The weapon flew back to him, and he caught it, just as the other two creatures leaped forward, throats growling and jaws snapping.

He met the first one with a blow to the chest and grimaced as he felt its bones crush and snap beneath the power of the hammer. However, the third creature bowled him over, knocking Geer from his hand. He grappled with it, rolling over and over. Terrible teeth snapped inches from his face, and long claws sought to tear at him.

In that moment, something seemed to awaken deep within him – something that had nearly lain dormant throughout his life, but had always been there, and only seemed to show itself in moments of great need. A surge of tremendous strength washed over him, and with a mighty heave, he threw the monster from him and it went rolling across the forest floor, slamming into a great tree. It stumbled to its feet, lifted its head, and howled a deafening howl. Distant calls answered it, and it howled again.

Adol snatched up the hammer and let it fly with all his strength. It struck the creature, knocking it senseless, then flew on, and with a sickening *crack,* collided with the tree behind it. There was a snapping and grating sound as the massive tree shattered. It cracked straight down the middle, and then broke in two. Down it came, and Adol ran from its path as its dry branches swept downward with the moaning sound of an anguished wind, struck the earth, shuddered, and then lay still. The hammer of Geer circled back through the air and returned to his hand.

Adol looked about, listening. A huge full moon was rising now, cresting the horizon above the forest. The barren trees were cast like black skeletons against its great white face, and as he gazed at it in awe and wonder, for a moment, he forgot the creatures, forgot that he had stepped through the mirror, and simply stood in the silence, bathed in a shaft of soft light that shone through a gap in the trees. A strange sensation swept through him, a sudden sense of participating in a primordial event that had occurred for untold ages – of being in an ancient place that whispered secret tales of long forgotten years. He hardly dared to breathe, every part of him unwilling to step away from that profound moment.

But then a thought broke through the spellbinding experience and the strange world around him rushed back in. Dark shadows lay still as death all around, and a feeling of heaviness hung in the air, almost like that of the Dismal Bog back home, but more profound. A sense that this place was *alien* took hold. Where was the familiar face on the moon and why was it so big? It was bright and strange – different from any moon he had ever seen, and it illuminated the whole world with a soft light. Where was he?

He looked about, peering through the trees, and saw something hanging on a low branch. He went to it, pulled it from its place, and held it up to the moon. He recognized it immediately – it was Colleen's sash.

His mind whirled. How could she be here? The thought of his little girl lost in these woods with such horrible creatures all about nearly burst his heart. Yet, he had seen her get on the ship. She was in Wales now, at school. Surely, this sash could not be hers. He examined it again, and there was no mistake. Had Colleen come here before, and lost it then? She would have told someone of this place – this dead wood that was haunted by evil beasts. He clutched the sash close to him, and then stuffed it into his shirt. He had to know if his daughter was here, and he had to know now.

The raw power and strength he had felt moments ago still coursed through his veins, and he felt as though he would burst if he did not somehow expend it. Howls in the night drew near, and he had a sudden urge to burst through the wood and pursue them, to hunt them down and chase them to their foul dens in search of Colleen. But he steadied himself, and began to look for signs of a trail, anything to indicate that she had been here and walked away of her own accord.

Within a few moments, he saw something else that made his eyes go wide. For very clearly, on a patch of soft ground where the bright moonlight spilled through the trees, there was a hoof print, and the mark of a young boy's shoe. Badger? That would explain his disappearance. Someone else was here as well. A young boy. Henry? Frederick? No, not Henry - the shoe print was too large to be his. Frederick then, or perhaps one of the neighbor boys?

Adol urgently stooped low and looked about. There was another hoof print a little ways off. In fact, the leaves were clearly disturbed in that direction, although the trail was many days old.

With the howls of night-creatures drawing closer, Adol McGunnegal sped off into the night of a strange land in search of his beloved daughter, not knowing that he had stumbled into the Land of the Little People.

Chapter 20 – Grip

Colleen awoke to the sound of Dvalenn snoring loudly. The Wigglepox family and Oracle were nowhere to be seen.

Perhaps they're still in some cubbyhole in the tree, she thought.

Through the knothole high above, she could see the fading light of dusk. Then she remembered Nous, and wondered if he was all right. And what about Grip?

She rose and stretched, then shook Dvalenn to wake him. The old dwarf opened his eyes, smacked his lips, and sat up, looking around the tree.

"Oh! I dreamed I was still sleeping next to that tree in the gorge. Dreadful, just dreadful!"

"Well, the sun looks like its setting. I think we should be going, but we need to find the Wigglepoxes and check on the goblins," she replied.

Dvalenn wrinkled his nose and said, "If you ask me, Colleen, those goblins will only do us harm. There's no sense in taking them with us. They'll only betray us to the Witch. I hope they left while we slept."

"Dvalenn, I think that Nous is actually grateful that we saved his life. He hasn't quite figured that out yet, but I think he will," she replied.

Just then, Mrs. Wigglepox, Lily, and Rose came out of a small hole.

"You know, Colleen," she said, "Dvalenn is probably right. The goblins may very well betray us. In fact, they most certainly will. We have never, in all our history, known of a good goblin."

"But Nous seems different, Mrs. Wigglepox," argued Colleen. "I just wonder if something is *shifting* deep down inside him. Maybe he can't leave the service of the Witch on his own, but maybe we can help him. In the meantime, he can help us. He knows all about the Witch's operations."

"So do I, in a way," said Dvalenn. "I say we leave them here. Let them fend for themselves. That's what they're best at."

"No, Dvalenn. At least Nous is coming with us," she said firmly. "And we can't just leave Grip by himself if he's not well."

"I certainly hope you're right, Colleen," said Dvalenn. "As for me, I'll be keeping my eyes on them, and a good staff in my hand."

It was just then that Oracle came tumbling out of a hole in the tree with a queer giggle, as though he had come down some great sliding board and was having a bit of fun. He grinned as he picked himself up and brushed leaves from his gray cloak.

Dvalenn shook his head in bewilderment at the old leprechaun. Then he looked up at the fading light coming through the knothole and said, "Best be off as soon as possible, ladies, so how about a bite to eat?"

They ate a hasty supper from their supplies, packed up, climbed into the wagon, and then Mrs. Wigglepox spoke to the tree, and it slowly groaned open with a great sad wail, as though it was mourning for the cruelty of life and the loss of its mate.

Colleen flicked the reins, and Badger pulled the wagon out. No sooner had they left, the great tree slammed shut with such force that it sounded as though it had snapped in two. Badger surged forward, and Colleen had to rein him in.

They rolled back toward the pool of Ooze and the dead Sentinel Tree. There they saw Nous crouched beside the pool and Grip submerged to his neck in it, staring at them with a look of malice.

Nous stood as they approached, and Colleen reined the wagon to a halt. Grip only scowled, but was still as a stone. Dvalenn gripped his staff as Colleen climbed down from the wagon and walked over to Nous.

She touched him gently on the arm and smiled. “I'm glad you are all right, Nous. I was worried about you.”

She turned to Grip, whose head seemed to be floating on the surface of the black pool. Colleen could not help but begin to giggle, and then laugh.

“Grip, you look positively hilarious in that pool! It looks as though you've become a disembodied head just floating there!”

Dvalenn snickered, and then began to laugh as well, and a moment later, the Wigglepoxes joined in. Nous looked from one of them to the other, and then looked down at Grip's head.

“Grip, you do look like a floating head,” said Nous.

He spurted out a laugh that came awkwardly at first, and then more easily, until all six of them were truly laughing together at Grip's ridiculous frowning face bobbing on the surface of the stinking pool.

In that moment, it was as though a tension that had been building for days snapped, and all of the stress, fear, and foreboding that had weighed upon Colleen vanished away as she, the dwarf, the goblin, and the three little people giggled at the funny sight. Oracle peered over the edge of the wagon, a wry smile on his wrinkled face.

Grip, however, sneered at them all and growled, “Go ahead and laugh now. Soon enough, you won't be laughing. The Witch knows of your presence here by now, and she will be hunting for you. We will track you and hound you and capture you and take you to the black pits, where you will spend the rest of your days slaving for our king.”

The reality of their situation rushed back in on them, and only Nous continued to giggle a bit, and then even he stopped.

“Ah, Grip, they ain't done us no harm. Fact is, this Colleen here saved our lives. I think she might be a goblin friend, I do. Not like those others who do us harm,” said Nous.

"So, Nous, you are a *friend* of these foreigners? I'm sure the King and the Witch will be very interested to hear that," replied Grip, and he pulled himself from the pool of Ooze.

His body was much like Nous', skinny and mottled gray-green, and now covered by the same black leeches that had fastened themselves to Nous.

"Nous, you come with me," said Grip. "You know our orders."

Nous looked from Grip to Colleen. He gazed down at the bubbling pool, then back at Colleen again.

"Orders, Nous!" growled Grip. "You go with them and it's over for you!"

Nous now looked curiously at Grip's body and at the black slugs that hung limply on him.

"What'd we ever get by following *her* orders?" said Nous, half to himself and half to Grip. "Seems to me all we ever got was this Ooze. Look at it – full of worms. And it stinks."

"You speak of the *Ooze* like that!" shouted Grip. "Have you forgotten that it is the *gift* of the *Great Worm* to the Goblin people? What else could give us such freedom, such power, such intoxication, such delight – and how else could we *live?* Don't be an idiot, Nous. You can see just as well as I can what the Ooze does for us, and what it does to our enemies. It killed this evil tree, but gives us strength and life!"

Grip, animated in his defense of the Ooze, positioned himself between the others and the pool, as if to defend it. Colleen was amazed that the goblin would be so passionate about this stinking pool of death.

She climbed back up in the wagon and said, "We're leaving, Nous. Please, will you come with us? Grip... you could come too. I think that if we could just break the Spell of the Witch somehow, and if you stopped bathing yourself in that awful stuff, you would find out that you haven't been living at all, but withering away. Look at yourselves – you goblins are nothing but skin and bones and covered by... by *worms,* of all things! I'll bet every one of those things is leeching the life right out of you. There has to be a better way for you. Won't you come with us and help us find it?"

All this time, Oracle had been peeping over the side of the wagon watching the whole exchange. His eyes were fixed on Nous.

Colleen held out a hand to the goblins, but they only stared at her, as if considering what she had said.

Suddenly, Grip spat toward Colleen in disgust and sneered.

Nous looked at him, then back at Colleen, at the Ooze, at Grip, and then at Colleen again. Then he took a sideways step toward her.

"Nous, get back here!" shouted Grip.

He stopped and looked back, hesitating, thinking, debating with himself. Then he turned his back on the pool of Ooze, ran forward, and leaped into the wagon.

Colleen flicked the reins, and Badger began to pull.

"You'll be sorry, Nous!" shouted Grip. "When the burning sun dries up your flesh like cracked leather, and you have no Ooze to run to, then you'll remember my words!"

As they rode away into the Burning Sands and the sunset filled the western sky, Colleen looked back one last time at Grip. As the day ended, and night took the world, Grip slid his skinny body back into the pool. The black worms that covered him seemed to shake with delight as he sank down into the stinking slime, until once again, only his head remained floating on the surface. This time, Colleen did not laugh, nor did any of the others. They only rode on in sad silence.

She looked back once more and saw Grip shut his eyes and slide completely beneath the black muck. There was a frantic commotion of worms in the pool, and a bubble rose from where Grip had disappeared. It burst its stink on the surface, and then the pool was still.

Chapter 21 – The Burning Sands

The evening sky was a fiery red as Badger pulled the wagon south and a warm wind blew from the desert as they came to the top of the first sand dune. Colleen reined him to a halt for a moment as they looked out over the vast desert. They could see nothing but dunes before them, and the road was completely lost from sight, buried long ago beneath the blowing sands.

"We'll keep the sunset to our right as long as we can," said Dvalenn, "and then we'll have to rely on the stars to guide us southward."

Colleen nodded, flicked the reins again, and Badger pulled them down the dune. The sand was difficult even for the great horse to pull through, and the going was slow. However, Badger showed no sign of tiring, although he strained mightily up and down the dunes. The Spell still hung in the air, although it seemed to come in waves as if it were rushing past them on its way to the forest. The night grew cold as the moon rose, and each of them wrapped themselves as best as they could in their cloaks.

Hour after hour, they rode on, speaking few words until Colleen began to grow sleepy. When she felt she could fight it no longer, she handed Dvalenn the reins and said, "Would you mind driving for a bit? I just need to lie down for a few hours."

Dvalenn glanced back. Oracle lay in the hay at the front of the wagon, sleeping, and Nous was sitting in the far back corner, his arms wrapped around his knees.

"Just watch that one," he whispered. "I don't trust him."

Colleen climbed into the back of the wagon and sat down next to the goblin. They sat in silence for a few moments, and then Colleen said to him, "Nous, why did you choose to come with us?"

Nous did not answer at first, but gazed up at the brilliant stars that shone overhead. Then he shrugged and said, "Nous wonders."

"About what?" she asked.

"The Colleen," he replied.

"Me?" she asked.

"The Colleen is very strange," he said.

Colleen realized that the goblin was actually having a conversation with her.

"Why do you say that, Nous?" she replied.

He thought for a moment and said, "The Colleen has been... been..." and then he could not seem to find the right words to say.

"I care about you, Nous," she said. "I care what happens to you."

"Yes, very strange," he replied.

"I would like to think that you care about me too," she said.

He looked at her sidelong, and then turned away.

"Nous is tired," he said, and curled up in a ball in the hay.

Colleen watched him for a moment and then curled up next to him and was soon asleep.

She awoke some hours later to Nous shaking her.

"The Colleen must wake up! Wake up!" he whispered sharply.

She rubbed her eyes and looked around. They had stopped, and Dvalenn was not in the driver's seat. After a moment, she saw him. He was on the ground digging in the sand and looking very excited.

"Dvalenn, what is it? What have you found?" she called.

He seemed startled by her voice, and jumped up, holding his hands behind his back.

"Oh ... oh, nothing," he said. "Just... giving Badger a rest, that's all."

"What have you got behind your back, Dvalenn?" she asked.

Dvalenn shuffled his feet and looked down and said, "Nothing, nothing, guess we better be going."

"Dvalenn!" scolded Colleen. "Let me see your hands."

He slipped both hands into his pockets, which Colleen noticed were bulging even more than before, then brought them out empty, and smiled. Then he quickly climbed back up into the wagon and flicked the reins.

Colleen noticed that the Wigglepoxes were all sound asleep on the bench, and Oracle snoozed in the hay. Dvalenn looked back at her, grinned, and then kept right on driving as if nothing had happened.

She was not sure what to make of all this, so she whispered to Nous, "Nous, what was Dvalenn doing?"

"Stones," he replied. "The dwarf was picking up shiny stones."

"Whatever for?" she asked.

"His kind likes shiny stones, it's said," replied the goblin.

"For what?" asked Colleen.

"It's said they just carry them about and shine them and collect them and hide them away in their caves. Then they grow fat by sitting and counting them. And when they've grown fat enough, we goblins come and take it all away from them!" Nous cackled.

Dvalenn turned his head and eyed Nous suspiciously, then turned back and drove on.

"Do you think that might be what happened to Dvalenn's brother, Fafnir?" asked Colleen.

"Maybe. Might have been before my time," he replied. "Anyway, we just take such things and give them to the Witch or throw them into the Ooze. Orders, you know."

"You throw precious stones into the Ooze?" asked Colleen incredulously. "But why?"

"Orders. It makes the Ooze better," he said.

"Nous, where does this Ooze come from?" asked Colleen.

Nous grinned wickedly and said in a low voice as if he were sharing a great secret, "From *us!*"

He cackled, then said, "It drips from us, we scrape it from ourselves and, bit by bit, fill the Ooze pits. Sometimes, it sinks into what we touch, and especially if we *bite* it! *Then* the Ooze takes root in what we bit. It starts to become like us."

He had showed his yellow fangs at the word *bite,* and Colleen shuddered.

"But surely your people weren't always like this, were they?" asked Colleen.

Nous looked serious then, and said in a low voice, "There are stories that say the goblins did not always have the Ooze. But when the Great Worm came, it gave us the Ooze, and we ever after possessed it."

"And what is the Great Worm?" asked Colleen.

"Nous does not know," said Nous. "Nous has never seen it."

"But wouldn't you like to be rid of this horrible stuff?" she asked.

Nous' expression changed from shock to suspicion, then to anger, and then serious. Emotions flowed across his face like a tide, and for a moment, Colleen was afraid that he might leap at her or fly into a rage. However, he seemed to settle down after a moment, hissed, and said, "It is the Ooze that lets us *live*! Without it, we would dry up and die. Nous has seen it once."

"One of your people *dried up?*" asked Colleen.

"That's what we call it. Stay too long away from the Ooze and at first you grow ugly. Scars, like poor Grip had from the evil water, start to form. That poor gloat that dried up - his ears and nose rightly fell off his head. His whole body was one big scar. He came to the pits talking like a mad goblin. Said he had been out in the desert for forty years, and had met a hermit and lived with him. He had bathed in the Evil Lake, and said the Ooze had died in him. Said he came back to take anyone who wanted to follow him out into the desert to get rid of the Ooze. Said there was some sort of oasis out here where it could happen. Poor thing." Nous shook his hooded head.

"Did anyone go with him?" asked Colleen.

"Noooo. Who would want to? Besides, we threw him into an Ooze pit. When we pulled him out three days later, nothing had happened to him. Fact is, all the worms in the pit died. Ruined a perfectly good Ooze pit. The boss was rightly angry with him and had him killed then and there. Said he would pollute the whole pit if we let him live," replied Nous.

Colleen, shaken by the cruelty of the goblins, wondered what had actually happened to the goblin that had been freed of the Ooze.

"Nous, you said there was an oasis that the... the mad goblin had been to. Do you think we could find it? Did he mention where it was?" asked Colleen.

"Don't know," replied the goblin. "North of the Wizard's Castle, I think. Goblins do not go that way."

"Then we just might come across it!" she said.

Nous seemed to shudder and drew his cloak tighter around him, but said no more.

She watched him for a moment and then climbed back to the front of the wagon and told Dvalenn that she would drive for a while. He nodded, handed her the reins, and climbed to the back, staying as far away from Nous as possible. He then gathered his own cloak about himself and fumbled in his pockets. Oracle awoke and climbed to the front with Colleen, being careful not to disturb the Wigglepoxes.

The night grew steadily colder, and the chill crept beneath their cloaks and into their bones until Colleen was shivering and praying for the dawn as the hours passed by. Oracle sat silently by her, wrapped in his own cloak, staring at the distant horizon as they traveled on.

Suddenly, there was the sound of Badger's golden horseshoes on stone, and the wheels of the wagon clattering. The Wigglepoxes awoke, and Colleen reined the horse to a stop. The sand had given way to a stone pavement, and all about them were broken and jagged walls, giving the impression of decaying teeth jutting upward from the land.

Colleen urged Badger on, and as they slowly moved through the ruins, a great arch loomed before them, black against the night sky. Colleen pulled up to it and gazed at its spectacular height. Unlike the rubble around them, the arch was still intact, seemingly untouched by time or the scouring winds of the desert.

“Dvalenn, Nous, look at this!” she said, waking the dwarf and goblin, who had both been asleep.

They all stared at the strange sight, but Dvalenn leaped from the wagon and ran forward to the arch. He touched it, caressing its smooth surface, then turned back to the others and said, “It is the Arch of Regin, my brother. This place was his house.”

“Dvalenn, we have to keep moving. We can't stop here and explore,” said Colleen.

“Oh, but it will be dawn soon. We need shelter, and here we might find it, or at least some shade under the arch,” said Dvalenn.

Colleen looked at the sky. Indeed, there was a glow in the east, the first hint of the coming dawn.

“Well, I suppose you may be right. Who knows when we might find shade again today,” she replied reluctantly.

“Good!” said the dwarf, and began to examine the structure.

Colleen pulled the wagon under the arch, then climbed down and unhooked Badger. There was no grass for him to graze on, so she took some of the hay from the wagon and gave it to him to eat.

“Colleen,” said Mrs. Wigglepox, “would you mind carrying us about in your pockets for a bit?”

“Of course,” she replied and, one by one, carefully put them in the pocket of her green cape.

Mrs. Wigglepox then whispered to her and said, “I'm still not so trustful of Nous, you know. He is a goblin, after all, even if he's like no other I've ever heard of.”

They watched as Nous climbed out of the wagon and crawled under it, curling into a ball, his robe wrapped tightly around him.

“We must hide from the burning sun,” he mumbled into his robe.

Colleen was about to reply when there came a “Whooohoo!” from behind them. Even Nous uncurled himself and looked. It was Dvalenn, and he was dancing about under the arch, looking very excited.

“Whatever is the matter?” asked Colleen.

“I have found it! The secret ...” Then he stopped, seeing Nous staring at him. “Oh, er, nothing,” he said, and walked away from the arch, kicking at stones and picking up a few and cramming them in his already stuffed pockets.

"The dwarf is mad," growled Nous, and curled back up under the wagon.

As soon as he was sure Nous was not watching, Dvalenn tiptoed back to the arch and frantically waved for Colleen to come and have a look at what he had found.

"Look! It's the secret door that my brother made in the arch, still here and hidden," he whispered.

He pointed to some engraved dwarven runes in the side of the Arch. Colleen looked at the runes and then at the dwarf. His old face was full of excitement.

"What was this thing for, Dvalenn?" she asked.

Dvalenn looked over at Nous and then said, "It is magic. See all around? Alas, the House of Regin has fallen, but the arch has not! The magic he wove into this stone still holds fast, and this – this is the secret door that leads down into his tunnels and chambers. Once they led down to the river, and from there..."

Dvalenn paused again, looked in Nous' direction, and whispered even lower. "And from there, the tunnels ran all the way to the Wizard's castle."

"Are you saying that we could follow Regin's tunnels under the desert?" asked Colleen.

"Yes!" he whispered, almost squeaking with excitement.

"And who knows what magic things wait in his workshops," said the dwarf. "We might find things of great power with which to fight the goblins and the Witch."

For a moment, Colleen was quite intrigued by the idea, but then Mrs. Wigglepox spoke up.

"But is this door big enough to take Badger and the wagon through? And are the tunnels still intact after all these years?" she asked.

"No," said Dvalenn. "The door is not big enough."

He looked sad for a moment, and then a glimmer shone in his eyes again.

"Badger might fit without the wagon, though," he said.

He paused, looked over at Nous again, and frowned.

"But I will not allow the wicked goblin to enter the last vestiges of my brother's house!" he hissed. "He and his kin and their witch are the cause of this!" He spread his arms wide at the ruinous scene all around them.

Colleen looked about her at the broken remains of the House of Regin. The silence and emptiness of the place was only broken by wisps of wind that kicked up little dust devils amid the crumbling walls. She looked in his pained eyes and felt pity for him.

"I'm sorry for your terrible loss, Dvalenn," she said. "But we must go on together. Something good is happening to Nous. We have to give him a chance. And besides, he knows the Witch's lair and how to get in there. He is our one hope of rescuing my mother!"

Dvalenn's face grew hard.

"No. He has only been half-friendly to you because you saved his life. But he has done nothing good for me at all, nor will he ever wish to. He is a goblin, Colleen. You don't know their kind. You've never been in their pits of gloom, nor labored under their whips. I have been there, and I will never trust them. Once a goblin, always a goblin," he said.

"Please, Dvalenn, Nous is changing, I can see it!" she said. "We need to give him a chance. Yes, he is a goblin. But that's the only life he has ever known. Don't you think that maybe, just maybe, if we show him a better way, and show him that we're willing to live that way ourselves, he might actually leave behind his goblinish ways?"

Dvalenn sneered. “It will take more than a good example to change their kind. You'd have to do a whole heart transplant on them to change what they are. They're wicked to the bone.”

Colleen was silent for a moment, then said, “Mrs. Wigglepox, what do you think?”

She looked thoughtful for a moment and then said, “I have never heard of a goblin turning good, Colleen. They have terrorized my people for hundreds and hundreds of years. They serve the Witch and themselves and no one else.”

“But Nous himself said that there was once a goblin who did just that! I know it seems impossible, but I believe in him,” she said.

“Colleen,” said Dvalenn, “we are here to rescue our families from these goblins. Can we really risk taking a goblin with us? You've seen how he treats me. If I were to find one of my brothers in their black pits, do you think that Nous would help me bring him out? No, he would betray us all in a moment.”

Colleen looked at the goblin, who was still curled up under the wagon.

“Doesn't anyone care what happens to him?” asked Colleen sadly.

“I care,” said a little voice from her pocket.

“And me too,” said another.

It was Rose and Lily. They had been listening quietly to the whole exchange.

“I don't want to act like a goblin, Mother,” said Rose. “They would leave us behind, or worse, if they were in our shoes. I think we ought to act like leprechauns, and help out poor old Nous if we can.”

“That's right, Mother,” said Lily. “Aren't we supposed to wish good for others? And what good would be our wishing if we didn't *do* something too?”

Mrs. Wigglepox was silent for a moment, then took her daughters in her arms and hugged them.

"Forgive me, children. You are right. What good would it be to be a leprechaun if we didn't wish what is good and right for people, even our enemies," she said. "I say Nous comes with us."

"Leoples!" said Oracle, grinning at the Wigglepoxes.

"Well, what of it, Dvalenn?" asked Colleen.

The dwarf looked hard at the goblin once again. He seemed to struggle within himself for a long time.

But then he set his jaw firm and said, "No. I have decided. The goblin will not enter the House of Regin."

"Dvalenn, please," said Colleen.

But Dvalenn turned to the wall of the arch, and gestured over the runes that covered it. A door silently slid aside, revealing a dark green staircase that descended down into the darkness.

Oracle stepped forward and in a serious voice began a little rhyme.

"Weighed, weighed, the giponderous stones,
From pocket to heart their burdensome goes.
Hear them call? Let them fall! Their greedousness dropped!
Only then, then, Dvalenn's way won't be stopped."

"Dvalenn..." said Colleen, pleading.

The dwarf glanced at Oracle and frowned, and then looked at Colleen, turned, and walked into the darkness, his pockets sagging under the weight of the many stones that he had stuffed into them. The door slid silently shut behind him. Colleen stared at it for a moment and then sighed a heavy sigh. "I hope he comes back by evening," she said.

The sun was rising now in the east, and she felt very tired, so in the shade of the great Arch of Regin, they settled in to try to sleep through the heat of their first day out in the Burning Sands.

Chapter 22– Dvalenn's Decision

Dvalenn's pockets sagged heavily as he made his way down the stairs. The walls of Regin's tunnels glowed with an eerie green light that somehow emanated from deep within them. He had walked for over an hour, ever descending down, down into the depths of the earth. He was very tired, and the weight of the stones in his pockets was wearing on him.

"Got to keep going," he said to himself. "Too late to go back now."

He trudged on for some time, and then said, "But what about Colleen and the little people, you old fool. You've left them with a goblin!"

Downward he went, and then said, "They were fine without you before, they'll be fine without you now. And no goblin will set foot in these hallowed halls. Might be the last place in all the land that their foul feet have not polluted."

On he went.

"But she's just a little girl!" he said to himself.

Downward...

"More than that, any fool can see - there's a power in that one. And if we find Regin's Workshop, we can help her out better."

Downward...

"Right, then."

Onward he padded, until after a long while, he came to the last of a thousand stairs, and a wide chamber of many, many doors opened before him. There were so many doorways in the immense room that he could not count them all. Dvalenn sat down on the steps and looked about the glowing room.

Which would it be? he wondered. *Might as well try them all.*

One by one, Dvalenn opened the doors, counting them as he went. The first led to complete darkness. No glowing hall lay beyond. The next was a stair, also leading down into darkness. And the third likewise opened into complete blackness. On and on he went – ten doors, then twenty, then fifty – all leading into impenetrable night that his eyes could not pierce.

"Where did you hide it, Regin?" he shouted into the darkness as he opened door after door.

Sixty doors, seventy... ninety. Dvalenn was panting now, leaning heavily on the glowing green wall.

"Where is it?" he whispered through his labored breath.

At last, he came to the final door, next to the stair that he had descended in the first place. He gripped the handle and pulled. It was locked. He examined the frame, the handle, the door, the floor, the walls, anything for a clue to open the door. But he could find no keyhole.

Suddenly, Dvalenn felt very tired. And so old! How old was he? He could not remember. But a great weariness seemed to be coming upon him.

"Where is the key, Regin? Where did you hide the key?" he said, trying to shake off the heaviness.

And then he saw it. A tiny, tiny inscription on the doorknob, which read:

"To find true gold, you must dig deep."

"This must be the door!" he whispered.

But for the weariness that he felt, and the burden of the stones in his pockets, he would have leaped into the air.

Hardly containing his excitement, Dvalenn recalled the ancient dwarven magic that so very long ago he and his brothers had used to shape things of beauty and might, for locking and opening, for finding and hiding. He hastily breathed the words of opening, and the lock on the door silently opened before him. Beyond it was a roughly cut room barely ten feet wide and long with no doors leading from it. In one corner were propped a pick and shovel and a bucket.

"What is this?" said Dvalenn indignantly. "Where is the gold and treasure of Regin?"

He waddled over to the tools and noticed that in the bottom of the bucket was a rolled up scroll.

Carefully, he picked up the old parchment and began to unroll it. He licked his lips as the first words appeared in the dim green glow of the chamber. It read, *The Dwarven Way – The Sayings of Regin.*

"Ah!" he said aloud. "This must be Regin's treasure map!"

He turned the bucket over and sat on it, hunching his shoulders, and allowing his gray beard to drag on the ground.

Eagerly, but with care, he unrolled it further. The page was inscribed with golden ink, and read:

True Gold

Gold, gold, scattered like sand,
Deep beneath the troubled land.
Dig, dig, toil and mine,
Only then will you see it shine.
Wash, wash with water so clean,
Then burn it 'til no dross is seen.
Give, give, to the craftsman to fix,
To fashion vessels, censers and candlesticks.
Find, find that which you seek,
For not of earthly gold do I speak.

Dvalenn looked puzzled, and then brightened.

"Ah, Regin was a clever fellow. Spoke in riddles to hide the location of his treasure!" he said to himself.

He unrolled the scroll further. A second inscription appeared and read:

Greed

Dark is the Dwarf who falls to greed,
Who bears within, that bitter seed.
An all-consuming fire it grows,
Until a dragon's heart he knows.

Dvalenn hurriedly unrolled another bit of the scroll. There was yet another saying, then another, and another, one entitled *"Desire,"* another *"Gems,"* another *"The Pit,"* and all sayings that Dvalenn could not comprehend the meaning of.

Surely these must tie together somehow – these riddles and sayings must lead to the treasure that Regin had found, and surely hoarded in these chambers somewhere, he thought to himself.

He unrolled the whole scroll to the very bottom and read it. It was not a rhyme or saying as the others had been, but a note that read the following:

"*To my brothers:*

Our brother, Fafnir, has discovered the final end of all earthly desires. I tried to dissuade him, but he has plundered my house and his. Here in this bucket I leave all that is left to me, and I find this more valuable that all my lost treasures.

I am delving deep now. Deeper than I have ever dug, to find the secret treasures that lie beyond the reach of pick and shovel.

Follow in my footprints, if you dare. You can bring only yourself. Nothing else can pass this way. It will cost you all to find what is most precious."

Dvalenn looked down at the floor and, for the first time, he noticed footprints that seemed to be etched into the floor. They led from the door and directly to the wall, and there stopped. He went to the door and put one foot in the first footstep, then in the next, then the next, until he was standing in the last set of footprints in front of the wall. He reached out his hand, and to his complete surprise, it passed into the rock. He moved forward an inch, and his outstretched arm passed further into the stone before him. Slowly, he moved forward, his eyes wide in amazement. He stretched out his other arm, reaching, and began to enter into the solid stone of the wall.

Ah, Regin what magic you possessed! he thought.

But suddenly, he found that he could go no further. Something was blocking his way. He pushed, but felt as though something was pushing him back – by his pockets. He looked down and saw that his bulging pockets would not pass into the stone. He pushed harder, and harder, but try as he may, he could not move any further into the wall.

Dvalenn leaned forward, pressing his face into the stone, and as he did, a strange vision came to his eyes. There, just within the rock, was a white stone path that led away through a beautiful, shining pillared hallway that grew wider and wider as it went, until far in the distance, he could see a marvelous white city that shone with a brilliant radiance. Again, he pressed forward, trying to force his way through the wall of rock, but again, his stuffed pockets prevented him.

He pulled away from the wall and looked at it. Why did he feel so tired? He sat down on the bucket again and stared at the rough wall. Gathering his strength, he stood uncertainly and stumbled forward, arms outstretched. But once again, his stuffed pockets prevented him from going on completely.

Realizing what was happening, he reached into one of his pockets and pulled out a handful of stones. He looked down at them and, for the first time, noticed that they were nothing but worthless gravel. No gold, no silver, no precious gems.

He hesitated, staring at the common stones. Why had he picked them up? He couldn't remember. But there had been a reason. And why did he feel so tired again? He put the stones back in his pocket and paced slowly about.

Regin had found it... he had found what every dwarf had heard of from the time their mothers told them bedtime stories. He had found the White City of Dwarves – the place where all dwarves could go if they could just find the way. But it was said that one only found it at the end... at the end of their life.

That final thought struck him like a hammer blow. He had come to the end. He had a choice to make now. The Lady Danu had hinted at this. He could go to the White City, and live there forever, or walk away and roam these dark tunnels in search of treasures of his own making. And Oracle – that stupid little leprechaun and his ridiculous riddles – he had said something about stones and letting go.

But couldn't I just take these few things with me? he thought.

He pulled the gravel from his pocket again and picked through it. Surely there was something of real value here. He knew there was. There had to be. He had borne the burden of it all these miles. But for some reason, he couldn't think of why it had been so important when he picked it up.

Then a thought struck him. He got up, turned the bucket over, and began to empty his pockets into it. Soon it was filled to overflowing, and it was *heavy.*

Dvalenn trudged over to the wall, carrying the bucket. But it would not pass through the wall. He turned around and tried to back in, and indeed, without all of the stones barring his way, he was able to slip easily through the wall and into the radiant white hall that lay just beyond. But when he tried to pull the bucket through, it would not budge.

Exhausted, he sat down in the white hall, one hand feebly gripping the bucket of gravel on the other side, and stared at the distant White City. It shone like a radiant sun, its brilliant walls beckoning to him, and sparkling fountains glittered in its courtyards. Then he saw them – dwarves – hundreds of them, all dressed in festive colors as they walked among the fountains and statues and other structures that were becoming clearer to his eyes the longer he gazed toward it. A great desire to join them rose in his heart, and he felt as though he might burst if he didn't.

"*Just let go of that old bucket of worthless stones!*" said a voice inside his head.

Slowly, he slackened his grip and, one by one, his fingers slipped from the handle until just the tip of his index finger still touched the handle. But just as the bucket was about to fall, Dvalenn seized the handle, gripped it all the more, and stepped back into the darkness.

Regin's scroll lay unrolled on the floor at his feet. He stared at it and read the last words of his brother again.

"*...It will cost you all to find what is most precious.*"

For a moment longer, he stared at the words, then at the gravel.

Then, in a moment of decision, he looked up at the ceiling, gazing upward through the rock and earth, and said, "Forgive me, Colleen! My time has come."

Then he heaved the bucket of stones at the far wall and ran for the secret doorway. He did not stop as he passed through the wall, but with a flood of relief and joy, ran on and on to the White City of Dwarves.

Chapter 23 – Farewell to Dvalenn

Dvalenn did not return that day, and as the blazing sun beat down on the ruins around them, Colleen barely slept. The heat was unbearable, even in the shade, and more than once she got up and drank some of Doc's draft or the Lady's water.

Nous lay in the darkest corner of the Arch of Regin, and kept moving to stay in the shadows as the sun rose high and then sank in the western sky.

The Wigglepox family did their best to rest under the driver's seat of the wagon, where Lily's wagon had yielded up yet another surprise. There they found a hidden compartment that had tiny beds within it, and these they gladly crawled into and slept quite comfortably, with Mrs. Wigglepox saying again and again, "That was some wish, daughter, some wish."

Oracle also rested in the shade of the Arch, his old head lying upon a stone, and Badger stood above him, his head hanging low.

But when she could no longer lay in the heat, Colleen rose one last time and began to prepare something for them to eat.

"Nous, are you awake?" she said.

Nous stirred from his shady spot and uncurled himself.

He glanced at the sky and said, "The evil sun still shines."

"I know," she said, wiping sweat from her forehead. "But I thought you might be hungry. Dvalenn hasn't come back yet."

Nous crept over to the wagon and looked at the things that Colleen was unpacking. The aroma of Doc's mushrooms and the Lady's provisions wafted up from the sack.

"Stinks," said Nous.

“Well, it's all we have,” said Colleen, “plus these roots and nuts. You should eat something wholesome, you know. Look, it's really good.”

She took one of the stuffed mushrooms and popped it in her mouth, savoring the flavor.

“Yum,” she said, and picked up another and offered it to Nous.

Nous carefully took it and rolled it over and over in his hand. Colleen noticed that his hands were filthy and that dirt was caked under his yellow fingernails.

He sniffed it, wrinkling his bulbous nose, and screwed up his face.

“Oh, try it, Nous. You just might find that it's good,” said Colleen.

Nous squinted his eyes shut and popped the mushroom in his mouth. He stood motionless for a moment, grimacing, but then his expression seemed to soften, and he began to chew.

He slowly opened his eyes, and they grew wide, and a look of wonder crept over his face.

“Haven't you ever had mushrooms before, Nous?” asked Colleen.

The goblin shook his head and continued to chew slowly, then swallowed. A rare look of delight crossed his face, and he reached into the sack and pulled out another mushroom, and ate it.

“Mushrooms, yes, but not like this!” he said.

Colleen laughed and said, “What do goblins usually eat, Nous?”

Nous stopped chewing for a moment, and looked at her.

“The Colleen does not want to know,” he said.

“Well, what about something to drink, then? We have the water from the Lady, and...” began Colleen.

“No! Nous will not drink the evil water!” he said firmly.

Colleen took a drink from the water sack. It was warm, but delicious and refreshed her completely.

“It's wonderful, Nous. I think if you tried it, you might find that you like it, just like the mushrooms,” she said.

Nous hissed and turned away.

“Well, how about some dwarven brew then?” she offered.

Nous sniffed at the brew and then took a drink, then another.

“See, you like dwarven mushrooms and dwarven drinks,” said Colleen. “They're really not such bad folk, now are they?”

Nous snorted and put the sack down.

“We have stories about the dwarves – evil stories. They have been enemies of the goblins since we had stories to tell. They do nasty things to goblins, just like the little people do,” he replied.

Colleen thought about this for a moment and then said, “Nous, do your people have any stories about the world of Men, where I come from?”

Nous looked sidelong at Colleen for a moment and then said, “Goblins in the land of the Little People have not met many humans. Nous has only seen four.”

“Four?” asked Colleen.

“Four. The Colleen, the boy, the hag, and the Pwca-killer,” he replied.

“Nous, you've mentioned the Pwca-killer before. What is a Pwca?” she asked.

"Pwca was our goblin Captain," he replied. "The Pwca-killer was an evil Witch that made him vanish."

"You mean there was more than one witch in this world?" asked Colleen.

"The Pwca-killer witch appeared and attacked us. But we captured it and took it to the Goblin King," replied Nous.

Colleen thought for a moment and then said, "Nous, what did the Pwca-killer look like?"

"Ugly," he grunted.

Then he looked at her sidelong again and then, almost seemingly embarrassed, mumbled, "Looked almost just like you, just bigger."

Then he looked at the ground and kicked a stone.

Colleen smiled, and then a thought occurred to her.

"Nous, you said that the Pwca-killer looked like me. How so?" she asked.

"Same hair. Same face. But bigger," he replied. "Same as all humans. Ugly."

"Where did you catch her, and where did you take her, Nous? Was she all right?" asked Colleen.

She was sure that Nous had been one of the goblins to capture her mother.

"We caught the Pwca-killer by the mirror in the woods. Took it to the black ship. It escaped twice, but we hunted it down. Fast, that one was. Had to call on another goblin band to help catch it. But we found it. Nasty thing. Fought hard," he said.

"Was she all right when you captured her, Nous?" asked Colleen again. She was beginning to worry.

"Knocked it cold!" declared Nous triumphantly. Then he narrowed his eyes and hissed.

"We'd have done worse, but the Witch's orders were not to hurt any big people too bad and to bring 'em to her straight away," he said.

"Nous, I can't believe my mo... that the Pwca-killer... would actually kill anyone. Are you sure that's what happened?" she asked.

"Pwca jumped onto the Pwca-killer when it appeared in the woods, and it threw him into the mirror. Poor Pwca – vanished! Threw him into the Abyss, I say," growled Nous.

"Nous, Pwca isn't dead. Pwca is back in the World of Men! He's been sneaking around our farm for months now – we just didn't know what he was.

"He went through the same mirror that Frederick and I came through, just the opposite way! In fact, I'm quite sure that Frederick and I saw him. He almost came back through with us," said Colleen.

Nous screwed up his face, trying to comprehend.

"The Colleen came through the mirror from the world of Men?" he asked. "And Pwca is there now?"

"Yes, Nous, we accidentally fell through. I think my ... I think my *mother* came through the same way. I'm sure she didn't mean to throw Pwca through the mirror. She was probably just surprised, and he managed to fall through to the other side before the mirror shut down," she said.

Nous thought for a moment and then, to Colleen's surprise, began to chant a strange chant. His voice was raspy and cold as he sang, and a weird look was in his eyes – something wild and primal.

"When opens once again
A portal to the World of Men,
Then let all goblins sing!
And battle horns, let them ring!

For at long last the door
So long hidden 'neath forest floor
Shall open for them then,
And ancient kings shall rise again.
Goblin armies shall be free
To claim new lands amidst the sea."

He stopped his chant and looked solemn.

Colleen stared at the goblin for a moment and then said, "Nous, where did you learn that from?"

"Olden times," he replied. "Handed down from olden times. Don't know who spoke it first."

Colleen glanced at the sky and decided to change the subject. The idea of armies of goblins running freely through the Gate of Anastazi down in old Doc's caverns was, to say the least, scary. What if they did invade the world of Men? She decided that there were some things she would keep to herself and not discuss with the goblin.

"Nous, back when we were tied up in the wagon, I remember the other goblins talking about some sort of rebellion in the pits, and that a sorceress had risen up and was fighting against the Witch. What do you know about that?" she asked.

"Not much," he replied. "Lies started by the little people. I've not been there for a long time."

"But what do the other goblins say about it all?" she prodded.

Nous glanced around and then lowered his voice to a harsh whisper.

"They say it all started half a year ago or so. Nobody knows where she came from. Just appeared in the pits. Then prisoners started disappearing. The Witch herself got involved, and there was some sort of fight. Huk, the Captain of the Pits got killed, they say, from a blast of fire from the Witch's staff that was aimed at the Sorceress."

Nous looked about again and lowered his voice further. “Then, they say, the Sorceress made the pits come to life. Like some giant rock creature, they say, and the Witch... the Witch had to flee.”

Colleen wondered what this could mean. If the Witch was so powerful, and had defeated so many of her enemies, who was this Sorceress?

“Nous,” she said, “we've got to find out more about the Sorceress somehow. She could be an ally.”

He narrowed his eyes at her and, for a moment, she was afraid he was going to grow angry. But the look passed, and he said, “The Witch has served the Goblin King for long years. Her power is in fire. Nothing she sets her fire to can survive, not even this Sorceress.”

They both fell silent for some time, and then Colleen looked at the sky.

“We better get going soon,” she said. “It's getting dark. I do hope Dvalenn comes back soon. I don't like the thought of leaving without him. I suppose we ought to wait a while yet.”

They waited, and time slipped away, but still Dvalenn did not return.

“Do you think we should leave yet?” Colleen asked Mrs. Wigglepox.

She looked thoughtful and then replied, “Yes. I think that Dvalenn has decided not to return to us. But I feel that he has somehow found himself. It's not a bad thing, Colleen. Something good has happened to him, I think.”

“What about it, Oracle?” asked Colleen.

Oracle then did a very strange thing – he took Colleen by the hand and drew her down next to him. He then stooped down with his face to the ground, shut one eye, opened the other as wide as he could, and, with his nose in the sand, stared downward, as though he were trying to see deep underground.

Colleen giggled at the funny sight, thinking that he was simply performing one of his antics. But then she thought better of it and followed his lead. Still holding his rough, leathery hand, she closed her eyes and focused. Immediately, she found herself seeing a vision of deep tunnels and long stairways. Down, down her mind descended, and she felt as though Oracle was leading her, his gentle presence simple and without guile, and for the first time he seemed untouched by the Spell.

Suddenly, she saw Dvalenn. He was struggling with something that looked like – yes, it was a bucket of stones. She could also see the White City, and knew that the dwarf was at his final decision point in life – that he could choose to hold on to his earthly treasures, or release them and finally go to the halls of his fathers.

The moment came, and Dvalenn made his choice. She watched, and a smile beamed on her face. Oracle giddily laughed, and Colleen could not help but laugh with him.

"He made it!" she said. "He made it home!"

After a moment, the vision faded, and Colleen sighed heavily.

"Time for us to go as well," she said, and, rising from the ground, went to pack the rest of their things.

The sun was setting as they set out southward. Colleen looked back at the dark shape of the Arch of Regin and wondered if they would ever pass this way again.

She felt a twinge of loneliness without Dvalenn, and a little apprehensive at the thought of traveling with just the Wigglepox family, a mysterious old leprechaun, and a goblin. But she was more determined than ever, now that there was more news of her mother. So southward they rolled, the mighty Badger pulling their magnificent wagon through the Burning Sands.

Chapter 24 - Pwca

Pwca the goblin sat for some minutes in the basement of the house, breathing heavily. His bat-like ears moved up and down in time with his chest, and his scraggly black strands of hair hung limply over his gray-green face.

"The big one got itself a magic hammer, it does," it said to itself. "But it won't survive the *stalkers.*"

He grinned at the prospect.

"But Pwca needs more friends. Allies. Yes, Pwca must go back and bring more – more than just the evil little ones."

He stood and paced about the basement, thinking. Now that the man was out of the way, he was free to do as he wished. A thought struck him and he stopped pacing.

"Magic hammer..." he said aloud, and slowly a toothy grin spread across his deformed face. "Magic hammer to break the chains..."

He lifted the crystal ball before the mirror. The dark wood opened before him, and he quickly slipped through and put the crystal back in his cloak. As the mirror swirled, Pwca dashed behind the wall and peered out, looking into the darkness. To his amazement, several stalkers lay dead in the leaves, and a great tree lay split in two, fallen in the forest, with a third stalker lying dead at its base. Pwca frowned. They had been nursing that tree with bits of Ooze. Now they would have to start over with another one.

Looking about, he slunk from behind the wall and examined the ground, then the dead beasts.

So, the man survived, thought Pwca.

The goblin was surprised, but now he was even more interested in the hammer that the human bore.

More howls sounded in the distance. Yes, the stalkers would be tracking this man. And Pwca would follow them. Off through the woods he flew, dashing from tree to tree, pausing to listen, and then running on, sometimes on all fours, and sometimes upright. All the while the howls drew nearer, and soon he came to what he knew was the main trail through the forest that led to the goblin encampment. The Troll Bridge was up ahead, so he slowed his pace and drew up behind a tree, peering out at the two bridges.

There, standing on the farther wooden bridge, was the man. Four stalkers had him trapped on the bridge, two on either side, and Pwca knew that more would be coming, likely the entire pack, which in these parts numbered at least twenty. Pwca watched, transfixed, as the huge beasts howled in delight and slowly moved forward for the kill.

With a movement so fast that the goblin could hardly believe his eyes, the great hammer flew from the man's hand, striking one beast on the far side of the bridge, knocking it completely off the bridge with a yowl of pain, and sending it crashing into the river below. The hammer flew on and circled back, striking the second stalker in its path. The creature crumpled and lay still, and the hammer returned to the man's hand.

He turned and, with a great bellow, swung upward as one of the two remaining beasts leaped upon him. He caught it under its chin and sent it spinning backward into its companion, and both of them went careening over the railing of the bridge. There was a splash as they struck the water below.

The man looked about, but saw no more opponents. His jaw was set, and his face was grim and resolute as he crossed the bridge and continued on up the road into the dark night.

Pwca slunk from the trees and went to the edge of the bridge, then peered down into the darkness of the gully. The river gurgled in its course, but amid its babbles came another sound – the sound of heavy, rasping breathing. He strained his eyes, and there by the stream bank he could dimly make out the shape of the two stalkers that had fallen. One of them was stirring now, wagging its head as if trying to get its bearings. It lifted its head as if to howl, then its voice was cut off, and Pwca saw a great shape towering above the beast. There was a whimper, the stalker went limp, and the giant shadow dragged its victim away toward the Troll Bridge.

"*The old troll!*" hissed Pwca. "*He'll dine well tonight!*"

Pwca started to cross the wooden bridge in pursuit of the man, but then another thought struck him. He stared up the river at the Troll Bridge. The troll had already disappeared into the shadows beneath it. Silently, he slipped back the way he had come and crept up next to the Troll Bridge, listening intently. There were muffled sounds of chewing, and the occasional *snap* as something was broken beneath the bridge. Pwca waited until the sounds died away, and then slowly, carefully, he inched his way down the steep bank beside the bridge.

When he was sure he was in a place where he could easily run, he called out, "Troll! I have a proposition for you!"

There was no sound.

"Troll!" called Pwca louder. "I wish to speak with you! In the name of the Witch, I ask for a parley!"

Still, no sound was heard. Pwca wondered if the old thing had fallen asleep after its meal, and was just preparing to slip further down the bank when, with no warning, the gigantic face of the troll rose before him, and two great arms lunged at him. The green monster bellowed a dreadful cry as it came at him, mouth still fouled with its last victim's remains. Pwca leaped into the air just in time, barely saving himself, and scrambled up the bank. To his surprise, the troll did not follow, but stared up at him, gasping as if catching its breath.

Then it spoke.

"What … is it … the goblin … wants," it said through gasping breaths.

Pwca stared down at the creature. It was massive and green and bore a chipped and broken skin of scales. Its claws were long and ragged, and its bulbous bald head looked rather like a misshapen blob sitting upon a thick neck. Its pinched eyes seemed too small for its large face as they stared back at him.

“I wish to free you from this land of the Little People,” he said.

“Free … me...” said the troll flatly.

“Yes, free you. Take you from this dreadful place. Take you to a place where you can have meats other than fish and worms and stalkers and goblins.”

“You … lie …” it said. “Come … down … and I will … have you … for dessert.”

“You know of the mirror in the wood?” asked Pwca, now fingering the crystal ball in his pocket.

“Mirror …” breathed the troll.

“Yes, the one some ways down the trail – the one that's been there for ages and ages now. But perhaps you have forgotten. Perhaps you are too old and feeble of mind to remember it,” said Pwca.

The troll growled and spat, and foul things flew from its mouth.

“What … of it?” it said.

“I have obtained the key to open it!” he declared, and pulled the crystal from his pocket, holding it up to the night sky.

The moon shone down upon him, striking the crystal ball and seemingly illuminating it so that it glowed with a blue-silver light.

“Where … did a … goblin … get … that?” it wheezed.

"Ah! Does it matter? Come with me and I will show you what it can do! We shall go together to the world of Men, and there you will be free to hunt!" declared Pwca.

The troll was silent for a moment and breathed heavily.

"And what … does the … goblin … want from me?" asked the troll.

"Just your strength," said Pwca. "There is a little thing that I need moved. A mirror on the other side – a heavy mirror, too big for one poor little goblin to carry. Help me and I will give you more than you can dream of. Come now, a new age is about to be born in the world of Men, when old things shall awaken and walk the earth once more! Creatures of the night are gathering, gathering around a great and terrible Presence. Come with me, and you will feel it! You will worship it!"

Pwca was growing exuberant, but the troll just stared at him for a moment, then looked back beneath its bridge.

"Long … years … I have … lived … beneath this … bridge," said the Troll. "I … built it … so long ago … It is mine!"

"Ah, and you may keep it if you wish. Once we have the mirror, all the bridges in all the worlds will be yours! Only come with me and see," answered Pwca.

The old troll hesitated and then said, "I will … come and … see. And if … you lie... I *will* … eat you … for … dessert."

The green creature, at least ten feet tall, slowly climbed the bank and then stood towering over the goblin. It was thick and broad, with legs like tree trunks, and a broad barrel of a chest that hung with aging fat and muscle.

"This way," said Pwca, and led the way down the trail.

The ancient troll followed, breathing heavily, and after a long while, they came to the mirror in the wood.

The troll looked at the dead stalkers and sniffed.

"The man – he killed them with his magic hammer. We must stay away from him, yes, until *we* can get the hammer. Come and watch!" said Pwca.

He pulled the crystal ball from his pocket again and held it up. Instantly, the mirror before them swirled, and there was the basement of the McGunnegal house, dark and still.

Pwca stepped through.

A look of surprise crossed the troll's fat face.

"Come!" said Pwca.

The troll bent low and passed its hand through the mirror, then with great effort, squeezed through, its chest and back scraping the mirror's sides as it entered the basement. It looked from side to side, then, seeing a dim light filtering down from an open door up a stairway, pushed through completely.

Pwca put the crystal ball away.

"Now for our little agreement," he said to the troll. "You see this mirror? We shall have it for our own. Just pick it up and carry it up these stairs, across a field, over a wall, and into a bog where the Presence is. Then! Yes, then we shall bring the creatures of the night to the Presence, and the new age shall begin!"

The troll stood breathing heavily for a moment, considering. Then it gripped the heavy mirror with its powerful arms, lifted it, and followed the goblin up the stairs. The wooden steps groaned and cracked under its weight, and when it reached the top, it would not fit through the doorway with the mirror. The troll breathed heavily for a moment, then with one mighty blow, it smashed the doorframe, sending splinters flying into the kitchen. Up it came, a thing of horror and might that had not stalked the green earth for many an age.

The goblin cackled with glee as it led the troll to the back door, which it also smashed open with its massive fists, and, wheezing as it went, followed the goblin step by step. Together, they disappeared over the wall and into the Dismal Bog.

Chapter 25 – Trouble in Ireland

All day, the McGunnegals, Frederick, Gwydion, and Professor McPherson sailed northwest toward Ireland. An extraordinarily strong and steady breeze had been with them, and the *Unknown* skipped lightly over the sea northwestward after they had rounded the bend of Wales. They spent considerable time talking and learning and cleaning, with a noontime break during which Gwydion had produced the most amazing meal of soup and bread and cheese that they had ever tasted. Gwydion and Bib spent hours working together and talking about the advancing technology of the present age and about magical things of ages past.

"From what you say, Bib, magic seems to have faded from the world to a thing of legend and myth – the stuff of bedtime stories and fireside tales. I wonder what happened?" said Gwydion.

"Do you mean that it wasn't that way in your day?" asked Bib.

"Oh, there have always been legends and myths," he replied, "but when the Gates were open, the gifts and powers of the races were a thing of everyday life, at least for the folk that we met. But there were few of the race of Men who had such abilities. It was only after the mingling of the races that some were born with the gifts."

"Do you mean that after this Anastazi the Great opened the Gates, and the various peoples walked in each other's lands that some folk of the race of Men started to *become* magical?" she asked.

"No, no, I didn't mean that, though I have heard such rumors. What I meant was that the races *mingled.* Anastazi himself took a human wife. Their children bore the traits of both human and elven peoples," replied Gwydion.

"Do you mean that *you* have *elvish* blood in you? Are you related to this Anastazi the Great?" asked Bib, amazed.

"To answer your second question, no, I am not related to Anastazi the Great, unless it might be through an ancient bloodline of the elven folk. But my father's father's father was a great elven lord. Njord was his name. He loved the sea, it is said, and left the Emerald Isle to find lands of his own. My grandfather, Freyr, took most of our folk – all except my father and mother, that is, and went in search of free lands. It has been many years since I saw him last," replied Gwydion.

He paused, and then said, quieter, "Many years."

Bib was about to ask him another question when the voice of Frederick called from high above. He was in the crow's nest and had been watching out over the sea.

"I can see land ahead!" he called.

"Already?" said Professor McPherson from the ship's wheel. "Truly, we are sailing fast!"

Indeed, as they gazed out over the bow of the ship, they could see the coast of Ireland steadily drawing nearer. Soon it loomed large before them, and the professor called them to make ready for docking. Frederick climbed down as the ship glided into the same harbor that Captain Truehart had sailed from some ten days before. They raised their sails, and two rowboats met them. After securing ropes to the ship, they slowly made their way to the docks.

As they went ashore, Frederick was reminded that the Irish people were starving, undergoing one of the worst famines in their history. The men standing around the docks were thin, and some appeared to be sick. Emaciated children stared with hollow eyes, looking on as the little group made their way down the docks. He silently wondered how long they could endure such hardship.

They soon found the dock master, and the professor spoke to him about the ship and how long they would be docked there. They then found a farmer with a large wagon who was heading their way and hitched a ride, with the professor and Gwydion sitting in the front and the rest of them in the back. Gwydion sat watching the landscape roll by as they made their way toward the farm, but the children talked in whispers among themselves.

"It will be wonderful to see Father again," said Henny.

"Yes," said Bib, "and the farm. There's so much to talk about, and I'm sure the professor and Gwydion and Father will know what to do once all the plans are made. We'll catch that goblin and make things right in the land."

Soon they came to a crossroads, and the farmer said, "I'll let you out here. Tell your dad that Emmit says hello and that I hope he's well. These are hard times. Hard times."

He shook his head sadly.

"This will be fine, sir," said Aonghus. "It's only a few minutes more. Many thanks."

They piled out of the wagon and waved good-by. The farmer turned to go, but paused, then said, "You all watch yourselves. Some folk about here are blaming your family for the blight. Strange things have been seen on your farm – strange things. Not that I believe all the stories, but I'm just a-warnin' ya." He turned and headed down the lane to the right.

"What's that supposed to mean?" said Bib.

"I'm not sure," said Abbe. "Let's just get home."

As they walked along and neared the house, Henny tugged on Aonghus' sleeve and said, "Aonghus, can you carry me? I'm scared."

Aonghus picked her up and said, "What's wrong, Sprite?"

"Something's bad," she said. "The farm doesn't look right."

But the farmhouse was still some distance away, and it looked the same as always. The old brown wooden house and its dark thatched roof stood next to an old oak tree, a pile of firewood still lay stacked to one side.

Yet as they drew near, something did feel wrong. They hurried on down the road and passed through the gate. All was quiet. Too quiet. A wind blew across the yard, licking up a whirlwind of dust before passing on over the fields.

"Dad?" called Abbe as she ran to the front door.

They all followed behind. The door was ajar, and when they entered, a frightening sight met their eyes. The house was wrecked. Furniture was overturned, a chair was smashed, and as they went into the kitchen, they found the cellar door ripped from its hinges and broken into splinters.

"Dad?" called Aonghus.

Immediately, they began to run through the house, calling for their father, almost panicking with fear, but suddenly, Gwydion called out loudly, "Stop!"

They all stopped, shocked at the commanding voice that the old man had used.

"Quickly, come here," he said.

They returned to the kitchen where he stood, and looked where he pointed. There on the floor by the remains of the cellar door were huge muddy footprints leading away from the cellar and toward the back door. The prints were at least two feet long, and where toes would have been there were scrapes and marks on the wooden floor, as though claws had rent the old planks under some tremendous weight.

"What is it?" asked Bran, leaning close. "This mud looks to be maybe a day or two old."

Gwydion leaned down next to him and examined the marks.

"Come, all of you. Stay close. Do you have any weapons here?" he said.

Aonghus ran upstairs and returned a moment later with a staff and Bran's hunting bow.

"The upstairs is a mess too," he said grimly.

Gwydion looked at the staff and bow doubtfully and said, "Follow me."

The back of the house was no better off. It looked as though something huge, too big to fit easily through the door, had made the doorway bigger by simply smashing through the wall. A terrible thought struck Frederick.

"Oh no," he said aloud.

They all stopped and looked at him.

"Frederick?" said the professor.

"The mirror!" he said, a look of horror on his face. "What if the goblin opened a doorway into some other world and brought something terrible through, and got into the house?"

"Then we need to go and see this mirror," replied McPherson.

They hurried across the fields and to Grandpa's house. Lighting a lamp, they went down the cellar, and Frederick led them to the place where the mirror had stood.

"It's gone!" he said.

They looked at him skeptically.

"It was here, I swear!" he said. "I'm not lying!"

Gwydion looked grim. "If it was the mirror of Mor-Fae of which you speak, one goblin could not move it. It would take many. But I fear that Frederick may be right. Something else may have come through. Something far stronger. We must stay together."

They left Grandpa's and went back to the farmhouse and gathered in the broken kitchen.

"Where's Dad?" asked Henny, pulling on Aonghus' sleeve.

"We're not sure, lass," he said. "But you know Dad. He can take care of himself better than any man alive. I'm sure he's out looking for this goblin thing."

"But the house..." she said, a frightened look on her face.

"Never mind that," he replied. "I know it looks bad, but you can bet all this happened while Dad was away doing something. He might come back any minute, or maybe..."

"Or maybe he ended up there too," cut in Frederick.

"End up there?" said Professor McPherson.

"I mean maybe that goblin *did* open the door to the Land of the Little People. Maybe it brought back something... like a troll. We met one there. I remember it. It was *huge.* And I remember seeing its footprints in the mud. They were about the size of those marks on the floor. Maybe Mr. McGunnegal followed the goblin into that land, and maybe he got trapped there," said Frederick.

"Then all the more reason we hunt down that thing and get both the mirror and the crystal ball back," said Bran.

"Perhaps," said Professor McPherson. "Or perhaps we should split up. Frederick, you said that this Lady Danu told you that you were to find a king in the sea?"

"Yes," he said. "I'm sure that I am supposed to sail out there and find him."

"No," said Aonghus. "I think we should stay together. If that goblin is going about bringing other evils into our world, we've got to stop it."

"And how shall we do that?" asked Gwydion. "It has the crystal ball – the key to the mirror – and with that, it can travel to any world, and bring many things here that have not walked in the world of Men before. I have seemingly slept long, and I do not know what has befallen the other worlds. But I do know that three of the eight worlds fell into darkness in my time, and a shadow had fallen over four others."

"The eight worlds?" asked Bib. "What are they?"

Gwydion was about to answer when Frederick cut in.

"Under the hill lay eight doors.
Some lead to sun, and some to moors."

"What did you say, Frederick?" asked Gwydion.

"It's the rhyme," he replied.

"Tell me of this rhyme," said Gwydion.

Frederick cleared his throat and began.

"Under the hill lay eight doors.
Some lead to sun, and some to moors.

In one, you find the Little Folk,
With treasures hidden under oak.
There I found the lady sleeping fast,
And broke the spell that had been cast.

But, no princess prize was she,
Indeed, a witch turned out to be.
Oh, what treachery was this,
That I should wake her with a kiss?

Door two finds Trolls, their cruel hearts long
To rob and steal and do folk wrong.
Once architects and builders tall,
Now under bridges they do crawl.

A third finds gold and gems and ale,
And treasuries and spear and mail.
Magic ax and armor bright,
And carven halls of dwarven might.

Four is where the Giant roams,
Beware him lest he crush your bones
Into his bread and nasty meal
To feed his lusty gullet's zeal.

The fifth you must not pass, be sure!
For demons wait beyond that door.
Your soul they seek! From them I fled!
Do not open! This I have said!

The sixth leads home, remember it when,
You wish to return to the world of Men.
And there find rest and peace at last,
When you return from the looking-glass.

The seventh finds Elf and tree and song,
Spells, and laughter all day long.
Bright never-dying folk and friend,
And maids so fair your heart will rend.

Open eight and find sure gloom,
An ancient plague, the goblin's doom.
And there the Worm that brought the blight,
Calling all into its pits of night.

Behind these doors such perils lie,
And lo, no keys to these have I!
Yet to these worlds I yet have passed,

Through a simple looking-glass.

The portal to a perilous maze
Into which I have dared to gaze.
No simple trek around a wall,
But beyond it I have placed it all -

A king's ransom, oh, and so much more!
Things of might and magic stored.
Things too great for mortal men,
Things so great that I, a brigand, send

Them far away from mortal lands
Into, I hope, far wiser hands.
Yet three things I dare not leave
Lest too, our world, become bereaved.

The first, this map to mark the place
That leads beyond our time and space.
The next an orb so small, yet rare!
With it you travel, but oh, take care!

And last, a looking-glass to see
Wherever the traveler may be.
And at special places you may pass
And step through the looking-glass.

What secret powers these things possess,
None have fathomed, none have guessed.
Yet with simple folk who have no cares,
I leave these things from wizards' lairs."

They all looked at him and were silent.

"It's on the map above the fireplace," he said.

"Those are the Eight Worlds, aren't they?"

"There is a map?" asked Gwydion.

Aonghus led them into the living room, but to their further dismay, they found the map was gone.

“It took the map too!” said Abbe.

“It would seem that our goblin is gathering many things to itself. But to answer your question, yes, those are the Eight Worlds – of Little People, Trolls, Dwarves, Giants, Orogim – I believe the rhyme called them *demons,* although they are not – Men, Elves, and Goblins. They are the eight that Anastazi the Great opened doors to, although perhaps not the only eight that exist. Who can say? But where did this riddle come from? What is this map of which you speak?” asked the wizard.

“It's an old thing,” said Bib, “passed down from generation to generation in our family.”

“It was drawn by Atsolter the Pirate,” said Frederick. “He got the crystal ball somehow and went to those worlds, I suppose. He’s the one who wrote the rhyme.”

“Was that all that the rhyme said?” asked Gwydion. “Please, tell us this riddle once again.”

Frederick recited the whole thing to them again, and they listened carefully. When he was done, they were all silent for a long moment.

“I say we find this goblin here and now,” said Aonghus, “before it causes more trouble.”

“And what of Colleen?” asked Professor McPherson.

“We take one day. One day to track down this thing and make it give us the crystal. If we can't find it in one day, then we set sail and return no later than four weeks. But if we find its lair, we seal it up, and make sure it can't get out,” he replied.

“Aong, we tracked that thing for weeks and weeks, and never found it,” said Bran.

"We have a bigger trail to follow now," he replied. "And we didn't have a wizard with us then."

They all looked at Gwydion. His dark eyes returned their expectant gazes, but he was silent.

"Very well, then, but there is something you need to know about this place, if indeed this is the same place where once I dwelt. There is something that we, that is, the wizards, buried here long, long ago. It may lay still beneath the earth," he replied.

"What is that?" asked Bran.

"It was an ancient evil. We... chained it," he slowly replied.

A sudden wind whistled through the broken kitchen door, and a shiver ran down their spines.

"What was it?" asked Henny, her eyes wide.

"A black thing," he whispered. "A terror that fell upon the world of men and ravaged it. We warred against it for long years, and at last, we captured it, and would have slain it. But one among us forbade its destruction. So, deep beneath the earth we chained it, and there kept it far from the lives of simple men. And there it may yet dwell, haunting the world with its nightmares and nameless fears, but impotent to do ought else."

"Gwydion," said Aonghus, a thought coming to him, "there's a bog just south of here. It's an evil place. There's something about it that makes your blood run cold and fills your heart with fear. The farther you go in, the more you feel it."

"I've been there too," said Bran. "Right in the middle of the bog there's a broken place, and a cave of sorts that descends down into blackness. I'm sure that's the source of it all."

Gwydion took a deep breath.

"Then that is where the goblin will be," he replied. "This terror that I speak of will draw all such creatures to itself. Let us hope that it, itself, has not been wakened."

"I don't like the bog," said Henny. "Dad said not to go there."

Aonghus knelt down next to her and looked into her blue-lavender eyes. Her golden hair hung down across her rosy cheeks, making her look cute and lovable, but her face bore a worried expression.

"Don't you worry, Sprite," he said with a smile. "I think Dad would approve. What we're doing now is really important, okay?" He tousled her hair and said, "We'll be fine."

"I think that we should not waste any time," said Professor McPherson. "But I do not think we should send the girls into the bog. Nor do I think it safe for any of us to go there. If there is a goblin and a troll, and this nameless terror that you speak of, and now who knows what other creatures, could we face them alone? How do we plan to get the mirror and the crystal ball back from them? Will we fight them? And if so, then with what?"

They were quiet for a few moments, and then Aonghus spoke.

"Bran and I will. We know this bog pretty well, and we know exactly where to look for this goblin. And we know some hiding places where we can spy things out. The professor is right – we shouldn't take a whole troop of us blundering into the heart of the bog, just to be spotted by these creatures and ambushed," he said.

"Now hold on, Aonghus," said Abbe. "I want to go too. Believe it or not, I've been in there myself a time or two."

"You... when did you go wandering in there?" he asked.

"Never you mind," she replied. "But I know a thing or two about it as well."

"No, Abbe. I need you to stay here and watch over the others. If there's trouble, you'll know what to do," he replied.

She started to protest, but then stopped, seeing both a stubborn and pleading look on his face.

"All right then," she said grudgingly. "I suppose we can try to fix up the house a bit."

"Frederick and I will stay with the girls and lend a hand with the house," said the professor. "No, Frederick, no protests. Perhaps you and I can talk a bit while we work."

"I think that I shall accompany you to the bog," said Gwydion. "But we should return well before dark. That should give us four or five hours yet. And we may wish to consider staying on the ship this evening. It may be difficult to secure the house in its present condition."

So the girls, Frederick, and Professor McPherson set about cleaning up the house while Gwydion, Aonghus, and Bran headed across the farm toward the bog.

"Everything has changed here," said Gwydion. "Once there was a great white castle with marvelously tall towers. Every one of its stones was enchanted and carved with runes of great power against the evils that stalked the world in my day. The Council of Wizards met there, and peoples of many worlds came and went, and the McGunnegals were..."

He stopped and looked at the boys.

"I don't know why I never thought of it before, but there were McGunnegals who lived on the outskirts of the castle. They were … big men. Do you know your family history?" he asked.

"Some of it seems a bit vague when you go back more than six or seven generations," said Bran, who had studied the history of both the McGunnegals and the McLochlans. "There are weird stories on both sides, though. Family stories of strange things happening, I mean. But the oldest stories say that the first McGunnegals were *really* big, and came to Ireland thousands of years ago. We have a graveyard, but only the McGunnegals are buried there, no McLochlans."

"Indeed? I would like to see it, perhaps tomorrow. I wonder if you are related to the McGunnegals that I once knew?" replied Gwydion.

"Well, it's a pretty common name," said Aonghus. "Could be no relation at all."

"Perhaps," said the wizard, and they walked on in silence.

When they came to the wall, Aonghus said, "Well, here we are. The bog is on the other side."

Gwydion examined the stones piled up to form the wall and shook his head.

"There is no doubt," he said. "These are the broken stones of the Wizard's Castle."

"Well, whatever it was, it happened a long time ago," said Aonghus. "This wall has been here as long as anyone can remember."

"And is there a way through?" asked Gwydion.

"No, we just climb over," said Bran, and he nimbly mounted the wall and sat on top with a smile on his face.

But when he looked out over the bog, his expression changed, and a look of shock replaced his smile. The others followed him up, and when they looked south, their eyes grew wide, and a feeling of dread crept over them. There, like a vast sea, stood a dense gray fog, with only the very tops of barren trees reaching their twisted branches beyond the dank roof. And it stank.

"What has happened?" whispered Bran. "It was always a bit misty, and always smelled of decay, but never like this!"

"Some devilry of that goblin, I'll wager," said Aonghus. "Just like the black rot that's killed our crops."

“There has been a plague?” asked Gwydion.

“Oh yes, started last year when our mom disappeared, and that thing first came,” replied Aonghus.

“Devilry indeed,” said the wizard. “We must be cautious. Can you lead us through this fog?”

“I never get lost,” said Bran. “I'll lead us.”

Down they went, descending into a cloud of mist that swirled about and clung to them as they walked. With the mists, there was also a feeling of uneasiness all about them. A feeling that they were being watched and that something else was here as well – the dark brooding presence that they had so often felt before when they dared to walk the bog's paths.

“It will take a bit to get to the center,” whispered Bran. “I say we move carefully and quietly. I never did like the feel of this place, but even less now.”

The others nodded and followed him, with Aonghus behind Bran, and Gwydion bringing up the rear.

The fog was as thick as pea soup, and even Bran paused every twenty paces or so to get his bearings. An acrid smell permeated the dank air, sinking into their clothes and hair until they were wet and stank.

As they slowly moved toward the bog's center, they began to see what they thought was movement – small dark creatures that peered at them from the rotting weeds, but which vanished in a swirl of mist when they paused to look closer. And as they went on, the sense of uneasiness began to weigh heavily on their minds, like a black dread that was growing as thick and heavy as the fog.

Suddenly, all three of them stopped, although they did not know why. But whether it was by some instinct or a sense that the air around them had quite noticeably changed, they immediately gripped their weapons and turned back to back. Bran notched an arrow to his bow and held it ready, and both Aonghus and Gwydion gripped their staffs.

Then they heard it – an eerie cry in the distance, coming through the mists like some great dying beast's final wail. It rose and then died away with a haunting echo through the dead trees. Both Aonghus and Bran felt their blood run cold at the sound. They looked at each other and then at Gwydion, but the wizard was staring into the fog, his eyes wide, and his face grim.

"What was that?" whispered Bran. "I've never heard that in the bog before."

"Hush!" hissed the old man.

He appeared to be listening intently. Then, with a suddenness that startled them, he moved.

"Into the trees, quickly!" he rasped and ran into a thicket of gnarled willows and tangled brambles.

They followed him, and all three of them crouched down and peered from behind the twisted trunks. A moment later, there was the sound of something coming toward them. It made no secret of its presence, for it was stomping heavily through the muck, making its own path by breaking branches and trampling the underbrush. There was another sound as well – a sound of *flapping*, like the beating of many, many wings.

Then they saw it. It came through the fog like a lumbering giant, at least ten feet tall, and its breath came in great wheezing gasps. Although it was man-shaped, it was no man, for it had a thick green hide and a massive head, with a great deformed nose and ears and beady yellow eyes. Its legs were thick and squat, and its feet clawed with sharp yellow nails. It was clad only in a ragged brown waist wrapping, and in its great fist, it bore a tree trunk at least eight inches thick and six feet long.

All around it flew bats. Hundreds and hundreds of them fluttering about, forming a great swarming shadow that blotted out what little light of the sun filtered through the fog. And beneath this canopy of darkness, all about it on the ground, small black creatures scurried, although they could not make out what they were. It was like a scene from some dark nightmare, but Aonghus and Bran knew that it was all too real.

On it came, directly toward them, and through the gloom that surrounded the creature, they could see that it was looking this way and that, as if it were searching for something. A broken yellow fang protruded from its bottom lip, and a line of thick drool ran down its wrinkled chin. When it reached the place where they had left the trail, it suddenly stopped, looking at the ground. The bats whirled in a wild frenzy all about it, and the black creatures on the ground scurried about, somehow following the mad dance of the bats.

Then the creature lifted up its head and gave a great cry. Whether it was a battle roar or howl of defiance, they were not sure, but in that moment, it turned in their direction, roared again, and charged. Instantly, the bats flew into an even greater frenzy, spreading outward and above them like a black roof. With three great bounds, the creature was upon them, swinging its massive club as it came.

Even as it took its first step, an arrow from Bran's bow whistled through the air and struck it clean between the eyes. To his astonishment, the arrow bounced off. Seeing this, Aonghus leaped from behind the tree. The beast turned on him and swung its club down in a killing blow. But Aonghus sidestepped and brought his own staff up under the beast's chin with a tremendous *whack.* His staff broke, and the creature stumbled backward with a howl. Instantly, it recovered with a roar, baring its huge broken fangs at him.

Aonghus suddenly found himself surrounded by a swarm of black bats. They whirled round and round him, scratching at him with their hooked claws, trying to tear at his face and arms. He instinctively swatted the creatures away and, in that moment of distraction, the creature was upon him. It picked him up with its two massive hands by the shoulders and brought him close to its great bulbous head that was nearly as big as his chest. It stared him in the eyes for an instant as if pondering how it might eat him, and then opened its great maw wide. Aonghus retched as its fetid breath came in great wheezing gasps and, for a moment, he wondered if this would be the last thing he saw – the gross gullet of an unearthly monster.

But the thing did not eat him. There was a sudden bright flash, and the creature stood still, gripping him in its stony hands, its face frozen. Then he realized that something had changed. He looked about and could *see*. The bats were gone, and in their place was a great swarm of flies buzzing about.

Bran stood poised behind the creature, his knife drawn and raised above his head, ready to strike it in the back, a look of fear and astonishment and surprise all at once on his face. He hesitated for an instant, then, leaping upon the thing's back, he brought the knife down, hard. The blade struck and threw sparks, breaking its tip, but the creature still did not move. Gwydion casually walked over to the beast and placed a hand on the outstretched arm that still gripped Aonghus.

"What..." began Aonghus.

"Trolls do not like the sun," he said, rapping on its head with his staff.

"Trolls!" said Bran, coming to his senses. "This is a troll?"

He slid off its back and cautiously walked about it, watching its face. It looked just as gruesome as it had a few moments ago, but was as still as a statue.

"It is indeed," said the wizard, "and as I said, they do not like the sun. It makes them rather... stiff."

"More like turned to stone," said Aonghus, struggling now in the huge hands of the troll, and still staring down its wide-open mouth.

His feet were dangling above the ground, and his arms were pinned to his sides.

"Well, big brother," said Bran, now beginning to laugh. "Let's see you muscle your way out of this one!"

Aonghus furrowed his eyebrows and gave Bran a stern look.

"Now see here," he said. "I was nearly eaten by this thing a moment ago and you stand there laughing. And would you *please* get these flies off my face!"

Now Bran did laugh, and Gwydion could not help but chuckle.

"Here, Aonghus," said the wizard. "Let me help you a bit. We better get you out of there before the sun goes down and the troll revives."

"This thing is going to come back to life?" asked Bran.

"Oh, it may indeed. And I would suggest that we be far from here when it does," replied Gwydion. "In this fog, I do not know if the troll has turned permanently to stone or not."

The wizard looked about and found a broad leaf, picked it, and brought it back to the troll.

"Any shade may turn this stone to flesh again. If it does, break free as quickly as you can, Aonghus," he said.

He nodded and Gwydion held up the leaf, casting a dim shadow on the gripping hand of the troll. Almost immediately, the fingers began to stretch and flex. Aonghus pushed hard, dislodged his trapped shoulder, and dropped to the ground. A swarm of flies buzzed away into the bog and scores of black beetles dashed away from where he landed. Gwydion pulled away the leaf and the hand froze once again in the dim light. Aonghus rubbed his upper arms and shoulders.

"That thing was *really* strong," he said. "I've never felt anything like it."

"Trolls are not easily dealt with. Let us be thankful that we met it in the daytime," said Gwydion.

"But the bats..." said Bran. "What happened to the bats? They were there one moment, and then next they were gone, and just a bunch of flies were left in their place."

"And those black things on the ground... you turned them into beetles, didn't you?" said Aonghus.

Gwydion only frowned. He was looking at the flies that were now congregating on the troll's head and shoulders, and the beetles that were now crowding about its huge clawed feet. The troll began to twitch.

"We must go back," said the wizard.

"But we've got to find that mirror, and that goblin thing," protested Bran.

"Yes," he replied. "But don't you see what has happened here? The goblin has already traveled to another world and brought back this troll. We do not know what other things it has brought back. This may be the only one, or there may be scores of such creatures waiting for us ahead in the fog. And believe me, there are worse things than trolls among the worlds."

"Are you saying that there could be a whole *army* of these things multiplying in this bog?" asked Aonghus.

"I have no idea," he replied. "But we three will not wish to find out by ourselves, especially as the light begins to fade."

"But what are we to do?" asked Bran. "What of the mirror?"

"What if we fail in this? What if we go deeper into this swamp and fight what awaits us there and fail?" said Aonghus quietly, "What will become of the girls, and Frederick, and the professor... and of Ireland?"

"And what if we wait too long, Aong?" replied Bran. "I say now is the time to strike, before they can grow their numbers. We've got a wizard with us, don't we?"

"You have," said Gwydion. "But I am still only one, and I dare say that this goblin is capable of a bit of dark magic as well. You saw the bats."

They were silent for a long moment and then Gwydion said, "This is your farm and your homeland, and it is your battle. I will help in any way that I can. But here is my counsel. Warn the countryside and villages that an evil has entered the bog. They must band together and even call the authorities in the land. Tell them to use this *technology* that this age possesses to arm themselves.

"But we cannot risk a prolonged battle with dark forces swarming out of a magical gateway from other worlds. I think that this goblin is cunning, but also greedy. It *has* brought creatures from other lands, such as those black things you saw at the feet of the troll. They are creatures of darkness that we would not want to meet when the sun goes down – gremlins of great mischief.

"This troll, however, was not an ordinary one. Did you hear how it gasped for breath? It was either ill or very old. This goblin is bringing creatures here that it can control. I would say that it desires power – power for itself. It would be unwise to force its hand into bringing something larger and more dangerous. I think that it will be some time before its plans are fully laid. But I also suspect that its lair will be well protected. We may well encounter greater perils than this troll if we continue on."

"Then what shall we do?" asked Bran.

"Warn the farms and then sail for Bermuda. Your sister still needs rescuing. And there may be help unlooked-for there. Perhaps we can open a door of our own," he replied.

Aonghus and Bran looked at the huge troll. It was now beginning to move its beetle-covered feet.

"If only Father were here," said Bran. "He would know what to do."

"Yes," said Aonghus, "he would. But he's not, so here's what I say we do. We check with the neighbors and see if they've seen him. If he's off somewhere, he would have left word with someone. But if he's somehow gotten into some other land, then all the better we find a way there quick as may be.

"Let's wait one day, and if Dad doesn't show up, we warn the neighbors that some bad folk have taken up in the bog, and they best arm themselves, then we sail for Bermuda."

Bran thought for a moment and looked toward the middle of the bog through thickening fog, as if considering their options. Then he nodded.

"All right, then," he said. "Let's get out of this place."

As quick as they could, they made their way back to the farm, and none too soon, for even as they left the troll, the flies and beetles returned in force and began to cover its entire body. Bit by bit, its fat and muscle began to quiver and move.

By the time they reached the wall, the sun was moving down toward the horizon. They climbed up and over, and felt immediately safer as they dropped down into the farm. Soon they were back at the damaged house, where they told their tale to the others, leaving out the part about Aonghus nearly being eaten. The girls listened intently, their faces full of worry.

As the sun set and the shadows lengthened, they heard off in the distance a howling roar. Aonghus and Bran looked at one another knowingly. The troll, no doubt, stalked the bog once again.

That night, they set a watch, Gwydion and Professor McPherson first, and then the boys. But none of them slept well, for strange sounds came echoing across the farm from the south. Dark things were on the prowl.

Morning came, and they fixed a meager breakfast, after which Aonghus and Bran took off, running to the neighboring farms and inquiring about their father. Soon they returned with bad news.

"No one has seen Dad for some days," said Bran, "and he left no word with anyone. We've warned all the farms of trouble brewing, and that a band of ruffians is laid up in the bog. They'll be arming themselves, and they're calling the authorities as well."

"Then I think if we are not to be delayed with many inquiries and questions about it all, we ought to be going very soon," said Professor McPherson.

"Yes, indeed you should, as quickly as you can," said Gwydion.

"You said *you* should," said Frederick. "Aren't you coming with us?"

Gwydion was silent for a few moments, and all eyes turned to him.

"No," he finally said. "I think it best that someone stays here and makes sure things do not get out of hand. As well-meaning as your neighbors and authorities might be, I think that there may be some work for a wizard to do, and there is a great deal that I need to learn. So much has changed since I was... away."

"But we may need you, Gwydion," said Frederick. "What, with this Witch and all that – oughtn't we to have someone like you to set things right?"

"Maybe," he replied slowly, "but something tells me that I may be needed here even more. Someone *should* hunt for this goblin. I will do what I can."

When they began to protest further, Professor McPherson spoke.

"I think Gwydion is right," he said. "Someone should also look over your home for you. We can tell the neighbors that you have lent out your house to a friend while your father is away for a time, to keep an eye on things until the authorities can take care of the situation in the bog."

"Indeed," replied Gwydion, "and I shall do more than look after things – I shall do my best to fix them. I have some skill in carpentry and stonework. I will see what I can do to fix your house up as good as new, and with your permission, I will add a few, shall we say, improvements."

They were all sad about Gwydion's decision to stay behind, for they had become very fond of the old man even in the few short days that they had spent together. It was as though they shared some kinship that they could not explain. But they gathered together what few things they needed, and by noon were ready.

They said one last goodbye to the farmhouse, hating to leave it in such a wretched condition. But they shut the gate behind them and headed down the dirt road back toward the village and the ship.

Gwydion waved to them from the door and watched as they disappeared around a bend. He stood gazing after them for a time, thinking. Who were these amazing children? Could they be related to the McGunnegal family that he once knew? There was a resemblance, but also a resemblance to another family – a family that had vanished from the face of the earth – or so he had thought. After some time, he turned and walked back into the house and surveyed the damage.

"*They* will be coming," he said to himself, "and this old place is no defense. It ought to be torn down."

He sighed, looking at the broken and dilapidated walls. "But, let's see what can be done."

He held aloft his staff, and a soft white glow began to shine from its carven top...

Chapter 26 – The Storm

Frederick stood on the bow of the ship, watching dolphins leap beside them as they sailed southwest toward Bermuda. They had delayed as long as possible, but could find only six more crewmen, all Englishmen, to join them on this journey, and so had set sail, trusting that their nine crewmen and the able-bodied McGunnegals and Frederick would be enough.

"After all, there is hope for fair seas this time of the year," said the professor, "and the *Unknown* is a small ship, in any case. She doesn't need a large crew."

They had been sailing for a full day now, with good strong winds and favorable weather, and the old ship slicing smoothly through the waves. Professor McPherson said that if this wind kept up their whole journey, they would make it to Bermuda in less than ten days, but he thought it unlikely that their luck would hold, and the winds would not shift or even die.

"Strange things happen in the open sea," he had said. "We'll just have to hope that Providence is with us, and we make good time."

The McGunnegals and Frederick had occupied themselves with their chores about the ship, straightening things up, winding ropes, scrubbing the decks, and generally getting the ship in order, all the while listening to stories of the sea that the crewmen told.

"You're an amazing lot, you are," said Professor McPherson as he watched them all work.

Frederick had done his part, but his eyes were ever drawn to the sea. Something about it called to him – its vastness and depth. It held secrets that no man had ever beheld, and the legends surrounding it inspired him like nothing else could.

Each day, the professor gave them lessons about navigation by compass, by the stars, by the sun and moon, about knot tying, fishing, gathering water, sea life, and many other things as the hours rolled by. They all amazed him with how quickly they learned and remembered everything that he said to them. By the end of the second day, they knew every aspect of the ship – how it was made, the type of wood that was best for such ships, how the prow and rudder and masts and shape of the hull all contributed to the Clipper ship's great speed.

They had sailed for many hundreds of miles now, but no land was in sight. The sky was a brilliant blue, and the noon sun was warm and friendly.

Frederick found that what he loved most was gazing out at the water. His thoughts often drifted to Colleen and the little people, and he wondered where they were and hoped that they were all right.

"We're coming, Colleen. I promise," he whispered.

Suddenly, something caught his eye, and his attention came into sharp focus. Off in the distance, there seemed to be a gray line at the horizon. He stared at it for several moments and saw that it seemed to be growing. An odd sense of dread began to grow in the pit of his stomach, and he backed away, then turned and ran to the tallest mast and began to climb the rope ladder to the crow's nest. Up he went, climbing as if he had done it all his life, and then jumped into the nest and gazed southwest where the darkness seemed to be gathering. Wind licked at his dark hair – not the steady breeze that they had been sailing with, but a wild gust.

"Professor!" he called down to McPherson, who was standing behind the wheel and chatting with Aonghus.

He looked up from the deck and waved at Frederick.

"Professor!" he called again. "There's a storm ahead!"

Everyone stopped what they were doing and turned to look up at him, and then where he pointed. Professor McPherson and several of the crewmen quickly went to the bow of the ship and looked out. The dark clouds were very visible now – an angry wall of forbidding blackness that seemed to be rushing toward them.

One of the crewmen turned to another and said, "It's the bad luck of the Irish, I say. If I hadn't needed the cash, I would never have come."

"Enough of that!" said the professor. "This is no time for such bigotry!" He paused only a moment longer and then shouted, "All of you come here! Frederick, come down quickly!"

They gathered around him, a foreboding in their hearts.

"Forgive me, my friends. This storm will not be a kind one. We are not in the season for hurricanes, but I fear that we are quickly approaching one. We must tie down everything quickly. Don't worry about the cargo hold – that was secured before we left. But everything in your quarters and everything on deck must be tied. We will try to go around the storm, but we must prepare for the worst. Put on your life vests now, and let's get to work."

The crew looked at one another with dark expressions, but quickly hurried to make the ship as secure as might be. Each of the McGunnegals and Frederick had been assigned a place on the deck that was their responsibility, and each of them had a partner – Aonghus and Henny, Bran and Bib, Abbe and Frederick – and so they quickly tied down everything that was movable or took it below deck.

The sails were flapping in the wind when they finished, and a dreadful wall of black clouds loomed nearer. Professor McPherson had turned the ship east in hopes of sailing around the huge storm and perhaps gaining sight of the coast of France or Portugal, but the darkness seemed to pursue them. Soon the first sheets of rain could be seen, great gray washes falling from the forbidding clouds, and whitecaps began to break against the prow of the ship.

Professor McPherson gathered the children around him and said, "Don't be afraid – we will ride out the storm. We have a good old ship that's weathered many a gale and an experienced crew, and we have a lifeboat if things should turn bad. Remember all I have taught you.

"But now, time is short. We must tie up the sails and let the ship be driven by the storm. We will need to watch for land – for any lighthouse. I will need two sets of eyes to help me with that, and one set of hands to keep things tied down. Ladies, I will need you all below deck to keep all the hatches secure and watch for leaks. Bran, Frederick – you will be my eyes. Aonghus – you will be the rope man. I want you to stretch a rope between each mast so that you can move between them freely. Now, men – you will tie yourself to a rope and tie that rope to the rope between the masts. Off you go now."

They all nodded and hurried to their places, while the professor gave further orders to the crewmen. Abbe led Bib and Henny below, and there they busied themselves making sure all was secure in the cabins and in the galley. No sooner had they huddled together in their cabin, holding tight to the main post that supported the ceiling, when a great wave lifted the ship and dropped it back down upon the sea.

On deck, Frederick and the others watched as Professor McPherson angled the ship to meet the wall of dark rain. It slammed into them like a great hammer blow that nearly knocked them from their feet. They pierced the wall of the hurricane and were immediately drenched and blinded by the torrents that rained upon them.

"Hold your positions!" shouted McPherson above the howling wind. "And watch the sea!"

Great waves bore them up and down in the maelstrom, and more than once, Frederick could see Aonghus, his red hair plastered to his face, gripping the ship's rail with one hand while tying down some stray rope or line with the other. The crew labored manfully against the storm, but there was dread in their eyes as it grew worse.

Suddenly, a sail tore loose and began to flap in the wild gusts. Three crewman, which, he could not tell, untied themselves from their safety lines, climbed the mast through the raging wind, and secured the sail. Together, they descended, watching one another, ready to grab hold should their crewmate slip. But as their feet touched the deck and they reached for the safety line, a tremendous wave washed over the ship. All three men were there one moment and gone the next.

“Man overboard!” Frederick screamed. “Man overboard!” But his voice was lost in the storm.

Aonghus had seen what had happened as well, and rushed to where the men had been. Frantically, he looked into the sea, but they were nowhere to be found. Grabbing a life preserver with a line tied to it, he threw it blindly out into the waves, hoping beyond hope that perhaps they might see it and grab hold.

“Grab the line!” he shouted into the wind. “Man overboard!”

Another crewman rushed to his side, and now Frederick had made his way there as well.

“A wave just took them!” shouted Aonghus. “They’re… gone!”

Aonghus began to untie himself, but the crewman stopped him.

“You can’t save them, lad!” he shouted. “They’re… Look out!”

Without warning, a gigantic wave lifted the ship high into the air, and then sent it careening downward at breakneck speed into a deep troth. Mountains of water surrounded them for a moment, and cries of fear from the crewmen rose above the din of the storm.

Again, they were borne upward by a behemoth wave, and again, they dropped. Every one of them gripped the nearest piece of the ship for dear life as the maddening roller coaster of the ocean threw its worst at them. Then, as quickly as they had come, the towering waves were behind them, carrying away any hope of rescuing the lost men. The stinging spray of the sea swept away the tears that might have flowed as both Aonghus and Frederick stared with empty hearts into the gray of the storm.

The wind howled, the waves crashed, the ship creaked and groaned as though it were in the throes of death. Yet somehow, they sailed on, and still, the storm did not abate. Hour after hour, it raged, carrying its insignificant prey, where, they did not know. All sense of direction was lost to them, yet still Professor McPherson manned the wheel with tireless determination, a grim but defiant look upon his face.

Day turned into night, and, exhausted, they clung to the ship. Frederick's mind began to play tricks on him, and more than once he thought he saw a glimmer of light through the driving rain. But when he looked again, it was gone. He could hear nothing now except the hiss of rain and wind and waves, blending together in a cacophony of wild noise that dulled his senses. Yet he stayed at his post, weary, cold, and wet, his body's strength long gone, but his eyes riveted to the raging sea, searching for some horizon and light that was beyond his vision in this storm.

Then there was a hand on his shoulder, and he turned to see Aonghus standing behind him, holding his safety lines.

"Come!" he shouted.

Weakly, he released the rail and tried to follow Aonghus as he turned to go, but he was immediately swept from his feet. Aonghus grabbed him as he slid by, lifting him to his feet. Together, they held onto the ropes until they reached the first mast. He could see Bran now standing by the door that led below deck, waiting for them, and Professor McPherson still on the upper deck gripping the wheel, his jaw set and his face dark. He and two crewmen appeared to be having an argument, although they could not hear their words above the storm.

"The professor wants us to get below and rest if we can! We rest now, and then relieve some of the crew in a few hours!" shouted Aonghus.

He opened the door, and they hurried in. In the hall, they quickly untied themselves and shut the door.

The storm was silenced to a dull roar, and now the terrible groaning of the anguished ship could be heard, a twisting sound that came up through its belly and ribs like the magnified creaking of a hundred trees blown about in a gale. They hurried to the girls' cabin, but did not find them there.

Bran called out, "Abbe! Bib! Henny! Where are you?"

"In here – in the galley!" called Abbe.

Down the hall they went to the galley, where a fearful sight greeted them. Water two inches deep covered the floor, and they could see it running through a crack in the ship's hull.

"We heard a terrible snap, Aonghus," said Bib. "We ran in here and found this!"

"We've got to patch it somehow!" he said urgently.

"Screws and pitch!" said Bib. "These ships carry them, I'm sure!"

"What..." began Abbe, but Bib cut her off.

"There should be some sort of wooden beams that have screws on top – they're meant to support the hull and decking in times like this. And there ought to be some oakum – rope soaked in pitch, a hammer, and tools that look like chisels, and a barrel of pitch that we can seal the leak with. Check in the supply area," she said urgently.

"Shouldn't we go aloft and get a crewman?" asked Abbe.

A crewman, however, appeared in the doorway and looked in. He was soaked and weary, but when he saw the crack in the hull, his eyes went wide.

"She won't last in this storm with that rip in her belly. If you want my advice, you best grab some line, a sack of grub and water, and make for the lifeboats. This lady is going down!" he said.

He then grabbed a crate of food and ran from the room.

"No time! Hurry!" said Bib. "Find those tools and beams!"

Indeed, the water was pouring in now. Frederick, who was closest to the door, ran out into the hall to the supply room and Bran followed him. They looked about, and sure enough, lying against one wall were four long beams that had iron screws protruding from the top. Together, they picked one up. Frederick found its weight almost unbearable, exhausted as he was, but somehow they maneuvered it through the hall and to the galley. Aonghus then went to the same room and retrieved a large barrel of black pitch and a mop, along with a length of oakum and a box of tools.

"We'll need a T-board for the top," said Bib. "Something we can put the screw-end on. Go find it while we pack the crack with oakum."

Frederick stumbled back down the hall as the ship lurched sideways, and found several small boards, which he grabbed and took back to the galley. Bib seemed to be in complete control of the situation as she directed Abbe and Henny to saturate the top of the T-board with pitch, while the boys hammered the oakum into the crack.

"This stuff is supposed to go in hot, or at least warm," said Bib as Aonghus drove the last of the sticky rope into the leaking seam, "but this will have to do."

At her direction, Bran and Aonghus took hold of the beam and positioned the screw end against the crack, then the other end of the board against the opposite wall.

"Now turn the screw until it's tight!" she ordered, and Aonghus began to turn the big screw while the others held it in place.

Soon it was secured, and the crack stopped gushing water and only trickled a bit.

"Now seal all around it with the pitch," said Bib, and Abbe and Henny took mopfuls of the black tar and jammed it all around the beam.

The leak stopped, and they cheered.

"I think we won't need that lifeboat just yet! But, better check the rest of the hull where we can," said Bib.

Two other leaks were found, and two more screws and the black pitch were used to secure them.

When at last they felt as though they could breathe a little easier, Abbe said, "You boys need some rest. You look exhausted! Go on then, we girls will keep watch over the hull. Get some sleep if you can."

Grateful, the boys went to their cabin, put on dry clothes, and lay down on their beds. But the rocking and creaking of the ship did not help them to rest. Had the beds not been made with railing all about, they would have rolled right out and onto the floor. But so great was their weariness that they somehow fell into a fitful sleep.

The girls, having completed their survey of the ship, and being satisfied that there were no other leaks for the moment, peeked in the boys' cabin and, seeing them asleep, quietly shut their door.

"Poor things," said Henny. "They worked hard up on the deck."

"Up on the deck!" exclaimed Abbe. "Professor McPherson is still up there!"

It had been over an hour since the boys had come down, and now they were fearful for the professor.

"I'll go and check on him," said Abbe.

"No, Ab," said Bib. "Let me go. You know I'm a bit more sure-footed and a better swimmer, if it comes to it."

"No matter, Bib. I'm the oldest, and it's only right that I go. Stay here with Henny," she replied.

Bib was not happy but, with a frown, agreed with her older sister.

“Tie in, then Ab, and do be careful,” she said.

Abbe tied one of the ropes around her waist and looked at her two sisters.

“Wish me luck!” she said, and opened the door.

Immediately, the howling rage of the storm hit them, and Abbe rushed out, slamming the door behind her. Bib breathed a prayer after her and she and Henny waited.

Out on the lower deck, Abbe was awestruck by the fury and raw power of the storm that raged all about them. It was pitch black now, and only the continual flashes of lightning illumined the rocking world about her and allowed her to make her way to the ladder that led to the upper deck. Slowly, carefully, she climbed, clinging to the wet rungs of the ladder until she felt the top and pulled herself up. A flash of lightning illumined the deck, and in that moment, she saw the brazen image of Professor McPherson gripping the wheel of the ship. An oil lamp was secured to a post by his side, casting an eerie glow over his face in the darkness.

She moved across the deck, trying desperately not to slip, but with every wave, she slid about, unable to gain any sort of footing. Finally, she managed to half crawl, half stumble her way over to the professor and gripped the railing that surrounded the platform on which the wheel was set. In the dim light of the lamp and through the lightning flashes, she could see that he had tied himself to the railing on either side of the wheel.

“What are you doing up here, Abbe?” he yelled through the wind when he saw her.

“Checking on you, Professor. We were worried. Can you come below and rest?” she yelled.

“No, I must stay at the wheel and guide the ship!” he called back.

“Guide it to where?” she asked.

He pointed at the railing in front of them, and there, set in the wood, was what appeared to be a compass of sorts, although it was intricate and beautiful and had a strange design.

But Abbe had no time to admire it, and she said, "What is it, Professor?"

"It will guide us out of this storm!" he said. "But I must stay at the wheel and follow its direction."

"Guide us out... Professor, a compass just ... Oh, Professor, please do come below, you must rest!" she called.

"No, Abbe! Get below. I will be fine! I will get you to safety! I promise!" he said.

Lightning lit up his face. He was stern and full of determination. He looked in her eyes for a moment, then said, "I will not fail you. Now go and rest while you can. If I need you, I will rap three times on the deck."

Abbe looked at him once again in the dim glow of the lamp and then nodded.

"We repaired several leaks in the hull, sir," she said.

He looked alarmed for a moment, and then smiled and said, "So, I brought the right crew, after all!"

Abbe looked about the ship as lightning suddenly lit its decks and masts.

"Where is the crew?" she yelled. "Professor, I don't see the crew anywhere!"

Then she noticed that one of the lifeboats was missing.

"They have abandoned ship," he said, a look of resignation on his face. "Fools! Our best hope was to stay together with the ship. But their fears overcame their reason. We must not allow the same to happen to us. We must stay the course and hold together!"

Abbe's heart sank. How would they sail the ship without the crew? She turned to go, not knowing what to say, and she made her way back to the ladder and then down to the door. Bib and Henny were waiting for her when she opened it.

"Oh, Abbe, you're drenched!" said Henny.

"What about the professor?" asked Bib.

"He's still at the wheel and he won't come below. He says his compass is guiding us out of the storm. I do hope he's all right. But he looks dreadfully tired. But there's worse news. The crew has abandoned ship!" she said.

"What!" said Bib. "Why? We fixed the crack!"

"I don't know!" she said.

"Do you think we ought to wake the boys and have them go back out there?" asked Bib.

Abbe took a deep breath and steadied herself. "Not yet. Let them rest for a bit if they can. What can they do anyway? But we need to keep watch for any further leaks. We'll take turns. I'll take the first watch, then you, and then Henny and me again," said Abbe.

Bib and Henny nodded and went to their cabin, curled up together in one bed, and tried to rest.

Abbe stalked the corridors and other cabins with an oil lamp, watching for any sign of more water. Outside, the storm raged on, and the ship pitched and turned, creaking and groaning like a thing in pain. The hours rolled by, and Abbe felt as though she could not keep her eyes open any longer. She went to their cabin and found Bib and Henny hugging each other, fast asleep on Bib's bed. She did not have the heart to wake them, and so decided just to rest her eyes for a bit.

"But only for a few moments," she said to herself and stretched out on her own bed.

But the weariness and stress of the day took hold and soon she was fast asleep.

Chapter 27 – The Eye

"Frederick! Frederick!" someone was calling. He opened his eyes and remembered where he was. Aonghus stood over him. All was quiet.

He rubbed his eyes and said, "How long?"

"Not sure, lad. But we'd best get back up on deck and check on old McPherson," he replied.

"Right," said Frederick, and steadied himself as he stood up. Then he realized that the ship was no longer bobbing like a cork, but seemed still as death.

"What's going on? Is the storm over?" he asked.

Aonghus said nothing, but beckoned for him to follow.

Bran was up as well, and together, they left their cabin and went out into the hall.

Aonghus knocked on the girls' cabin door, and when no one answered, he peeked in and called, "Abbe?" There was a sudden gasp as Abbe jumped out of bed.

"Oh my!" she said. "What's the time?"

Bib and Henny woke as well, and sensing the storm was over, they sat up and looked about.

"What's going on?" asked Bib. "Is it our shift to keep watch?"

"I think we've all been sleeping too long," said Aonghus. "We're going up and checking on things. It seems terribly still."

"We'd best come as well," said Abbe.

Together, they went down the hall and opened the door that led to the deck. To their surprise, bright sunlight streamed in. They hurried out, and the sight that greeted them stopped them in their tracks.

The deck of the ship was a mess, with torn tarps and frayed ropes strewn about. Both sails hung limp and ripped, their tie ropes broken and dangling. But the dark clouds were some distance from them, and blue sky shown above.

Slowly, they walked onto the littered deck, and then Henny cried out, "Professor!"

They could see him on the upper deck. He lay limply upon his wheel, his knees buckled under him, and the ropes that he had tied about himself holding him up. They rushed up the ladder and to his side. Aonghus untied the ropes that held him and carefully laid him down on the deck.

"Professor!" he called. "Professor!"

For a moment, he did not respond, but then his eyes fluttered open and focused. He squinted at the sky, then at all of their faces. He smiled slightly, and then in a hoarse voice said, "Help me sit up, please."

"I think we rode the storm out through the night, Professor," said Frederick.

Professor McPherson touched his sides where the ropes had rubbed his skin raw, and he winced.

"Help me stand," he said.

Aonghus and Bran carefully lifted him to his feet. Unsteadily, he braced himself against the wheel. Then he looked out at the sea, and the distant clouds. Slowly, he turned his head left and right, and then turned and stared behind him. They followed his gaze. There were clouds all about them – walls of clouds.

Professor McPherson's face grew dark again, and he leaned heavily upon the rail. His chin dropped to his chest and he shut his eyes. Then he took a deep breath and looked at the children.

"Whatever is the matter, Professor?" asked Abbe. "We've come through, just as you promised, haven't we?"

He sighed heavily and then, with great weariness, said, "We are in the eye of the hurricane."

"What's the eye of the hurricane?" asked Henny.

"It's the middle of it, Henny," he said. "We've only come halfway through."

Chapter 28 – The Ghost of Lugh

Colleen, Nous, Oracle, and the Wigglepox family rode steadily southward as the night wore on. A brilliant full moon, and a sky of a million stars shone above them, shedding cool blue light down upon the brown desert floor. Nous rode in the wagon as usual, lying on his back and gazing at the stars, his black hood thrown back, and his bulging yellow eyes seeming to glow in the pale light. Mrs. Wigglepox was telling Colleen a story of the desert – of a mouse that ventured into the Burning Sands and returned with strange stories.

“The mouse said that there are spirits in the desert,” she said, “and that they are not all kindly. Still, the desert can do wonders for those who seek to find themselves, so long as they have a guide.”

“Why would we need a guide?” asked Colleen. “Couldn't we just keep heading south?”

“Well, the mouse said that the desert has a way of scouring away the Spell. But it also said that it holds rough places and pitfalls and quicksand and monsters, and that hunger and thirst are everywhere. A guide would be an invaluable asset. It also said that the magic of old is out there. The Wizard's Castle still stands, and there is a wishing well that the Spell has not stopped up.”

Colleen pondered this for a long moment, wondering what it might mean, and then a thought struck her and she said, “Mrs. Wigglepox, this mouse – could it talk? I mean, can you speak to animals?”

“Well, of course, dear,” she replied. “All little people can speak to the animals. Can't the big folk?”

“Not really,” said Colleen. “Although, I suppose if anyone can, it would be my sister, Abbe.”

“Oh!” exclaimed Mrs. Wigglepox. “You have a sister that can speak to the animals?”

"Well, she can't really *speak* to them as such. But somehow, they know what she wants. It's something less than speech and more than feeling, or so she says."

"Yes," said Mrs. Wigglepox, "that's the way of it. She must be an extraordinary person. I would so like to meet her one day."

"Oh, all of my brothers and sisters are rather special. They can all do the strangest of things," replied Colleen.

Mrs. Wigglepox looked up at Colleen from the seat where she was sitting with Lily and Rose and said, "Colleen, tell me, are there any odd stories about your family, perhaps other relatives, or ancestors?"

"Oh yes," replied Colleen, "all sorts of stories."

"Tell me one," she said.

Colleen thought for a moment and then said, "Well, my mom's cousin, Richard, who lives up north of us, is in his nineties, and claims to have heard voices in his well."

"In his well?" asked Mrs. Wigglepox.

"Yes. The neighbors all think he's getting a bit dimwitted, if you know what I mean. But a few years back, we went to visit him and he told us this story. He said he fell down that well when he was a boy, and there were weird symbols carved all over the inside of it. He was down there all night, and he said he heard voices – singing, in fact, coming from somewhere beyond the walls," said Colleen.

She paused for a moment and then said, "Truth be told, Mrs. Wigglepox, I snuck out that night and went to that well. I got in the bucket and lowered myself down inside. You might not believe it, but I heard singing down there too. I hauled myself right back up and ran back to the house quick."

"That is strange," replied Mrs. Wigglepox. "I've heard tales like that before myself – tales that say there are *thin* places where the echoes of other worlds can be heard. Maybe that old well is just such a place."

Colleen was fascinated by the thought. She resolved that if she ever got back home, she would go and visit her cousin Richard and make another visit to that well.

"Strange things are said to happen out here too," said Mrs. Wigglepox. "It's said that so much magic was unleashed in this place during the Cataclysm that it still lingers and swirls about at times. We must be careful."

They rolled on for some time in silence when suddenly, the wagon bumped, as if it had rolled over something. Then it bumped again, and then again. Nous sat up and looked about nervously. Badger was pulling them up a large dune, but they seemed to be hitting something round, like big logs, that were buried just beneath the sand.

Just as they reached the peak of the dune, a strange red mist swirled in the breeze all around them, and the sand began to tremble and shift, as if the whole hill were moving. Colleen stopped Badger, and they gazed about. In the silvery light of the moon, they could see a number of small dunes that lay to either side, and as they looked, they began to rise up, as though they were coming to life.

"Nous does not like this place!" said Nous. "He thinks the Colleen should get us away from here!"

"Right!" said Colleen. "Go, Badger!"

Badger pulled, and they began to roll down the shifting hill. Just as they reached the bottom, the sand dune moved violently, jolting the wagon and nearly upsetting it. Lily and Rose screamed and barely managed to hold onto the seat pad, and Oracle, who was sitting up front too, just caught Mrs. Wigglepox as she tumbled forward.

Badger neighed and pulled faster, and just in time, for as they rode away, the entire sand dune lifted into the air, along with half a dozen others, and the gigantic form of a man, seemingly made completely of sand, rose up and stood towering above them.

The giant monstrosity moaned a bellowing sound that spread across the desert like a great bass horn. It shook itself, raining down sand, moaned again, and then seemed to see them as they fled.

"Run, Badger!" shouted Colleen, and the horse shot forward.

Badger was fast, but the sands bogged down the wheels and slowed his pace. The giant came for them in great halting steps, sand flying all around it as it came. They could see now what they had rolled over, for the creature was actually a huge skeleton covered and filled with sand, and the dune they had climbed had been its massive rib cage. But Colleen could see something else now – something *within* the apparition's hideous bowels.

"Mrs. Wigglepox, there's something inside that thing. I can see it!" she cried.

The little lady stared wide-eyed at the towering monster, but said nothing. The creature bellowed again, and with a great leap, flew through the air and landed in front of them. Badger reared and kicked, neighing in defiance.

It laughed a booming laugh that echoed across the vast desert, and then it stooped down, its gigantic head drawing close to them, peering at them with blank eye sockets. Then it opened its great maw and bellowed, and a putrid wind blew from its gullet.

Badger backed away, and the little people climbed into Colleen's cape pocket. Nous curled into a ball in the back of the wagon, and Colleen stared into the face of a horror she had never encountered before. Her heart raced, and fear gripped her. She looked to the right and left in desperation, seeking a way of escape, but the giant skeleton planted a foot on each side and laughed again.

Then, to her surprise, it spoke. Its voice was deep and booming, but hollow, and they all covered their ears at the explosion of sound that thundered upon them.

"Who *dares* enter *my* realm!" it cried, anger and indignation in its voice. "These Burning Sands belong to *Lugh!*"

Mrs. Wigglepox poked her head out of Colleen's pocket, a look of astonishment on her face. Oracle, however, stood up on the seat, reached up to the giant with his cane, and poked it in the nose.

"Shame!" said the leprechaun to the giant, and it suddenly stood upright, surprised, it seemed, by the brashness of the little fellow.

Mrs. Wigglepox cried, "Colleen, run! We must run for it!"

Colleen saw a small chance, and she flicked the reins hard. Right between the giant's legs they flew, Badger straining with all his might.

"Fly, Badger, fly!" she cried, and the great horse stretched out his neck.

The race was on. Oracle tumbled into the back of the wagon and into Nous.

The sand man roared, a bellow of surprise coming from its lipless mouth, then turned about.

"You cannot escape Lugh!" it trumpeted, and lumbered after them.

"What is that thing?" cried Colleen, her hair and cape whipping wildly as Badger ran faster and faster.

"I think it is the ghost of Lugh!" said Mrs. Wigglepox frantically. "If it is, then his spirit never went over the Rainbow, and he has become a spirit of malice that haunts the place of his fall! We must run!"

"A ghost!" cried Colleen "How can we deal with a ghost!"

Nous now emerged from his balled up form and hauled himself forward. His black robe whipped about, and the few strands of hair on his head flew back.

"See!" he hissed. "Nous warned the Colleen not to go this way!"

Colleen glanced back. Oracle was splayed out against the back wall of the wagon, a wry grin on his face.

Badger had gained a good distance from the monster, but now it was catching up. Still, Badger ran, and never did a horse pull with such power and courage. But the wheels of the wagon slid in the sand, and as valiant as he was, he was losing this race.

"The Colleen must use her magic, she must! Sink it beneath the sands from which it rose!" said Nous.

Colleen shook her head, not knowing what to say or do, but the creature behind them bellowed again, and with a great leap, landed just behind them, spraying a great rain of sand over the wagon. But Badger ran on.

"You must!" cried Nous.

"I think the goblin is right, Colleen," yelled Mrs. Wigglepox, the wind nearly drowning out her voice.

"But how?" said Colleen desperately.

"Remember at the Lake?" she said.

Colleen paused, remembering how the spirits of the trees and lake had heard her voice, and responded to her call.

"Nous, take the reins!" she yelled.

Nous crawled forward, and she handed him Badger's reins. Then she climbed to the back, next to Oracle who was now peering over the back edge of the wagon. The great skeletal giant was just a dozen yards behind them now, its hollow face a terror to behold, and its coming was like the sound of a great storm in the desert.

Colleen knelt there, and then lifted her hands, her golden red hair flying wildly, her cloak whipping about her. She looked about desperately, trying to calm her mind and heart and see if there could be any help in this wasteland. But all she saw was sand and the terrible spirit pursuing them.

She desperately tried to calm her thoughts and, as the Lady had taught her, to hear the Great Song. And all at once, there it was – the shifting sands, the wind, the little beetles that inhabited the dunes, the lizards, the stifling air – all of these formed the choir of the desert, singing their part in the symphony of creation. Even the storms and the quicksand added their created voices to this choir, and there she saw her chance.

She attuned her heart to the music, found its melody, and shaped it in her mind. *Quicksand…*

To her utter amazement, the giant immediately stumbled and fell. Badger raced desperately ahead, and as the great beast plummeted downward, its gigantic skull crashed down, just missing the wagon and hurling sand upon them like a brown wave. It howled in rage, lifting itself upward again, but Colleen could see that now it was sinking down into a slowly spiraling whirlpool of sand.

"Nous!" called Colleen. "Look!"

Nous stopped the wagon as he turned and looked. The ghost of Lugh struggled mightily against the increasing tide of sand, and now its great body was submerged to its knees, and was sinking faster.

With a look of sheer hatred, it stared at Colleen. She could feel its loathing, its utter malice and desire for her destruction. It lifted its head and boomed out such an unearthly bellow that all of them except for Oracle stopped their ears and cried out in pain. Chills ran down their spines, and the horrible cry from the ghost echoed out across the wastes, causing the very earth to shift and quake.

Suddenly, from those trembling sands rose up more horrors. Skeleton after skeleton lifted itself from its long dead grave, twisted and grotesque forms rising upward with broken bits of armor and shields and swords, tattered black robes clinging in shreds to their abominable bodies.

“He has raised the dead goblins of old!” cried Nous, and covered his face in terror.

The army of goblin skeletons rose up and stood all about them as Lugh slowly sank downward in the swirling sands. Then the ghost spoke again.

“Stop your spell, witch,” it bellowed, “or I shall command my army to crush you and those with you into dust, and here your remains shall blow amid the Burning Sands until the world's end, and I shall take your spirits to the place of the goblin dead!”

The skeletal army began to march slowly forward all around them. Bone against bone, the scraping and clattering sound of their coming was weird and terrifying. But Colleen gathered her wits and again raised her hands. “Your army shall follow you, Lugh, down to the place of the dead where you belong!”

As if in response to her words, the sands began to move, but leaving the wagon on a still island amid a swirling storm. They watched bones and shields and armor and spears and swords clatter against one another as the sands swept them down, down, swallowing them into its depths. Lugh raged in frantic bellows as he too sank deeper. Then suddenly, with titanic, unworldly strength, the giant surged forward, wading through the whirlpool, fighting against its dragging force. They all watched in amazed horror as it began to draw near to them again. Then it laughed.

Nous' eyes were wide with fear, but then he narrowed them, and he snarled. Leaping from the wagon, he ran right to the edge of the swirling whirlpool of sand.

Colleen watched as he pulled up his right sleeve, and taking his index finger, he dipped it in the stirring dust. For a moment, nothing happened, but then a black streak formed in the current where his finger was, and spread itself outward, as if some dark dye had been poured into a whirling tub of water.

Round and round them, it stretched, and it began to grow, like black streaks in a brown mixing bowl.

Nous withdrew his finger, then pulled his sleeve up further and found one of the worms that dangled limply to his arm. He considered it for a moment, and then plucked it from its place. He held it up, staring at it in the dim light. Lugh was nearly upon them when the ghost's skeletal hips touched the outermost black streak. It stopped in its struggle, a look of surprise on its face, and glared down. Nous looked at the giant, at the worm, then at Oracle, and threw the tiny worm with all his might at the ghost. He turned and ran back to the cart and climbed in.

"The Colleen must make us a bridge, and we must fly!" cried Nous.

Colleen paused for a moment, mesmerized at what was happening to the giant. The black stain was wrapping itself about the great skeleton now, clinging to it, like some thick tar, and it seemed as though the little worm that Nous had thrown at it was growing larger and larger, swimming about the monster amid the black streaks like some shark circling its prey.

"What did you do?" said Colleen.

"No time! Run!" cried Nous.

"Through that?" said Colleen.

"Run!" said Nous, urgently.

Colleen whipped the reins, and Badger obediently surged forward into the trembling sands. Away they rode through a sea of goblin bones that reached out at them, grasping for the wheels of the wagon and trying to trip Badger as he ran. But the golden shod stallion thundered through the skeletal army, smashing them into the dust, crushing them beneath his mighty pounding hooves.

Suddenly, a skeleton gained the wagon. Oracle poked it in the eye with his cane and its head popped off, spinning on the end of the stick like a top, and its jaws snapping wildly. Its body staggered blindly across the wagon before falling off the other side. The old leprechaun flung the skull from his cane, knocking another skeleton from the rear of the wagon as it tried to climb aboard.

Then another was in, and Nous grappled with it. Its old bones broke at the joints as he wrestled it down, and soon he was tossing arm and leg bones out of the wagon at the clamoring skeletal masses as they surged around them.

But a moment later, they were clear of the valley of bones, and Colleen turned to look as Lugh howled one last time, his cry of frustration and anguish following hard after them. He had turned completely black now, a thick coat of darkness dripping from his half-submerged form. She watched as the worm, which had now grown enormous, leaped upon him, and as the ghost grappled with it, they both sank downward, hordes of goblin skeletons following after them.

Lugh's bellowing face was the last bit of him to sink beneath a swirling black sea until his cries were silenced beneath the Burning Sands, and the clatter of bones grew still.

Colleen ran Badger on for some time before bringing him to a walk again. She trembled as she did so, then stopped the horse completely and fought back tears of relief and fear.

After a moment, she took a deep shuddering breath and said, "Nous, what did you do back there?"

Nous grinned a devilish grin and then cackled, "Added a little Ooze to the mixing bowl, and a spawn of the Worm!"

Mrs. Wigglepox, Lily, and Rose re-emerged from Colleen's pocket. The leprechauns looked scared and worried. Mrs. Wigglepox looked particularly grave.

"Are you all right, Mrs. Wigglepox?" asked Colleen.

"I'm okay, and so are the girls," she replied. "But I fear that what was done back there may come back to haunt us."

"You mean the ghost might come back?" asked Colleen.

"Oh, I didn't quite mean it that way," she replied. "I meant that Nous put the Ooze into that whirlpool of yours, and one of those sickening worm creatures. It might have stopped Lugh, but fighting evil with evil never works. I hope nothing bad comes of it."

Nous screwed up his face and looked hurt. "See," he said, "these little people care nothing for goblin help."

"Oh, Nous," said Colleen. "I'm grateful for your help. I'm sure we'll be all right. See, we've gotten away from that thing back there, Mrs. Wigglepox."

"I do hope you're right, Colleen," she replied. "And, Nous, we do care. And I thank you for your efforts. But please, do not use the Ooze again. Only ill can come from that. Find some other power within yourself to help us along our journey. Deep down, I think the real, untarnished Nous dwells, the way the Old Goblins used to be."

Nous said "Hmph!" and turned his back, curling up in a ball in the back of the wagon.

Colleen took another deep breath and flicked the reins. She mused upon the strange things that had just happened to them, had happened to *her*.

Something inside her was changing, though she did not understand what it was. This land of magic and woe had awakened something within her, and it was growing stronger.

What *was* she becoming?

Badger trotted on through the moonlit night, and they rode on, each absorbed in their own thoughts, and Oracle humming a silly tune.

Chapter 29 - Up from the Deep

Professor McPherson leaned heavily on the wheel of his ship. He was exhausted. Aonghus immediately took charge.

"Professor, you are too spent to face another day and night of this thing. Show me what to do. I'll pilot this ship."

The professor looked at Aonghus with admiration and said, "You are right, son. I need you. I need you all."

He straightened himself, willing away his utter weariness and said, "All of you, look here. Do you see this compass? It is no ordinary compass. It ... it knows where to lead us. There is something strange about it. It is the very compass that I found long ago in a stone chest on... on the island where we are going."

"Shouldn't we make for Portugal, Professor, or Africa?" asked Bib. "The ship is a mess. We've already fixed one pretty bad leak, and who knows how well we'll fare when we hit that wall of rain and wind again."

"The storm drove us far out into the ocean, dear children. It shifted our course, and we're far southwest of where we were yesterday. It has, by some providence, actually blown us along the very course that we intended, although how, I do not know. I have never in all my days felt this ship move with such speed. I feared many times that the waves and wind would smash her to pieces. But I suppose your work below shored up the old girl. Destiny has driven us."

He managed a weak smile and then said, "But we must keep heading southwest. We ought to gain sight of Bermuda if we keep our course steady."

"But if we are this far west, perhaps we should try for the Americas," said Bib.

"I fear that for now, we are at the mercy of the storm, dear ones," he replied. "For now, we sail in the eye of the storm. Aonghus, Bran,

Frederick – there are spare sails below, but only a few. Hoist them while you can, and sail as the compass guides. Ladies – after these men take down the torn sails, mend the ripped ones if you can – they may be of use too. See now, let me rest while I may. Wake me when the storm draws near again."

He dragged himself below deck, paused for a moment to inspect their repair work, nodded, and then went into his cabin, where he lay down and immediately was fast asleep.

On the deck, Aonghus gave orders. "Frederick, go below and find those spare sails. Bran, Abbe, take the rear mast. Bib, you and I will take the main one. Henny, wait here and gather up the sails as we drop them down."

Up the rope ladders they climbed to where the ripped sails hung limply in the strange air of the eye of the hurricane. They untied the lines that held them and allowed them to drop down to Henny, who bundled them up and dragged them to a clear spot on the deck where they might be mended.

Frederick appeared, carrying a bundle. "I found two sails, or at least I think they are sails," he said.

Aonghus looked at the circle of dark clouds around them.

"Let's wait to put them up, and see if we can repair the old ones first. When we get through, I suspect we'll need the new ones," he said.

He took the wheel and looked down at the beautiful compass. Its golden needle pointed off to their right slightly, so he turned the wheel in that direction a little. As the ship turned, the arrow straightened, and he held their course.

As the others labored to repair the damaged sails, the wall of dark clouds before them drew steadily nearer and nearer.

"We've got one fixed, Aonghus!" called Bib.

Bran folded the repaired sail and climbed the main mast with Bib following close behind. Together, they secured it in its place once again, and none too soon, for the wind was blowing stronger now and filled the sail to its fullest. A moment later and the last sail was repaired, and they secured it firmly to the mast and watched it too fill with wind. The ship was leaping through the waves now. About an hour and a half had passed since they had entered the eye of the hurricane.

"Double check all the rigging, quickly, and all lines on the deck," said Aonghus.

"Shall we wake the professor?" asked Henny.

"Not yet," he replied. "All of you get below. I'll stand at the wheel."

"Not unless you tie yourself in like the professor did," said Abbe.

Aonghus smiled and said, "Right. Give me a hand here."

Then he assured them that he would be fine, and said, "Bran, come up in a few hours and we'll swap off. No sense in getting exhausted like McPherson did. We'll take turns at keeping the ship on course. Pray that the sails hold and speed us through this storm!"

The boys shook hands, and the girls gave Aonghus a hug. As the first drops of rain fell on the deck, they went below and checked the hull once again before going to their cabins to wait.

On the deck, Aonghus gripped the wheel. He gritted his teeth as the sky grew black and rain suddenly lashed down upon him like a whip. The sails beat in the wind again and again, and soon the ship was rising and falling over waves that could easily capsize them. But providence seemed to be with them, for the waves came head on and did not generally broadside the ship, and for this, Aonghus was thankful.

As they sailed deeper into the storm, the winds increased, and soon Aonghus knew what the professor had meant when he had spoken of the ship sailing at incredible speeds. The sails were strained to the breaking point, and within a half hour, the rear sail that they had sewn split apart once again and flapped uselessly in the torrent. But still, they sailed on.

Nearly another hour had passed when suddenly, there was a great lurch of the ship. Aonghus pitched forward against the wheel, and only his safety lines kept him from flying forward and falling to the deck below. It was as though the ship had struck something and come to a sudden stop.

Everyone below deck went tumbling from their beds, picked themselves up, and ran from their quarters and into the hall, and Professor McPherson flung open the door of his chamber.

"What has happened!" he called.

"We're not sure, sir," said Bran. "It felt as if we struck something."

"Tie in together, all of you," he ordered as he made his way to the door leading upward, then dashed out onto the lower deck.

The others quickly tied the rope that lay in the hall around each other's waists and ventured out onto the still rocking ship. They looked about in the gray light, but could see nothing out of the ordinary, other than the great waves smashing against the hull of the ship, the torn rear sail, and Aonghus still at the wheel, looking about just as they were.

Then, without warning, a huge red tentacle at least two feet thick and sixty feet long whipped up out of the water and over the side of the ship, its dinner-plate-sized suction cups gripping the slick wood. A second tentacle of even greater size shot upward on the other side and wrapped itself about the main mast. There was a sickening sound of splintering wood as the thick trunk of the mast split in half and broke, leaving a sharp jagged pole where the mast had been. The tentacle released the broken shaft and down it fell, directly toward the McGunnegals and Frederick.

"No!" cried Aonghus, and with a *snap*, broke the ropes that held him fast and leaped from the upper deck, catching the falling mast in his muscled arms. It barely missed them, but fell with all its weight on top of Aonghus.

The girls screamed his name, but could not reach his prone form, for at that very moment, a mass of tentacles swarmed up onto the deck, thrashing wildly, and a great bulbous head rose up from the raging waves. It was red and brown, easily fifteen feet tall and wide, and a black eye gazed down upon them with cold alien hunger.

Henny screamed and tried to run, but the rigging of the mast had fallen about them, trapping and holding them fast to their own safety line. Professor McPherson was at their side immediately, pulled a knife from his boot, and began to cut them free from the tangle.

"Get below!" he cried as he cut through their ropes, freeing them one by one.

Frederick was the first one free, and he hesitated.

"Go, I say!" commanded the professor, and Frederick turned and ran below, followed by Henny.

Suddenly a great tentacle whipped through the air and gave the professor such a blow that he dropped the knife and was thrown nearly overboard. He only barely managed to grab the railing and hung precariously over the side of the ship.

Bib grabbed the fallen knife and cut herself free, then handed the knife to Abbe. But just as she turned to run below, a waving tentacle seized her, wrapped itself about her waist, and heaved her into the air. She screamed as the creature dangled her high above the deck of the ship, and with snake-like constriction, it began to squeeze.

Bran grabbed the knife from Abbe, cut himself loose, and charged at the creature's massive head. Without regard to his own safety, he flung himself at it and drove the knife to the hilt into its rubbery flesh. A gross shrieking gurgle came from the beast as it hauled itself upward and revealed a great hooked beak at least four feet high and three feet wide, snapping like some loathsome deformed parrot.

Tentacles waved about the ship. The second mast snapped at the top, and the rigging fell to the upper deck.

Bran pulled the knife free and stabbed again, but this time, the creature seized him with one of its tentacles and threw him clean off the ship.

Abbe screamed as she saw her brother fly through the air and into the driving rain and raging sea, then disappear. She got to her knees, dazed, and then her eyes met the one eye of the sea monster.

Something clicked in her mind, and she could see – or feel – the raw animal instinct of this beast. It bore no malice – that was not an emotion it could feel. But she felt its primordial need to *feed* – and she knew that *they* were its prey.

But the creature also sensed something about *her*. And for a moment, it froze – its tentacles dangling weirdly in the air, as though somehow its simple mind had been put on hold in those brief seconds.

But then a faint cry tore her gaze from its great eye. Bib hung limply in the crushing grip of the monster. Anger at the creature and fear for her sister filled her mind, and with those raw emotions, she lashed out at it with her thoughts, or perhaps something beyond thought.

To her surprise, it recoiled in fear, and a great jet of dark ink sprayed the deck of the ship. Abbe stood, and advanced on the monster, her mind pummeling it, how she did not know. Opening its massive beak, it shrieked again and once again began frantically waving its tentacles.

Abbe's mind was bound to the beast's, and she would not release it. It struggled to escape, to flee from this unknown threat, back to the depths of the sea, but something bound it to this *presence* now gripping its mind.

Suddenly, someone ran past Abbe toward the great gelatinous head. It was Frederick, come from below deck with a shining sword in his hand. Right up to the creature he ran, and with a cry, he swung the sword. The tentacle that gripped Bib was severed cleanly off the monster's body. Bib plummeted to the deck of the ship, and only just in the nick of time, Aonghus regained his senses, saw what was happening, threw off the heavy mast that lay atop him, and caught his sister as she fell from the creature's grip.

Abbe's control broke, and the great black eye focused on this new attacker before it. The mouth opened, snapping with rage and pain, and half a dozen other tentacles whipped around, grappling with everything in their path on their way to Frederick.

SLASH, went the sword, and another severed limb fell writhing to the deck. *SLASH*, and there was a piece of another.

Then it had him, and Frederick felt the crushing grip of pure muscle as one of the thing's arms seized him and spun him around. Swiftly, it drew him in toward the snapping razors. Frederick's life flashed before his eyes as he drew nearer to a sure death. He knew that he would do one last great deed, and he held the sword ready as he was drawn toward the gaping gullet.

The great beak opened wide, and Frederick could see row upon row of spiked horns extending down its yawning orifice. Seconds later, he was inside the thing's mouth, kicking frantically as he felt himself being pulled downward into the sickening throat.

With all of his might, and with all the courage he could muster, he stabbed upward, toward what he thought must be the thing's brain. To his amazement, the sword burst into a hot green flame as it sunk deep into the monster's flesh, piercing clean through and out the back of its head.

Just as his sword sank deep, and it seemed sure the horrid beak would slice him in two as it snapped wildly open and shut, he heard a great cry – a war cry, like a man gone mad in the midst of fierce battle. He turned and saw, as the beak flew open for just an instant, Aonghus running toward him, the entire broken shaft of the main mast in his arms like some great spear, and his face ablaze with a ferocious anger. With a mighty *heave,* he drove the sharp end of the shaft directly into the eye of the beast.

As the black eye was pierced and the sword cleaved its tiny brain, the snapping beak froze open in a horrid, silent scream. Then it slowly closed in death, and Frederick was shrouded in thick gooey darkness. A weird silence fell over him as the outside world was shut out. The entire body of the sea monster shuddered, and thrashed one last time, and for a moment, he thought he would be sucked down the thing's throat and impaled on its sharp toothy spikes. Then all was still except for the unending rising and falling sensation of the ship on the waves.

On the deck of the ship, Abbe cried out in fear and rushed forward, “Frederick! Frederick!”

The huge body of the beast quivered grossly, its black eye pierced by the shaft of the mast. She watched as the last light of its primitive mind sparked once and then went out. She felt its death, and knew that something very ancient had just passed from the earth.

But what of Frederick? Aonghus seized the beak with two hands and ripped it apart.

Frederick rolled out of the thing's mouth, blood and goo from the monster covering him, and the sword still in his grip. A wave broke over the bow of the ship, bathing him in seawater, and washing away the filth of the monster. Slowly he stood, shaking, and smiled. Aonghus gave a sigh of relief and Abbe rushed forward to hug him.

“For a moment I thought...” she began.

“I'm all right,” he replied.

Their relief at seeing Frederick whole, however, lasted only a moment, for now they looked about the ship and the full gravity of their situation dawned upon them. Two tentacles lay severed, still slightly quivering, and the great bulk of the creature lay upon the bow, its remaining arms limp, some dangling over the ship's edge.

The masts were both shattered, and most of the lower deck lay in ruins. Somehow, the wheel had survived untouched.

But Aonghus took all of this in with a glance. Where was Bran? Henny? Professor McPherson? Was Bib injured?

He rushed to Bib's side, brushed the hair from her eyes, and said, "Bib? Are you all right? Please be all right."

She did not answer, so he gently lifted her in his arms and quickly took her below deck, Abbe following behind. He was relieved to find Henny in the girl's cabin, and he carefully laid his sister on one of the beds. She was still breathing.

"Watch over her. See if she has any broken bones," said Aonghus, then he hurried back out.

Back on the deck, he found Frederick trying to haul Professor McPherson up and over the ship's railing. Reaching down with one hand, he pulled the professor onto the deck where he immediately collapsed.

"It was all I could do to hold on, Aonghus. I tried – I tried so hard to pull myself up to help, but the waves..." he began, a pained look in his eyes.

"I know, Professor. Where is my brother?" he said.

They looked about, but Bran was nowhere to be seen.

Then Abbe appeared behind them and said, "Bib is going to be all right, Aonghus. But… but Bran... that thing grabbed him and... it threw him into the sea!"

She began to cry, and buried her face in his great chest, sobbing uncontrollably. Professor McPherson stood unsteadily and, holding onto the rail, made his way along the side of the ship, gazing intently out into the dark waves as the ship was tossed uncontrollably about.

“Get below, Abbe,” said Aonghus gently but firmly. “We'll find him. Be strong now and watch out for our sisters.”

Suddenly, Professor McPherson cried out, for there, swimming atop the crest of a wave, was Bran. He powered through the waves toward the ship, and the knife he had held was now clenched in his teeth. He reached the front of the ship where the sea monster's arms dangled, took the knife from his mouth, and stabbed it into the dead flesh. He climbed, using the knife to pull himself upward until he reached the outstretched arms of Aonghus and Professor McPherson. Over the railing he came, looked at the dead creature with its split head and the mast sticking out of its eye, then looked about the smashed and broken ship and said, “Well, who slew the beast?”

Frederick and Aonghus both grinned and pointed to each other.

“I'm glad you're all right, Bran,” said Frederick.

“It's lucky I found the ship!” he replied. “I was swimming and swimming, and with these waves and rain, couldn't see anything. Then I saw a flash of green light – and lo and behold, there was the ship right in front of me! Good thing that big tentacle was dangling in the water!”

Then they slapped each other on the back and shook hands and laughed for a moment. But then they looked about, and their smiles faded.

“Professor, what was that thing?” asked Frederick.

He looked at it for a moment, and then at them all, and said, “These are strange waters, and strange beasts live here. If I had not seen this with my own eyes, I would not have believed it. But I believe that you and Aonghus have just slain a kraken, if the description in old tales can be believed.”

“A kraken!” said Frederick. “But that's just a mythical...”

He stopped and stared at the huge creature that lay dead before them. It looked like a weird cross between an octopus and a squid, but huge. Its great brown beak lay open, revealing its spiked gullet, and its massive tentacles hung limply about the ship.

"It was very old," said Abbe. "Older than... than.... Its mind was so primitive, so..."

But she could not find any further words, and she walked forward to the hulk of the slain beast and touched its bloated head. Its great black eye, still pierced by the shaft of the mast, stared blankly at nothing.

Suddenly, a wave swept over the bow of the ship, drenching them and the huge body with spray. The kraken slowly, limply, together with its severed tentacles, slid from the deck of the ship and into the sea. There it lingered for a moment, its great arms splayed outward until another wave broke over its form and it vanished into the depths. They stared silently at the place it had been, the events of the last few minutes now emblazoned in their minds forever.

When Frederick finally tore his eyes away from the raging sea and looked again at the place where the kraken had died, he saw something. It was long and white, and he knew exactly what it was – one of the toothy spikes that he had seen in the thing's throat. He walked over to it and picked it up. It was over a foot long and two inches wide at the base. Its serrated edges and tip were sharp as razors, but it had a handle of sorts where it had been pulled out by the root from the beast's flesh.

"I will keep this as a token of my battle with the kraken," he declared and held it up to the sky.

The others stared at him, and wondered at how manly this boy had become – a long sword in his right hand and a jagged white token of victorious battle in the other. A wave broke against the ship, sending spray high into the air, casting his form as a dark silhouette against a backdrop of white foam and gray rain.

Broken and smashed, the ship rose and fell with the storm. Somehow, Frederick knew that they had to make it. Something was calling to him from out there – something that was going to teach him who he really was, and would shape his destiny forever.

Continued in "The Witch and the Waking Tree" ...

Author's Note

I hope you've enjoyed reading *Taming the Goblin*. My goal has been and always will be to provide great clean adventure stories for all ages that also whisper of deep things.

Please consider giving the book a review on Amazon. I would really appreciate it.

Book 3 – *The Witch and the Waking Tree*

Be sure to check out the next book in the series, *The Witch and the Waking Tree*. Here, Colleen and her band experience harrowing adventures as they encounter echoes of the Cataclysm that ruined the old world, a crack in time, the source of the Spell, a wishing well, the Pits of the Witch, and much more. Colleen finds her mother, and together they face the Witch herself, and wrestle with the terrible power that she wields.

Frederick and the other McGunnegals are also swept away in more adventures as a great burning meteor plunges into the sea, their ship is destroyed, they awake on a strange island, encounter an ancient king returned from death, find the Timeless Hall, and are reunited with Colleen in a final battle with the Witch and the goblins.

Both Colleen and Frederick also discover the secret to their ancestry, and why it is they are so *strange.*

An unexpected ending brings this first series of The McGunnegal Chronicles to a close, with an epilogue that promises more books to come. The adventures have just begun!

Thanks again, and enjoy reading!

Ben Anderson

Made in the USA
Middletown, DE
19 June 2016